HEARTWARMING

Snowed in with the Single Dad

—

Melinda Curtis

⬧ HARLEQUIN® HEARTWARMING™

Recycling programs
for this product may
not exist in your area.

ISBN-13: 978-1-335-51070-9

Snowed in with the Single Dad

Copyright © 2019 by Melinda Wooten

This edition published by arrangement with Harlequin Books S.A.

For questions and comments about the quality of this book, please contact us at CustomerService@Harlequin.com.

Printed in U.S.A.

"You're bored here."

"Incredibly." Laurel leaned forward. "How could you tell?"

"Besides the fidgeting? Maybe because you're butting into my business." Mitch grinned.

She seemed to be studying his face. "I thought we were having a conversation about how to find some peaceful common territory." She shook her head. "You know, when I was battling morning sickness you talked to me differently. But I guess that was before you decided I was Monroe-tainted devil spawn."

"Let's be honest..." Not completely honest. He wasn't going to tell her he wanted to lean forward and kiss her sometimes. "I realize my daughter is going to leave Second Chance one day. But I'd like her to be happy here before she leaves. And people like you and your family are trouble, so—"

Laurel drew a sharp intake of breath.

There was something about this woman that reached around logic and reality, that reached a place few women had been able to touch, that shook him to his core.

Attraction, his brain whispered.

Annoyance, he corrected stubbornly.

Because Laurel stood for everything he'd run from in Chicago...

Dear Reader,

Guess who inherited a town from her grandfather? Laurel Monroe and her eleven siblings and cousins! What did Second Chance mean to Harlan Monroe? Why did he leave it to his grandchildren? His adult heirs are going to find out. And while they're at it, they'll get a second chance at love.

It's a well-kept secret that Laurel Monroe sometimes stands in for her identical twin, famous actress Ashley. And usually it's no harm, no foul. But there's a reason Laurel is hiding out in Second Chance. She pretended to be her sister, and something went incredibly wrong. Pregnant. Fired. She needs a little TLC. She might not get it from single dad Mitch Kincaid, owner of Second Chance's only inn. He's not sure she's a good role model for his precocious twelve-year-old daughter. And he can't wait to get rid of her. Too bad the snow is so heavy all the mountain passes are closed...

I hope you come to love The Mountain Monroes as much as I do. Happy reading!

Melinda

Prior to writing romance, award-winning *USA TODAY* bestseller **Melinda Curtis** was a junior manager for a Fortune 500 company, which meant when she flew on the private jet, she was relegated to the jump seat. After grabbing her pen (and a parachute), she made the leap to full-time writer. Between writing clean romance for Harlequin and indie-pubbed romantic comedy, Melinda recently came to grips with the fact that she's an empty nester and a grandma. Brenda Novak says Melinda's book *Season of Change* "found a place on my keeper shelf."

THE MOUNTAIN MONROES FAMILY TREE

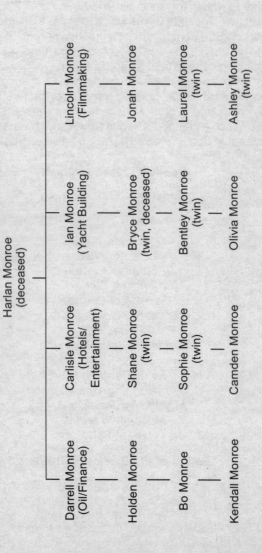

Harlan Monroe
(deceased)

Darrell Monroe
(Oil/Finance)

Carlisle Monroe
(Hotels/
Entertainment)

Ian Monroe
(Yacht Building)

Lincoln Monroe
(Filmmaking)

Holden Monroe

Shane Monroe
(twin)

Bryce Monroe
(twin, deceased)

Jonah Monroe

Bo Monroe

Sophie Monroe
(twin)

Bentley Monroe
(twin)

Laurel Monroe
(twin)

Kendall Monroe

Camden Monroe

Olivia Monroe

Ashley Monroe
(twin)

PROLOGUE

ONCE UPON A TIME, there were two little red-headed girls. Identical twins who lived in Hollywood, were best friends and wore princess dresses whenever they could get away with it.

Their parents were Hollywood royalty—a studio head and a talent agent. Said parents traveled, a lot. They entertained, a lot. But they also fought, a lot, which upset the girls.

Laurel was a girlie girl, in love with shoes and fabrics, hairstyles and makeup, peace and quiet. From an early age, she devoured fashion magazines and red-carpet shows. She begged the family maid to teach her how to sew, imagining a future where she created pretty dresses for celebrities. Making smooth, even stitches became a welcome escape from the household's chaos. But sometimes, there was no escape.

As for Ashley… She might have watched too many soap operas and romantic movies while the maid taught Laurel to sew. Those hours in front of the TV gave Ashley a fascination with people, their emotions and how they expressed them. The slightest of smiles, the well of tears, the shudder of bent shoulders. Body language said so much without saying anything at all. And pretending to be a character on-screen? That was sometimes better than being Ashley Monroe.

Like many identical twins, Laurel and Ashley learned early on that one could easily be mistaken for the other. And like many identical twins, they learned early on to take advantage of their mirrorlike facades and implement what they called "The Twin Switch."

The girls would have lived happily ever after in obscurity if not for their parents stumbling upon five-year-old Ashley reenacting a scene from a soap opera with what they said was amazing talent. Mama Monroe enrolled her in acting class, hired a writer to create a television series around her and devoted herself to making Ashley a star.

Which meant Laurel was often forgotten in her twin's shadow.

Unless she was needed to stand in her place.

CHAPTER ONE

"DON'T ENCOURAGE THE MONROES."

Standing in the kitchenette of the Lodge-pole Inn, Laurel Monroe stopped steeping her tea bag, stopped mentally mending the tears in the fabric of her life and paused, trying to place that voice.

Masculine.

Three men were living or staying at the inn.

Authoritative.

Two were natural-born leaders.

Presumptuous.

Given her father wasn't in town, that narrowed it down to one.

Mitch Kincaid, mayor of Second Chance, Idaho, and the man who ran the Lodgepole Inn. A month ago she'd thought Mitch had kind eyes. Three weeks ago he'd held her head when she'd been too weak to keep it out of the toilet. And then last week he'd cast shade on her family, the wealthy Monroes, not once but three times!

"Dad." A much younger, feminine voice reached Laurel.

"Gabby." Masculine. Authoritative. Presumptuous. That was Mitch, all right, talking to his preteen daughter. "We're not going to make friends with the Monroes. They need to leave town before it's too late."

Too bad for Mitch that the Monroes owned Second Chance. It was their town to ruin. Not that that was their plan. Not that they had a plan. Not that Laurel had a plan for herself, either. Not yet anyway. She'd make one after her doctor's appointment two days from now.

But the town...

Laurel still found the ownership part hard to believe. Years ago her grandfather had bought Second Chance—every ramshackle cabin, every building housing an underperforming business, every plot of land—which might have been a smart investment if Grandpa Harlan hadn't gone on to charge residents and those who ran businesses leases of one dollar a year.

Her beloved grandfather had left his hometown in better economic condition than he'd left his grandchildren. According to his will, the vast Monroe fortune was designated for Grandpa Harlan's four sons, but only if they fired Harlan's grandchildren, who all worked for the Monroe Holding Corporation, and evicted them from Monroe-owned residences.

Job? Gone. Rent-free condo? Gone. Trust fund? Never had one. And now she was pregnant? *Don't make friends with the Monroes?*

What did Mitch have against the Monroes?

The Monroes were the reason struggling businesses like the Lodgepole Inn weren't closed! The Monroes were the reason people like Mitch could make a living in the mountains!

"All I'm saying is I don't want you hanging out with the Monroes, especially Laurel." Mitch opened the door behind the check-in desk and saw Laurel.

Mouth dry, Laurel stopped dipping her tea bag.

They stared at each other in silence.

Mitch Kincaid carried himself like he should be wearing a suit and tie and standing in the corner office of a high-rise. Solidly built, tall and proud. Thick, dark hair cut short. Intelligent brown eyes that could easily read any situation.

But he wasn't wearing a suit or surveying the world from a corner office. Mitch wore a navy cotton sweater over faded blue jeans and stood in an inn built entirely from logs.

It was just that he wore the casual attire the same way he spoke. With authority.

Not that Laurel or her cousins acknowledged his authority as mayor. And maybe that was part of Mitch's problem. He had no control over what happened in town next and that seemed to be making him cranky.

Case in point, he made a grumpy noise to acknowledge Laurel.

"Bad morning, Counselor?" Laurel returned her attention to her tea, stung that she was the villain in this scenario.

And Mitch? He could've acknowledged her testy greeting with a muttered apology. Or a cocky eyebrow quirk. Instead, he went for a repeat of the grumpy noise.

Laurel had a grumpy noise, too. But before she could use it, the aroma of bacon drifted from the plate Mitch carried, turning Laurel's stomach—once, twice, a third time.

Baby doesn't like bacon.

Which was a shame, because Laurel loved bacon. Maple bacon. Smoked bacon. Crispy bacon with burnt edges.

Laurel disposed of the tea bag and willed her stomach to stop doing barrel rolls. "Are you going to eat that? As in immediately?"

"Is that Laurel?" Gabby poked her young face around Mitch's wide chest, lisping slightly from her new retainer. "Hi!" Gabby's smile was bright. Her intelligent dark eyes and quick wit seemed to be a gift from her father. Presumably, her long, straight strawberry blond hair was a gift from her mother, who wasn't around and apparently never had been. "Ignore him, Laurel." Gabby poked her father in the ribs. "His bark is worse than his bite."

"So you keep telling me." Laurel tried to discount the way nausea crept up her throat. "Are you going to eat all that bacon?"

"Smells good, doesn't it?" Mitch was no longer looking at Laurel or he might have noticed her green pallor. "Did you want some? I made plenty."

"No." Laurel took a step back and breathed shallowly.

Baby definitely doesn't like bacon.

Despite Laurel's best efforts, the aroma of greasy bacon filled her nostrils. Her stomach took a nosedive. "Could you...eat a little quicker?" She waved her hand in the air, trying to encourage Mitch to eat up.

Mitch gently pushed Gabby back and closed the door in her face, eliciting a muffled, *"Da-ad."*

"Ignore me and my bark, darling daughter." Mitch went to the check-in desk and deposited his plate there, sparing Laurel a half grin. "How are you this morning?"

If you smile at me like that any longer, I might forget you consider me and my family the plague of Second Chance.

People rarely considered Laurel trouble, if they considered her at all. She averted her gaze. "If you're asking, did I upchuck in my room last night? The answer is no. If you're asking if I might lose it now, well… Baby is undecided."

"Ah." Mitch bit into a piece of bacon and chewed slowly. He slid Laurel a look that said many things.

Thank heavens this Monroe won't try to snatch my bacon.

Thank heavens this Monroe didn't get sick in the bathroom I have to clean later.

Thank heavens this Monroe isn't bringing up the conversation she just overheard.

Laurel wasn't about to let Mitch get by on that last one. "Is there something you want to get off your chest?"

Your very tall, broad chest.

Baby was undercutting Laurel's perspective when it came to men.

Really, Baby was only undercutting Laurel's perspective when it came to *this* man. There was a handsome cowboy sitting in the common room recuperating from a nasty broken leg. Laurel's imagination didn't stray across appropriate lines when it came to Zeke. Nope. It was just Mitch who got under her skin.

"Off my chest?" Mitch took another bite of bacon. "Not a blessed thing." When it came to repartee, Mitch was a worthy adversary. Not surprising, given he'd been a defense attorney before he decided innkeeping was his calling.

"Dad, be nice," Gabby shouted through the closed door.

"I am." Mitch grinned like the evil overlord he probably thought he was. He turned back to Laurel, black hair glinting in the sunlight streaming through the window. "Are you going somewhere?"

"No." Laurel took a sip of her tea, breathing in the clean scent that masked the bacon. "Didn't you tell me the roads wouldn't be open until tomorrow?"

Second Chance was one of the snowiest places in America and was often isolated during winter. Outside, some drifts had to be at least eight feet tall.

"I don't expect the snowplows to make it over the pass until tomorrow. But…" Mitch gestured to her attire with a burnt piece of bacon. "You're dressed to go out on the town."

Silently cursing bacon, Laurel glanced down at her black geometric V-neck tunic and silver leggings. One hid her growing topside and one was forgiving of her expanding waistline. And her black leather booties… What did he expect her to wear? Clunky snow boots?

"Counselor—" she'd taken to calling Mitch that when she was annoyed because he'd taken to calling her Miss Laurel, like she was high society and he was her chauffeur "—you may have noticed I like clothes." Up until a month ago, clothes had been the way Laurel made a living—costuming actors for movies and styling her identical twin sister for the red carpet. "Dressing well isn't a crime."

It sometimes seemed it was around Mitch, whose plucky preteen daughter regularly wore ill-fitting, boy-cut blue jeans and T-shirts with iron-on transfers. Laurel would enjoy seeing the delicately blossoming beauty in a floral-print skirt and pastel blouse. Not exactly appropriate attire for the mountains in winter.

"I love the sound of kindly people exchanging kindly greetings in the morning." That was Zeke, recuperating cowboy and slinger of zingers.

"Good morning, Zeke." To avoid the lingering smell of bacon, Laurel carried her tea upstairs. "Clothes aren't evil. I'm not admitting defeat this round, Counselor."

"I wouldn't expect any less, Miss Laurel."

If Laurel hadn't been queasy, and bothered by her attraction to Mitch, she might have smiled.

The inn's stairs creaked as she climbed. The hallway upstairs listed to one side and protested every step she took. The outer wall was made of thick, stacked logs with gray chinking in between. The inner wall was flat-sanded wood, stained the color of redwood. It was a far cry from the Hollywood mansion of her youth.

Sorry, Baby. Mama won't be feeding you with a silver spoon.

Reality Check Number One. Laurel's share of Second Chance wasn't worth enough to buy silver spoons.

Take the Lodgepole Inn. It wasn't a five-star hotel. If it had a website, which it did not, it would have touted itself as "rustic"—code for outdated.

She opened a warped door that stuck and entered her room. It had faded brown carpet, a bed covered with an artfully crafted sunflower quilt, a woefully small closet and an equally small bathroom appointed with pink fixtures. From what she'd seen, the rest of

Second Chance was in the same—or worse—condition.

She sat on the edge of her bed and sipped her tea, staring at the pink rhinestone-studded evening gown she'd made for her famous twin's latest opening night.

Ashley! Ashley! Look over here!

The flash of camera bulbs had blinded. The pop of those same bulbs had made ears ring. The cries of the photographers had been deafening.

Reality Check Number Two. Ashley had never worn that pink dress.

Laurel had stepped into her twin's shoes, literally, and masqueraded as Ashley Monroe, up-and-coming starlet.

Laurel set her mug on the scarred bedside table and lay back on the bed to stare at the ceiling. Her days being a double for her identical twin in Hollywood were coming to an end. Soon, she wouldn't be able to fit into her sister's clothes.

Anxiety sat immobile on Laurel's chest like a semitruck stuck in LA traffic. Her sister was a joy, a talented actress and a delicate flower. Laurel had spent most of her life watching out for her. But...

Reality Check Number Three. Laurel was pregnant, and she hadn't worked up the courage to tell her family or the famous actor responsible for her pregnancy.

Her news… It wasn't likely to be well received.

Her news… It would make her the least popular Monroe with more than just Mitch Kincaid.

"WE'VE GOT TO get rid of the Monroes." A short time after Laurel had overheard his conversation with Gabby, Mayor Mitch Kincaid presided over an emergency council meeting held in the Bent Nickel Diner. "Them staying… It's not what Harlan wanted."

Or what he'd promised them ten years ago.

Promises? Mitch's father had scoffed at him from behind security glass. *You might just as well ask for rainbows.*

Honor a promise? His father hadn't known how.

Looking back, Harlan's promises sounded a lot like a pot of gold at the end of a rainbow.

"Harlan said by disowning his grandchildren and leaving them our town…" Ivy, who ran the Bent Nickel, paced behind the counter. "He said they'd agree with his stewardship and curate Second Chance remotely."

"While they made their own fortunes elsewhere." Mackenzie nodded. She ran the general store and garage.

"That's what Harlan hoped," Mitch reminded them. "Harlan banked on their hunger to make their mark in the world once he freed them from obligation to his fortune. But he didn't bank on Shane."

"He's a fixer, all right." Roy, the town handyman, pushed up the sleeves of his long johns until they disappeared beneath the cuffs of his blue coveralls. He blew out a breath. "And Shane Monroe ain't leavin' until he fixes this town."

"How's he going to boost our profits?" Ivy asked unhappily. "In winter, no less."

Second Chance had a unique rhythm. Seven or eight months out of the year, they did a brisk business in town, or at least enough commerce to get by. And when the passes began closing in winter, things slowed down. Snowed in, Second Chance residents spent more time with family, more time gathering and gossiping at the Bent Nickel, operating fewer hours or closing down altogether.

"Let's face it. Shane's fixes will likely improve his bottom line," Mitch added, not sounding any happier. "That is, if they aren't interested in leasing to us anymore and decide to sell the town." The coffee he'd been drinking felt like acid in his stomach. "But if it comes to selling, I'm sure they'll give us the opportunity to buy back our homes and businesses."

They stared at each other in silence, because none of them were convinced of that. The Monroes hadn't made any promises or guarantees.

"Home never looks the same after you leave." Those were the first words Harlan Monroe had spoken to Mitch. The millionaire had been standing next to a beat-up Ford pickup, gazing at the town's main drag with an air of sadness. "I suppose I'll need a room for a few nights, if you've got one available."

Mitch had just bought the inn. He was adjusting to life outside the courtroom and his role as a small-town single dad. Harlan's wife, Estelle, had just lost a long battle with cancer. Harlan was coming to terms with his own mortality and how to manage his legacy. A few nights' stay turned into a few weeks'.

Surprisingly, the notoriously media-shy Harlan had been a talker, particularly candid when he was one-on-one. He shared his past, his road to wealth and his hopes for his grandchildren, who he considered too privileged. And he expected frankness in return.

"And that's why I left Second Chance,"

Harlan had concluded his tale as he and Mitch sipped whiskey on the inn's back porch one night, serenaded by an owl in a nearby pine tree. "You know, I've never told my grand-kids that story. I love 'em, but try holding a meaningful conversation with a dozen kids staring at cell phones."

"You should tell stories like that to a biographer," Mitch had said. "If you tell them at all."

"Says the former lawyer with caution in his voice." Harlan had chuckled, a deep rumbly sound that hinted at fluid in his lungs. And then he'd switched gears. "None of the businesses in town seem at capacity. Tell me about your bottom line."

Mitch had.

"I want to invest in Second Chance," Harlan had told Mitch weeks later, his small satchel in hand. "I want it to live on, like my business legacy, but I don't want John Q Public to know." He'd explained his plan to buy up real estate in Second Chance and lease it back to residents. He'd shared his idea about guarding his legacy—the nondisclosure agreements with those who accepted his offer, agreements that would expire one year from his death, a date coinciding with the release of his authorized biography.

"Look." Mack tossed her dark braid over one

shoulder, bringing Mitch back to the present when her hair almost hit him. "Shane means well. He uses Mitch's snowmobile to deliver my grocery orders to folks without charge. My pocketbook isn't complaining about them staying longer, but…"

"They need to build lives for themselves elsewhere," Ivy said, her pacing stomping on Mitch's last nerve. "And forget about changing anything in Second Chance. We like our quiet winters. It's what's made this town like a family." She choked on the word and clutched her throat.

"Calm down," Roy said. "We'd all feel better if they skedaddled. But we ain't doin' so bad. One Monroe left already."

Mitch frowned. Granted, one of the Monroes—Ella—had left town nearly two weeks ago.

If Mitch had his druthers, he'd be rid of another Monroe. Not Sophie and her young twin boys, who posed no threat. Not Shane and his endless ideas about how to make the town a thriving metropolis—completely at odds with Harlan's wishes.

No. If Mitch had his druthers, it would be Laurel who left next, the petite woman with the vibrant red hair who sometimes looked as if someone had deflated her spirit. When

Mitch saw the unguarded side of Laurel, something inside him softened.

Mitch set his jaw. Now wasn't the time to be sympathetic.

Gabby showed too much interest in the redhead. Laurel might have arrived in Second Chance pale, pregnant and exhausted, but she had big-city, look-at-me style, like his ex-wife. And impressionable Gabby was enthralled, despite the fact that Laurel didn't fit in the Idaho high country. Her high-heeled, black leather boots weren't made for snow. Her paper-thin, black leather jacket wasn't made for temperatures below fifty.

For heaven's sake, she had an evening gown hanging in her bathroom!

Which Mitch only knew about because he had to clean said bathroom. Which, up until two weeks ago, Mitch could only reach by walking through the trail of clothes Laurel left on the floor, dropped—presumably— wherever she was when she undressed. Which—Mitch imagined, because he was divorced, not dead—was a process that wasn't conducted when she was standing still. Shoes had littered the space required to swing the door open and pants, leggings, sweaters and T-shirts fanned five to ten feet from there. Unmentionables of every color—indelibly marked in his memory—had landed closest to the bathroom door and the glittery pink evening gown.

Mitch pressed at the ache in his temples. He'd spent too many nights pacing, worrying, wondering what he could have done differently with Harlan's offer. "Granted, our deals with Harlan were a gamble to begin with." The buyout and low lease were like a golden ticket, one with an expiration date. When he sold, Mitch had figured after Harlan died, he and Gabby would move elsewhere. But he hadn't anticipated the town winning him over. "In Harlan's defense, no one could've predicted Laurel would arrive pregnant and be put on bed rest."

"Or that the other two would stay to support her." Mack rolled her shoulders. "We're lucky it's only the three of them. It could have been all twelve."

Harlan had assured them his grandchildren—who worked mostly high-profile jobs in the movie industry, finance, museums, oil, yacht building or luxury hotels—wouldn't want to stay in their small town.

"Three little birdies to force out of their comfy little nests," Roy pointed out. "And then things will return to normal, just like Harlan promised. You'll see." Mitch was having a hard time seeing anything other than disappearing rainbows.

"Return to normal? When Ella Monroe left, we lost Doc. Who will we lose with the next Monroe we get rid of? You, Roy?" Ivy stopped pacing behind the diner's counter and crossed her arms over her gray hooded sweatshirt, covering up the neon-yellow letters that spelled out *Best Mommy Ever.* "The next nearest handyman is in Ketchum and the nearest medical clinic is an hour's drive from here." The worry in Ivy's voice was hard to miss. It wasn't that long ago that her oldest had dislocated his shoulder and her youngest had sprained both his ankles. They were younger than Mitch's daughter and growing like clumsy weeds.

Laurel Monroe had probably never been a clumsy weed.

Something clattered in the diner's kitchen.

"Ow-woooo." Nick, Ivy's youngest, ran out in his *Star Wars* pajamas, holding his finger toward Ivy. His brown hair was in need of a brushing or a trim and it bounced with each urgent step. "Mom, I shut my finger in the microwave and dropped my plate of nachos."

Ivy picked him up and settled him on her hip. "Pumpkin, what have I told you about the microwave?"

Grinning, Roy elbowed Mitch and whispered, "What have you told him about eating nachos for breakfast?"

That comment earned the old man Ivy's evil eye.

"Not to use it!" the kindergartner wailed, fat tears rolling down his cheeks. "And I did and now my finger is broken!"

"Let me see." Ivy inspected Nick's intact digit. "Look. It bends. No bone showing. No blood dripping. You know what that means?"

Nick drew in a shuddering breath. "I… have to…clean up my *me-e-ess*." He tucked his head in the crook of Ivy's neck and cried some more.

Ivy kissed his thatch of wild hair, put him down and sent him back to the kitchen. "Thank heavens there are no customers around to witness that."

The Bent Nickel was the town gathering place, a time capsule with its checkerboard linoleum floors, green pleather and chrome counter stools, not to mention the yellowed pictures on the walls showing the town back in its heyday—cavalry units, trappers, miners, ranchers. The snow had been thick last night. It would take residents longer than usual to make their way into the diner for their morning news.

"No customers? Thank heavens there ain't no health inspectors around." Roy bowed his shoulders and sniggered, earning another glare from Ivy.

"We should get back on point." Mitch drained the last of his coffee, thinking of Laurel at home in Hollywood. He could picture her in slim-fitting blue jeans and a tank top, carrying coffee from some posh and popular place, red hair swinging across her shoulders with each high-heeled step.

Get back on point? Take your own advice, Kincaid.

"It's not like we can evict them." Roy rubbed a hand over his breastbone. "They own the place."

"Heartburn, Roy?" Ivy asked in a distracted voice, attention on the kitchen. "How much coffee have you had this morning?"

His pointy chin went up. "I'm allowed three cups."

"According to Doc?" Mack asked with a sly look Mitch's way. She enjoyed teasing the old man. "Or something you read?"

Roy's chin stayed up, but he didn't answer.

"What if the Monroes don't want to pay the doctor stipend anymore?" Ivy's eyes slanted with worry, her gaze still on her son.

"They're contractually obligated to provide

us with a doctor through the end of the year," Mitch reassured her, not that he felt reassured. "We just have to find a physician willing to come." Mitch had posted an ad for a doctor the day Noah left. "Let's not panic."

"Not yet anyway," Ivy grumbled, pushing her straight brown hair back from her face. "No one but Odette has wanted to see a doctor since Noah left."

"We'll find a doctor," Mitch pitched his voice to reassure the way Harlan used to on his quarterly visits. Their wealthy benefactor always seemed to provide Second Chance with what they needed, like a magician pulling a rabbit from a hat. "But the fact remains—the Monroes aren't leaving and they don't strike me as the kind of people who want to live in log cabins and outdated homes at a remote fork in the road."

Because that was just it. Second Chance wasn't anybody's destination. It was located where two narrow ribbons of highway intersected at the base of the Sawtooth Mountains. Drivers passed through on their way to Boise to the west, Challis to the north or Ketchum to the south.

Roy scrunched his face into a deeper cascade of wrinkles. "You think the Monroes want to turn this place into the next Challis?"

Ivy hugged herself tighter. "Or Hailey."

"Or Ketchum," Mack said glumly.

Those were some of the Idaho towns the rich and famous had bought property in to "get away from it all." The influx of wealthy residents had driven up real estate prices and given rise to restaurants with appetizers like black cherries wrapped in maple-drizzled bacon. Not that there was anything wrong with that type of food in Manhattan or Hollywood. But Second Chance was more of a loaded-nachos or twice-baked-potatoes kind of town.

"I could lose the diner." Ivy gripped the worn countertop with both hands, looking older than her thirtyish years. "I feel so stupid."

"Don't be. We all bought into Harlan's dream," Mitch said. He'd welcomed the infusion of cash. He'd bought a new heating unit for the inn, socked away the rest into a college fund for Gabby and then tucked his worries about making ends meet along with it.

"Second Chance is one of the few remaining towns in the state made up mostly of hundred-year-old cabins." Roy interrupted Mitch's wayward thoughts. "If we can't honor Harlan's wishes and run his family out of town, there ought to be something we can do to protect it legal-like. I won't let them tear down my place. I was born here, and I plan to die here."

Mitch opened his mouth, but nothing came out. Instead, an idea formed. A rough idea not yet ready to be put forth to the town council.

"You're onto something." Roy nudged him. "I can tell."

He was. "Maybe we do have something else up our sleeve." A final card to play if Shane couldn't be dissuaded from "fixing" Second Chance.

CHAPTER TWO

Two boys tumbled into Laurel's room with the enthusiasm only oversugared four-year-olds could bring.

They came at just the right time. Laurel had been practicing speeches on how to tell her family she was pregnant, each worse than the last. It didn't help that she kept getting distracted by the image of Mitch making bacon.

"Aunt Laurel!" the boys cried. She'd earned the title of aunt even though they were technically second cousins.

Laurel sat up on her bed, heartened by their enthusiasm.

"We're cannonballs." Andrew crouched and rolled across the carpet toward her.

His identical brother—Alexander, the twin with the cowlick at his crown—rolled on the other side of the bed.

"Look what I brought you and Baby—fresh fruit!" Cousin Sophie, mother of the minion twins, held up a small bunch of bananas and a large yellow apple. "Mackenzie at the general store got a shipment yesterday before the pass closed. Wow, she's a good salesperson. We barely got out of there without buying two more sleds. Did you call your parents? Or he who you refuse to name?"

That was Sophie, master of the conversational whip-around. The "he" in question was the father of Laurel's baby, a man whose identity she was keeping secret as long as possible.

Secrets made her head ache. Laurel rubbed her temples, remembering the night they'd met…

"Ash…" Wyatt Halford had believed he was on a date with Laurel's sister, Ashley. "I'm having a good time, but I have to admit. I'm surprised that you're so…so…" Wyatt had struggled for words and it had been endearing. His gaze lingered on Laurel's. His smile was completely natural. He hadn't glanced around the restaurant to locate the nearest camera or cell phone aimed his way. He'd been unlike any actor Laurel had been sent on a date with posing as Ashley.

Having grown up as a Monroe, Laurel wasn't impressed by beauty or wealth or celebrity. She didn't need what they had. Her job on these first dates was to discourage a second one. But Wyatt Halford…

"You're so…so down-to-earth," Wyatt had

said artlessly, flashing Laurel a smile that curled her toes. "Maybe it's because I hadn't realized you'd know the history of the action film genre." His claim to fame. "Or because I've never heard you laugh wholeheartedly. Or simply because you're wearing blue tonight."

"Teal," Laurel had whispered, won over. As kids, Mom had always put Ashley in pink and Laurel in a shade of blue or green.

On the night of her date with Wyatt, Laurel had argued with her mother about taking Ashley's place. She'd wanted to stay home and work on the pink evening gown pinned to the dressmaker's form in her bedroom. Eventually, Mom had won, as Laurel knew she would. In defiance, Laurel had worn a teal A-line dress, not black or Ashley's signature pink. And this man—this handsome, charming actor beloved by millions—had looked at Laurel and seen something other than the bright, shiny penny that was Ashley Monroe.

A simple dinner date had turned into a not-so-simple morning after, something Laurel had carefully neglected to mention to Ashley and her mother. And now nothing was simple.

"Earth to Laurel." Sophie snapped her fingers in front of Laurel's face.

"I'm going to tell them," Laurel reassured her cousin. It was a delicate matter. Wyatt still believed he'd slept with Ashley. How would he feel when he learned he hadn't? What would he do?

Sophie slid her red glasses up her slim nose and gave Laurel a look of disapproval, one that worked equally well on four-year-old boys and twenty-seven-year-old pregnant women.

Laurel squirmed. "I'll tell them after my doctor's appointment." Weather permitting. Her appointment was at least an hour's drive away in Ketchum. "With a medical all clear, I can go home and tell everyone in person." By then, she'd have her speech down.

Her head pounded. She wasn't looking forward to that discussion. Her father—who'd fired and evicted her in favor of inheriting millions—would worry that a man wasn't in the picture. Her mother—who considered Laurel her least successful child—would ask her *why* a man wasn't in the picture. Her brother Jonah would offer to pound the man who'd *once been* in the picture. Ashley would do some calculations and ask *if* Wyatt Halford *should be* in the picture. And then...

Everyone would realize that Laurel—the family member most likely to show up for someone else's crisis—was having a catastrophe of her own.

Her immediate family was in the entertainment industry. Dad ran Monroe Studios. Mom was a talent manager. Jonah, a script writer. Ashley, an actress. Laurel an on-set costume designer. Everything she did reflected back upon them. Impersonating a famous actress, sleeping with a famous actor and then having his baby was the kind of sensational news story Hollywood hungered for. It would overshadow every project, every business deal, every media interview her family was involved in from the moment the world found out about it. As for Laurel and her aspirations to be a red-carpet dress designer? Her revelation would bring rain on that parade.

"There's no shame in putting yourself first for once." Sophie was still riding the disapproval train, which was headed straight for Laurel. "Especially now."

Laurel refrained from mentioning that putting herself first was how she'd gotten into this mess.

The twins crashed into log walls on either side of Laurel's headboard and cried, "I beat you!" simultaneously. They flopped on Laurel's bed and continued to shout, "I won!" and "No, I won!" at each other.

"It was a tie!" Laurel drew them into her arms and gave them each a kiss. "A race too close to call."

"Behave, my adorable little heathens." Sophie set the fruit on Laurel's nightstand next to a large water bottle and an extralarge box of unsalted crackers. She pushed her glasses up her nose and gathered her brown hair from her shoulders as she peered at the stack of gossip magazines on the floor. "You need to get rid of these rags. That magazine article about Ashley making that pink dress." Sophie picked up steam. "That's just wrong. Don't let Ashley take credit for your talent."

"Let's not blow this out of proportion." Because the entire pink dress fiasco was Laurel's fault. She was going to have to clean up the dress mess, but it took a backseat to her pregnancy.

"Please. Ashley owes you a public retraction. When I think of all the times you saved her butt…" Sophie tugged down a new red-and-blue Nordic sweater she'd ordered online. She'd embraced mountain fashion in a way Laurel never would. "Listen to me. You've saved my behind a time or two. And there's a time or two more ahead, I'm sure. In fact, I'm waiting for you to get your sea legs back and help me explore the old buildings across the road before you leave." Which were rumored to be stuffed with junk and "treasure." Having been an art history major, Sophie considered

herself qualified to differentiate between gems and junk. "And we're going in just as soon as you get the all clear from the doctor."

"I can't wait." Actually, Laurel could. She didn't like the cold, cobwebs, bugs or *varmits*— as Roy over at the diner called the rats and raccoons he said inhabited the old trading post and mercantile. "You know, you won't find a da Vinci in there."

"A girl can dream." Grinning, Sophie pulled her boys off the bed. "Like you used to dream about weddings, wedding dresses, flower girls and ring bearers." She smoothed Alexander's cowlick.

"Weddings?" Alexander ducked from Sophie's touch. "Not that again."

"We had to hold ring pillows for hours at Uncle Todd's wedding." Andrew referenced their paternal uncle.

A wedding?

The semi returned to park on Laurel's chest, making her wheeze, making her head pound harder. Wyatt didn't want to marry her. As far as she knew, he hadn't even called Ashley or sent her flowers afterward.

Mitch would have sent flowers.

Laurel stifled a groan.

Mitch would have invited me to stay and then cooked me breakfast in the morning.

There was no stifling the groan this time.

"That's our cue to leave, Aunt Laurel," Sophie singsonged, herding the boys toward the door. "We'll return this afternoon for a book or a movie if you feel better."

Quiet descended. Laurel plucked at the seam of the handmade quilt beneath her, stared at the ceiling and contemplated her single status.

Not that I'm in love with Wyatt.

But no wedding bells meant single motherhood. Laurel sucked in a breath as she contemplated her future. Kids were a huge responsibility.

The semi took on additional cargo. It was increasingly difficult to breathe.

Women juggle careers and kids by themselves all the time.

That was what Sophie had done. She'd been the Monroe art collection curator until the reading of Grandpa Harlan's will. Of course, Sophie'd had permanent fatigue lines on her face that her cute glasses couldn't hide. And granted, she had twins, but that was little comfort. Twins and the Monroe family went together like mosquitos and still water.

Twins.

A second—*heavier*—semi parked on Laurel's chest.

What if I'm having twins?

Before Laurel had time to hyperventilate, there was a timid knock on her door.

"Laurel?" It was Gabby. "Can we come in?"

We? Gabby and Mitch? What happened to not encouraging the Monroes?

Laurel smoothed her hair, imagined Mitch's broad shoulders filling the doorway and invited them in.

Gabby entered first.

"Hope we're not intruding." An old woman appeared behind the preteen. She had a yellow knit cap on her short, coarse gray hair and wore three layers on top—a black turtleneck under a thin white sweater under a handmade, gray cable-knit cardigan that stretched to her knees. Her neon-red snow pants rustled with every step.

"Odette!" Laurel pushed herself up higher. She was surprised to see her, but unable to resist checking the empty hallway for one handsome, grumpy innkeeper.

"That's me." Odette blocked Laurel's sight line. The old woman was an artisan with yarn and cloth. She knit with precision. She quilted with small, even stitches, and paired fabric of different colors and prints better than some fashion designers Laurel could name. Before Laurel had known she was pregnant, she'd asked—more like begged—Odette to teach her how to quilt.

It wasn't that Laurel's sewing skills needed improvement. She was a master with needle and thread. It was that every fashion designer had a passion that drove them, an imprint that made their work immediately recognizable and gave it that special something. Laurel had yet to find her signature.

Clothes she'd made before flitted through her mind…

The sleek black pantsuit Laurel had made for her sister to wear to a charity luncheon.

The gauzy pink-and-white sundress Ashley had worn to a friend's beach wedding in the Bahamas.

A pink sheath. Rose-splattered pants. A brocade ball gown.

They'd all been nice. Well constructed. Well designed. But they lacked a je ne sais quoi— that special something that made one's heart light up with joy.

But when Laurel looked at Odette's quilts, she felt a stirring of something inside. A sense of excitement she hadn't felt before.

Odette dropped a tan canvas bag brimming with pastel yarn on the bed. "I've come for your first lesson."

"Can I stay and learn, too?" Gabby asked

in a small voice she seldom used. Few people cowed the spunky preteen.

Odette eyed Gabby severely as if the young girl had sassed her. "I tried to teach you once before." And by the tone of Odette's voice, Gabby had failed.

"I was just a baby then," Gabby said solemnly with that retainer lisp.

"That was last summer."

"Exactly." The girl nodded. "I was eleven."

"All right," Odette huffed, removing the knit cap from her coarse gray hair. It sprang free, revealing its true porcupine nature. "But this is your last chance."

Gabby thanked the old woman profusely.

Odette unloaded yarn balls and wooden knitting needles from her bag, tossing them on the bed the way children toss tissue from a gift box as they search for the prize at the bottom.

"Are there quilt quarters in that bag?" Laurel asked, thrilled to be receiving a lesson but confused by all the yarn.

Odette's shoulders stiffened. "You can't master quilting until you develop patience and precision."

Laurel had patience. For a week, she'd rested in her room all day waiting for her morning sickness to recede.

She opened her mouth to say something, but there was a warning in Gabby's eyes and the yarn balls on the bed and Odette's annoyance in the air, so Laurel swallowed back her curiosity and guessed, "You teach patience and precision through knitting?"

That earned her an approving nod. "Darn tootin'!" Odette finished unpacking the yarn and set her bag aside. Balls of bright purple, subtle teal, soft peach and oatmeal cream were scattered near Laurel's stocking feet. "We'll start with a scarf. Choose a color to begin."

Gabby nudged the pink aside and snatched up the vibrant purple.

Laurel picked a ball of teal, reminded that her career was at a standstill, of Ashley and Wyatt, and of truths that needed to be told. She had no interest in knitting, but if this was a test to move to quilting instruction and a mental space where she might discover an expressive passion for fashion, Laurel was determined to pass.

CHAPTER THREE

"HEY, MITCH." SHANE, Harlan's grandson, came down the inn's steps and headed Mitch's way a few minutes after the town council meeting ended. "I wanted to run something by you."

Of course, he did. Mitch drew a calming breath. The former hotel chain executive lay awake at night coming up with ideas to improve Second Chance.

Shane had a purposeful walk, a mind like a steel trap and a commanding presence. If Mitch were still a lawyer, he'd welcome a guy like Shane on his team.

Shane came to a stop in front of Mitch. "We've talked a lot about improving the income of Second Chance residents." He hit just the right note of camaraderie and business. "I want your opinion on the luxury development card."

The bottom fell out of Mitch's stomach.

Shane continued as if he hadn't just pulled the plug on Mitch's world, "My grandfather was sentimental. He never owned a cell phone or a computer. He conducted business with a handshake and a signature made by putting pen to paper."

Mitch nodded. All true.

"But he liked to make money." Shane tugged the ends of his too-thin jacket closer together. "And money can be made—good money—by building a luxury resort in Second Chance."

Mitch's heart fell toward his stomach.

"The last thing I want," Harlan had said to Mitch on more than one occasion, "is for this town to turn into a rich person's playground."

When Shane had first arrived in town over a month ago, he and Mitch hadn't hit it off. Shane didn't like how evasive Mitch was regarding Harlan's purchase of the town. Mitch didn't like how evasive Shane was regarding the family's plans toward the town. But recently, they'd managed to find neutral ground, mostly because Shane had admitted all twelve grandchildren had to agree about Second Chance's future and no one had mentioned anything about high-end development.

When Mitch didn't immediately answer, Shane asked, "What do you think my grandfather would've thought about a resort here?"

The snowflakes thickened. The wind gathered. Time might not have changed the town, but Shane Monroe might.

Mitch made a noncommittal noise and looked around the stretch of road that made up the heart of town.

Most businesses were located in historic structures dating back to the town's roots when it'd been established by one of Harlan Monroe's ancestors. The diner and general store had been competing saloons. The inn had been everything from a barracks to a brothel, although Mitch had argued the latter when Gabby put it in a paper for school. Other cabins and businesses about town had similar Old West histories.

During the town council meeting, Mitch had come up with an idea. Apply for historical significance. Could he convince a state board that the town's hundred-year-old log cabins were important enough to protect? Would that be enough to stop Shane from tearing them down and building his luxury resort?

"Mitch?"

"Well, Harlan…" *Shut up, Mitch.* "In my opinion, Harlan wouldn't…"

Shane's expression shuttered.

Shut up. Shut up. Shut up. Remember the nondisclosure agreement. The one he'd signed when Harlan purchased the Lodgepole Inn. And then there was the truce himself and

Shane. He had to be neutral and diplomatic. He had to—

"I hate the idea," Mitch blurted. "Who does it benefit? Not Mack." He pointed toward the general store, where Mack was creating a Valentine's Day display. "There's nothing high-end about what she sells. Or what Ivy serves. Or the accommodations I provide."

Shane drew in a breath as if preparing to speak, but Mitch wasn't done.

"Your grandfather didn't just care about the town. He cared about the people." A general statement, but one he hoped hit home. "About the community. Winter is our time to—"

"Objection, Counselor," Shane said, using his cousin's nickname for Mitch and holding up a gloveless hand. "Let me explain. Have you heard of the concept of due diligence?"

"I've heard of companies willing to take propositions off the table when they don't fit their philosophies. Fancy hotels and restaurants shouldn't be in Second Chance."

"I have eleven other owners to consider." Shane's words took on that high-and-mighty tone that grated on Mitch's ears. "If you think I can get a consensus without exploring all avenues, you're wrong. Now…" His voice hardened. "I asked you a question."

"In my opinion," Mitch said through gritted

teeth. "Your grandfather would fight luxury development to the bitter end."

Shane studied him for a moment before nodding, grinning wryly. "Agreed. I just needed to hear it from you."

"What?" With effort, Mitch pulled himself together. "Were you just yanking my chain?"

"Come on, Mitch." Shane laughed and turned toward the Bent Nickel. "You know the answer to that question."

He had been.

Mitch ran a hand over his face and then headed for the general store. He imagined the path to historical significance was paved with piles of paperwork, which would be easier to tackle later with a glass or two of wine, especially if Shane decided to pull his chain once more.

On his way back to the inn with a bottle of wine in hand, the wind picked up, rushing down the western mountain range on icy feet to dance around Mitch and any exposed skin it could find. It had been in the forties earlier, but the temperature was falling fast. More snow was coming.

"Please tell me that's a whiskey bottle you're carrying." Zeke Roosevelt sat in a wheelchair by the large stone fireplace in the inn's common room. His leg was in a splint and propped up. He wore a blue plaid shirt with pearly snaps and a pair of gray sweats with one leg cut off at the knee. His ever-present smile was worn around the edges.

The ginger-haired cowboy had been working at the Bucking Bull ranch north of town until he'd crashed his truck a few weeks ago, breaking his shinbone and sidelining him from the workforce for several months. Given the bunkhouse at the Bucking Bull had no kitchen and was separate from the main house, it would've been difficult for Zeke to recuperate on the ranch during the heart of winter. He'd checked in as a long-term guest, staying in one of the small downstairs guest rooms.

"It's wine." Mitch held the bottle so Zeke could see. "And I don't have to tell you what Noah said before he left about mixing pain meds with alcohol." That was a big no-no. Mitch crossed the foyer and went into the apartment he and Gabby shared behind the check-in desk.

Their living space was tight. A kitchen with a small table, a bathroom and two bedrooms. The common room served as their living room and had the inn's only television.

"I'm not taking the pain meds Doc gave me," Zeke called to him. "They give me bad dreams."

If what Zeke said was true, that explained the worn-out smile. His break had been nasty—bone through skin. It'd been set with plates and screws.

Ouch.

"Still not getting any wine." Mitch lifted the Crock-Pot lid and stirred the chili. Then he returned to the hotel desk and checked his email to see if anyone had answered the ad to replace Noah as Second Chance's doctor.

Not a single reply.

Mitch felt as tired as Zeke's smile. Could nothing go right today?

"Look, Dad." Gabby emerged from her room. Instead of toting her laptop, she held up a pair of wooden knitting needles and purple yarn with a couple inches of what Mitch assumed was a scarf. "Odette's teaching me and Laurel how to knit. I'm going to sit with her every day until we're done."

"That's nice of her." It was good for Odette to get out. The old woman routinely sewed all day, every day. "Are you going to work with Odette over at her cabin tomorrow?"

"No, Dad." Eye roll, eye roll, eye roll. "I'm going to be knitting with *Laurel* upstairs. Odette isn't coming back here until our scarves are finished."

"You're going to be knitting *with Laurel*…" Something inside Mitch sat up and blinked.

The fashionable Laurel was knitting? The two images didn't fit.

"Yes, *with Laurel*." Since Gabby's birthday over a week ago, which was when her braces had come off, she'd become touchy about the things Mitch said. She tossed her strawberry blond hair over her shoulder and waltzed past him into the front room, sitting on the couch near Zeke's wheelchair.

"Where's the love?" he murmured. Where had his precious little girl gone?

"Dad," Gabby said with the utmost teenage contempt. She glanced at Zeke from beneath lowered lashes as her cheeks turned a deep red. She had a crush on the cowboy.

Zeke was at least two decades older than she was, so anything romantic was thankfully ruled out.

"You can knit later." Mitch wasn't so old he'd forgotten the importance of a teenage crush, but he wasn't going to encourage this one. "We need to clean the rooms."

"Dad." Gabby's shoulders sank, and she frowned as if he'd suggested she clean the toilets with her toothbrush. "I'm busy."

"That you are." Mitch grabbed the basket of fresh linens on their kitchen table, an empty basket for dirty things, and a mop and a bucket filled with cleaning supplies from the nearby pantry. "You're busy cleaning rooms."

"Dad," Gabby grumbled, although she set her knitting aside and followed him to Zeke's small room and its full-size four-poster bed.

"You change the sheets and towels. I'll clean the floors and bathroom." He snapped on a pair of plastic cleaning gloves.

With the familiarity of practice, they went about their work and immediate worry over the fate of Second Chance faded.

The cowboy was neat, possibly because he was restricted to a wheelchair and bed. When Mitch no longer heard the sounds of Gabby changing linens, he stopped wiping down the counter and poked his head out the bathroom door.

His daughter was admiring Zeke's straw cowboy hat. And by admiring, Mitch meant she was lifting it from where it hung on a bed-post, looking like she intended to put it on her own head.

"Leave it," Mitch said, horrified. They'd had long conversations about a guest's right to privacy and here she was disrespecting that right.

"I'm done." There was mutiny in those two words, but Gabby put the hat back and smoothed the brown log-cabin quilt's corners. "What am I supposed to do?"

"How about talk to me?" *Like my little girl used to.* Mitch missed her chattering. He gathered the cleaning supplies. "Can you keep up with your homework *and* Odette's knitting lessons?"

"Dad," Gabby huffed, not that he blamed her. It was a silly question. "The only homework I haven't done is a history paper on the first governor of Idaho."

"A term paper?" The tension inside Mitch eased. That would require a big chunk of his daughter's time.

"We don't call them that." Gabby tucked the dirty linens into the empty basket, stacked it on top of the clean linens basket and carried both out, hurrying past Zeke without a word. She climbed the stairs with what looked like a drunken swagger. She'd learned long ago how to traverse the steps and the upstairs hallway like a ninja, avoiding squeaky floorboards.

Mitch's footsteps echoed unapologetically on the stairs.

Shane's room was next. The man's clothes hung in the small closet—expensive dress shirts, polo shirts and slacks. Slacks, not jeans. Mitch bet there was at least one tie in the man's suitcase.

Who brought business clothes to the mountains of Idaho in winter?

I did.

Mitch had kept five suits from his legal days. He even had some slacks—the same brand as Shane's—in a plastic bin at the back of his closet.

The difference is I don't wear them every day.

"Why don't you like Shane?" Gabby asked.

He reminds me of me, back when I was a lawyer with something to prove.

He's unpredictable and sets my teeth on edge.

Statements like that weren't something fathers said to their impressionable teenage daughters.

"I like Shane," he insisted instead. "We were just talking outside."

Gabby smirked.

"I like that he's neat," Mitch said, sounding almost as mutinous as Gabby had downstairs.

"I like that we changed his sheets yesterday," Gabby replied. They only changed the bed linens twice a week for long-term guests. Gabby sat down on the black, gray and white quilt, a modern kaleidoscope design. "Do you think I'm impatient?"

Mitch tried not to think about huffs and eye

rolls and changed the subject, switching to his helpful dad voice. "Are you going to need a trip to the library in Ketchum for this paper?" If so, as soon as the weather let up, they could spend a day away from Zeke and the Monroes. "We also haven't taken you shopping in a while. Are you growing again? Those jeans look short."

"My jeans are fine, Dad. And nobody goes to the library to research papers anymore. We use the internet." That earned him a huff *and* an eye roll. "What's wrong with you?"

I'm losing my little girl.

And if the Monroes disappointed Harlan and made it financially impossible to stay, who knew if he'd ever get her back. If they returned to Chicago, his ex-wife might take an interest in Gabby again, might drag her into the country-club scene, might try to put her on the beauty pageant circuit, might try to make her value bank account balances over self-worth.

"Nothing's wrong with me," Mitch insisted, swallowing back the what-ifs. "I'm trying to be nice and treat you to a bonus since we're having a good quarter. How about a trip to the bookstore?"

"You know I love the bookstore." Gabby swung her feet around on the bed so she could watch him finish in the bathroom.

"I know you love the bookstore," Mitch parroted back, heartened. He finished in the bathroom, gathered his supplies and led Gabby to the large corner room on the other end of the inn.

The wood floors creaked as he traversed the slanted hall.

"How much are we talking in terms of a bookstore spending limit?" Behind him, Gabby's footfalls were nearly silent. "One book? Two? Fifty dollars?"

While they negotiated, Mitch opened the door to the room occupied by Sophie Monroe and her two twin toddlers, who were still outside playing in the snow.

He and Gabby paused, letting the extent of the mess sink in.

The sheets and blankets were in a tangle on both beds. The pillows were piled in a corner as if someone had made them into a fort. Clothes and shoes were scattered everywhere. In the bathroom, all the towels were wet and sat in a mountainous pile.

Gabby slipped past him. "I may need a bonus just for cleaning this room."

She may be right.

They didn't waste more energy talking and went to work.

Beds made, bathroom and floors clean, wet

towels in the basket in the hallway, dry towels in their place, they moved to the final occupied room. Mitch always saved it for last.

"Come in," Laurel called before Mitch could knock, adding when he opened the door, "I heard you come down the hall." She didn't look up, didn't brush that red hair from her eyes. She sat on top of the sunflower quilt on the bed, bent over a pair of wooden knitting needles. She looped teal yarn around one needle, thought better of it and looped it the other way.

Mitch paused just inside the doorway, trying to reconcile the image of the stylish Laurel doing something as homey as knitting.

"Nice gloves." Laurel nodded toward Mitch's hands, sending the first salvo across his bow.

"Dad won't clean without them," Gabby said happily, earning her a frown from Mitch.

Laurel gave one of her distinctive laughs—*hardy-har-har*. As much as her clothes were sophisticated, her laugh was not.

He moved past his daughter into the bathroom, where he faced the shimmery pink evening gown.

"Pampering your skin is important." Laurel's voice sparkled with amusement.

Mitch bet if he glanced at Laurel, her blue eyes would be sparkling, too.

"Does your father also like manicures?" Laurel teased.

"He does not," Mitch said firmly, manhood imperiled. He moved the mop about quickly, being careful not to touch the dress.

"The sheets are fine," Laurel said to Gabby. "Like I said this morning, I didn't get sick in them or in the bathroom. Woo-hoo."

Mitch had to work hard not to smile.

Laurel's most admirable trait was her honesty. Mitch valued honesty in all its forms. Now that she was feeling better, her optimism continuously tried to sneak past the defenses he put up. So what if he admired her forthrightness? Didn't mean he lingered when he cleaned her room.

The mattress rasped as if Gabby had sat on the bed. "I can't believe you didn't know you were pregnant."

Mitch frowned and swung the mop with more velocity. The last thing he wanted was for Gabby to idolize Laurel, fashionista and soon-to-be single mom.

"Sometimes the truth sneaks up on you," Laurel said.

The mop handle tangled in the skirt of the pink dress. Frustration loosened Mitch's filter.

"I've been meaning to ask about this dress of yours. Does it need to hang here all the time? Are you getting ready to go to prom?"

"That dress wasn't made to hang, forgotten in a closet." There was starch to Laurel's words as if she'd gotten her back up.

Good. He had yet to see her riled. Witnessing a poor-little-rich-girl tantrum would take the shine off her for both Mitch and Gabby.

Gabby poked her head into the bathroom. "That dress is so pretty."

"And it's been hanging in here since she arrived." Mitch didn't try to hide his disapproval. Maybe disapproval was the way to squelch the attraction he felt toward this particular Monroe.

"I hate to tell you, Mitch, but your closet rod is shamefully low. I had to convert the bathroom to specialty dress storage." Laurel's tone was more suited for a put-down in judge's chambers than a room at the Lodgepole Inn. "If I hung that dress in the closet, the small train would brush the floor. Silk is a delicate thing—a delicate, *edible* thing—especially to Mothra."

Mitch choked on a snort of laughter. He hadn't expected a *Godzilla* movie reference.

"What's a Mothra?" Gabby swung on the door frame, smiling broadly, flashing her retainer wire and those straight teeth he'd paid a small fortune to fix.

"Mothra is a giant moth that starred in some B movies. The point is, moths plant larvae on clothes so their young have something to eat when they hatch. And moths love natural fibers like silk and wool."

"This I did not know." Gabby beamed. Deep down she was a nerd. "Did you wear this dress somewhere?"

"Um… I made the dress." Her voice lost its sparkle. "There's a picture of it in one of those magazines stacked on the other side of the bed. The one with the sexiest man alive on the cover."

"Why did you bring the dress here?" Gabby ran around to look through the magazines.

Mitch hurried to finish cleaning. He wanted to discourage Gabby's interest in less educational things, like video games and gossip magazines.

"I brought the dress here because…" Laurel paused. "What do you want to be when you grow up, Gabby?"

"Well…" The mattress springs creaked as his daughter sat on the bed once more. "I think being a lawyer would be cool because I could help people get justice."

Mitch's chest swelled with pride, even as he

made a mental note: *talk to Gabby about the pros and cons of the legal profession.*

"And then I have this rock collection and I like to look up why they all look different, so geology is in the running."

"Really?" Mitch froze midwipe of the toilet bowl. He'd had no idea she was interested in rocks.

Still out of sight, his daughter cleared her throat. "And then there's singing—"

Blindsided, Mitch blurted, "*Singing?* You never sing around the house."

"Dad," Gabby chastised. "Don't eavesdrop."

He dropped the cleaning brush into the bucket and came to lean a shoulder against the bathroom door frame. "It's impossible *not* to hear your conversation when I'm scrubbing the toilet."

"Pretend, Dad." Gabby had a stack of gossip magazines in her lap and a cynical shine in her eyes. "Pretend."

Laurel gave him a sympathetic look.

Mitch didn't want Laurel's sympathy. He wanted his little girl back. "Gabby, why would you want to be a shallow rock star?"

"As opposed to a shallow seamstress," Laurel murmured, referencing herself, he supposed. "Or a shallow innkeeper."

And now him.

"Whatever profession she follows," Mitch said, reaching for one of his oft-spoken refrains, "she'll still be the same person to me."

"Dad. Who said anything about rock? I listen to country." Gabby marched toward the door, magazines under her arm. "You are so out of touch."

Mitch groaned as Gabby ran away. The inn groaned as Gabby ran away, her feet pounding on the floor until she slammed a door downstairs. Laurel didn't groan. She studied Mitch.

Alone, Mitch and Laurel stared at each other.

Alone *together*, his heart began to pound.

CHAPTER FOUR

"GABBY'S ONE SHARP COOKIE." The beginnings of a smile teased the corner of Laurel's wide mouth.

Her kissable mouth.

She picked up one of three teal balls of yarn on the bed and tossed it from one hand to the other. "She knew you didn't approve of her reading my gossip magazines and she absconded with several copies."

Holy smokes. She had. Mitch had been too distracted by Laurel to pick up on that.

"Welcome to Gabby's teenage rebellion." Laurel scooted away from the headboard and faced him squarely, crossing her legs at the ankles, her knitting discarded. "We all go through it."

"You're saying I'll survive." Would he also survive the Monroes being in Second Chance?

Laurel nodded. "You know Gabby's not serious about any of those occupations." Laurel placed a pillow in her lap and rested her elbows on it, as casual with Mitch as if he'd been one of her best girlfriends. "She isn't going to hunt for rocks or take off one night to Nashville. She's going to fly rockets to Mars or find a cure for cancer."

The scary part was, Mitch agreed with his guest. His daughter had a curious streak. Point her in the right direction, and she'd accomplish anything she set her mind to. But she was also a gregarious child, easily distracted by the opportunity to be with people of any age.

And Laurel was the squirrel who was currently distracting Gabby. "Did you ask Odette to teach you how to knit?"

"In a roundabout way." She plumped the pillow, unable to sit still.

"You're bored," he accused.

"Yes. I'm counting down the hours to my doctor's appointment." Laurel leaned forward, gaze focused on his face, clearly intrigued. "You know, when I was battling morning sickness you talked to me differently."

Frustration clawed its way up his neck, given a leg up by a little bit of shame. "Let's be honest…" *Not completely honest.* He wasn't going to tell her he wanted to lean forward and kiss her sometimes. "I realize my daughter is going to leave Second Chance one day." Hopefully, not at the end of this calendar year when Harlan's protection ended. "But I'd like her to be happy and confident with who she is and how she dresses. When she looks at those magazines, she's going to be comparing herself to color-corrected, touched-up photos and begin to think she's lacking."

"You don't know that." But Laurel frowned.

"I do. My ex-wife was never happy in her own body." At the end of their marriage, she'd had a line of credit with a plastic surgeon as well as a personal shopper, aesthetician and physical trainer. He'd looked at Shannon but had been unable to see the woman he'd fallen in love with in law school. And she'd been unable to see the man disillusioned with the law and the trappings of wealth.

Mitch stripped off his gloves, pulling the cuffs around his palms and fingers so he could reuse them another day. He gathered the cleaning supplies, along with the basket of clean linens Gabby had left near the door.

"Counselor?"

Reluctantly, Mitch turned.

Her gaze was direct. Her eyes the soft blue of the paper stapled behind legal briefs. She had a little bit of makeup on, barely anything, really. She wore leggings and a tunic that covered everything appropriately. There was nothing come-hither about her appearance or the way she looked at him. Yet there was something about this woman that reached around logic and reality, that shook him to his core.

Attraction, his brain whispered, leading into thoughts of kisses.

Annoyance, he corrected stubbornly. She was the reason Shane was staying.

"Do you want some advice about teenage girls?" Laurel asked.

Mother of Pearl, no. "Do I have a choice?"

"Of course." He didn't trust her smile. "I can give you my thoughts today when it's just you and me. Or we can talk tomorrow when you clean. With Gabby."

Laurel would have made an excellent lawyer. She knew exactly how to box a person in.

"Some choice." He mentally girded himself. "Hit me with it, then."

"Go with the flow." Her voice lowered, softened, became an echo of her famous sister's. "What interests a newly minted preteen today probably won't interest her tomorrow."

"She's got a crush on Zeke," Mitch blurted.

"The ginger-haired cowboy downstairs?" Laurel went back to sparkling. "Two redheads. They'd make beautiful babies."

Mitch gave Laurel a hard stare. "Gabby's just a little girl."

Her sparkle dimmed. "That was a joke, Counselor."

"One that hit too close to home, Miss Laurel." He felt like rolling his eyes. Unfortunately, he didn't feel like leaving. He just stood there, juggling baskets and trying not to stare at her. The only thing he succeeded at was juggling baskets.

"I apologize for the redheaded baby remark. It was out of line." There she went again, being admirably honest. "You have a crush on her, don't you?"

"Who?" His eyes felt buggy.

"My sister." Gone was her wide, friendly smile. In its place was a small, rueful thing. "I've caught you looking at me every once in a while. You must be thinking of Ashley. My sister has a great presence on-screen and off. Guys fall for her all the time."

"I can assure you I don't have a thing for a movie star." He had a thing for *Laurel*. Made no sense on paper. Made no sense when he lay awake at night. Made no sense, period.

Laurel might have less outright charisma than her famous twin. But she glowed when something amused her. And that glow ignited something in his chest. Something he hadn't felt in a long time. Something he couldn't ignore.

But something he could refuse to act on.

"Since you'll be leaving town soon—" he refused to give up hope "—I'd appreciate it if you'd avoid putting ideas in my daughter's head," Mitch said as unemotionally as he was able to. "If you're bored, you should try that TV series with Wyatt Halford. I believe it's streaming online."

Laurel's smile stiffened.

SHANE GUNNED THE snowmobile he regularly borrowed from Mitch up the mountainside between two reflector poles that marked a driveway.

His due diligence included finding out whatever he could about Grandpa Harlan from residents who'd sold to him. He knew about the nondisclosure agreements, but he couldn't just sit around in the inn doing nothing. So he'd volunteered to deliver groceries. And it worked. Everyone he talked to let something slip.

Ahead, a figure stood on the narrow porch of a one-story log cabin, holding a shotgun. The weapon wasn't trained on Shane, but it was held in a way that it could be raised at any moment if need be.

Shane shivered from a combination of cold and the sudden prickle of adrenaline. The snowmobile surged forward—had he done that? He overcorrected and slid diagonally to a hard stop against a wide snowbank.

The figure on the porch laughed. "Are you sure you should be out on that thing unsupervised?"

"Are you Phyllis?" Shane eyed the shotgun. It was old. The stock was cracked. Chances were it was not be loaded, but he wasn't willing to bet on it.

"Folks around here call me Flip." She changed the grip on her gun. She didn't wear gloves. Her fingers were red from the cold. She didn't seem to care.

Loaded. Definitely loaded.

"Mack sent me. I've got your groceries."

Flip chuckled. There were deep age lines in her face and forehead. "Used to be a delivery boy was just that—a *boy*."

"I'm helping out." Mack ran the store and the garage. She had Zeke's truck on a lift in her service bay and had been grateful when Shane offered a few weeks ago to be her delivery boy. It allowed her time on Zeke's vehicle and Shane a chance to meet residents who didn't live in the heart of town.

Flip moved toward the door. "You can help me out by bringing those groceries inside."

Shane got off the snowmobile and opened

the storage beneath the seat. "Potatoes. Celery. Canned carrots. Peppers and onions. I'd say you're making stew."

"Venison stew." Flip opened the door. "You'd best get inside before you freeze to death. You Monroe boys never did have a lick of common sense."

"You've known other Monroes?"

"Please. Don't patronize me." She and her shotgun disappeared inside.

"Right." Shane carried the bag with her purchases.

Her cabin was warm and had paintings everywhere—hanging on the flat log walls, stacked on the floor and furniture. It smelled vaguely of turpentine.

He brought the groceries into the narrow galley kitchen, inching past an easel with a half-finished painting of a moonlit rose garden.

"Here." Flip pressed a coffee mug into his hands. "Coffee with whiskey. That should warm you up." She had limp grayish-brown hair, but sharp gray eyes that looked him up and down. "What are you? A poor Monroe relation? You can't buy proper winter wear?"

"Something like that." Shane had found early on that wearing his Nevada street clothes—slacks, polo shirt, serviceable jacket—got him entry into homes in Second Chance. And if the residents thought he was less of a threat because he didn't have the common sense to at least buy snow boots, so be it. He'd suffer the twenty minutes or so it took to ride the snowmobile from the general store to a house, and then back again.

"I didn't order wine." Flip held up the bottle of white wine Shane had bought. "Or cheese and crackers."

"It's your bonus for letting me in the door." Not everyone did. Shane removed his jacket and wandered the crowded, small living room, looking behind her paintings for photographs, trying not to think about how his toes stung from cold.

"You want to talk about Harlan." Flip opened a can of kidney beans with a hand-crank opener. "That's why you're here, isn't it? My friend Dori said you were heartbroken over your grandfather and looking for connections to the past."

Shane sipped his coffee. She'd been liberal with the whiskey, but it did the trick, sending warmth radiating from his chest. He took several more sips before answering, "Grandpa Harlan was an all-or-nothing type of guy. When it came to his childhood, it was more like nothing."

He'd taken all twelve grandchildren twice a year—camping, fishing, to the four corners of the United States. And when Shane was in high school, he'd taken him in. But he'd said nothing about his roots or where he'd grown up. And now Shane was sorry he'd never asked.

"Men of Harlan's generation didn't like to talk about their mamas or their upbringings." Flip moved on to open another can. She wore baggy blue jeans and a beige sweatshirt stained with different paint colors. "It wasn't considered manly."

"Did you know him? Before he bought this place?"

"Yes." Flip turned teary eyes his way. Not that she was broken up about Grandpa Harlan. She'd been chopping onions.

Shane set his coffee on the kitchen table, grabbed a tissue from a box on the windowsill and handed it to her. He washed his hands and relieved Flip of the knife. "I'll dice your onions. You heat up the skillet."

"First, grocery delivery and now kitchen service." Flip tsk-tsked. "Am I supposed to tip you?"

"Nope." He had a rhythm with the knife and didn't look up. If she expected him to grill her, she was going to be disappointed. He'd found more success letting people guide the conversation.

"You have culinary skill." Flip moved about the kitchen efficiently, adding oil to a deep frying pan and turning on the burner beneath it.

"My brother Camden is a chef." But Shane was competitive enough to have learned a thing or two himself. A skill that impressed the ladies. He switched to mincing garlic.

They cooked together, making small talk about the weather and the residents Shane had met so far. Shane opened the wine and poured them each a glass, biding his time. When the meat and smaller vegetables were browned, Flip put everything in a pressure cooker and stared at Shane.

"I sold to your grandfather because I don't have children." Her words lacked their initial sharpness. "My husband and I…" She gave herself a little shake. "I have no regrets. And you…"

"I have regrets," Shane admitted. "I wish I would have gotten to know my grandfather better. I mean, I knew him. I just…didn't know about Second Chance."

Flip nodded. "I was going to say you should talk to Gertie Clark over at the Bucking Bull."

She stared into her wineglass. "She knew your grandfather better than most."

"You think she'll talk to me?" More than the other residents had?

"She used to be quite a talker." Flip took a generous sip of wine. "And the Clarks didn't sell to Harlan."

Meaning they wouldn't have signed a non-disclosure agreement. Shane fidgeted in his seat, eager to take action. He'd seen the turn to the ranch and its closed cattle gate.

"You should talk to Gertie," Flip said again, sounding more like her prickly self. "But you'll have to get Franny Clark's permission first. Which you won't." She gave a little cackle.

"Why not?"

"Because..." Flip laughed some more, ruefully this time, never finishing her thought.

CHAPTER FIVE

Try that series with Wyatt Halford. Pushing her hands through her hair, Laurel's gaze swung around the room, seeking a target for her muttering. *Avoid giving my daughter any ideas.*

Like she had fashion cooties or something.

"Are you talking to yourself?" Sophie pushed Laurel's door open. "You need to get out of this room."

"I'm completely balanced and Zen-like." That sounded false, even to her own ears. Oh, Mitch had gotten to her, all right. She'd been unable to think of anything else since he'd left over an hour ago. "Do I look like a woman who's a bad influence on little girls?"

"You look like a woman who could use a hairbrush." Sophie darted into the bathroom to get one. "Is this about Gabby? She's the only little girl I know. You aren't a bad influence on anyone. In fact, you always try to put the well-being of others first."

"Almost always," Laurel said, inwardly cringing, thinking of the pink dress and how her pregnancy was going to upset the Hollywood Monroe applecart. She sighed, gaze landing on the hairbrush. "Don't tell me. Let me guess. I look like Bigfoot after a blustery day."

"Try Bigfoot with a bird's nest." Sophie approached, hairbrush raised.

"I can fix my own hair *and* mind my own business."

"And here I thought my boys were cranky." Sophie ignored Laurel's wishes and wielded the brush. "I put them down for a nap without Aunt Laurel movie time. They were so wound up they wouldn't listen to me outside. They nearly went sledding across the frozen Salmon River! They could've fallen through the ice. They could've drowned."

"But they lived to sled another day," Laurel said. *"Ow!"*

Sophie attacked a tangle with no care or finesse.

"Oh, good. You're both in here." Gabby appeared in the doorway, looking uncharacteristically shy. "Sophie, I have those extra towels you wanted."

"Put them on Laurel's bed for now." Sophie tossed the hairbrush on the quilt and pulled Laurel's hair to the base of her neck. "I'll take the towels to my room when I'm done braiding Laurel's hair."

"Okay." Gabby set the towels down slowly, revealing a gossip magazine underneath the stack. "Laurel, I love the picture of your sister in that pink dress." The teen turned the page so Laurel and Sophie could see the splashy headline: Is There Nothing Ashley Monroe Can't Do?

Ashley! Ashley! Who designed your dress?

In a blink, Laurel was back in the bright strobe lights of the red carpet. Another blink and she faced her twin, taking in Ashley's expression of shock and her mother's one of anger.

"Trash that." Sophie grabbed the magazine and tossed it in the hallway. "Sorry, Gabby, but we're mad at Ashley because Laurel made that dress and Ashley… Well, Laurel's family isn't appreciative of the sacrifices Laurel makes for them."

"Oh." Gabby shrank back in the doorway.

"We're not mad at you, honey." Laurel was quick to reassure her. "And only Sophie is mad at Ashley. The pink fiasco is my fault."

"Oh, stop being a martyr." Sophie's fingers stilled in Laurel's hair. She bent to push her glasses up her nose with her forearm. "I'm going to take a picture of you in that dress, one that shows you here in Idaho, because you'll need it for ammunition someday, I bet."

"I'm not wearing that dress again." Laurel shook her head. "Good luck finding a model."

"Well, I can't just take a picture of it on the hanger." Sophie finished braiding, took a rubber band from the handle of Laurel's hairbrush to hold her work in place and then went into the bathroom and returned with the evening gown. She held the dress up to her shoulders.

Over one thousand rhinestones were sewn in lines originating at the hemline. They glittered in the muted sunshine streaming through the window, making the dress look three shades lighter pink than it really was.

Laurel's throat threatened to close. Her first successful evening gown. Her masterpiece. She'd probably never make anything like it again. Because no one in Hollywood would hire her to create a dress or style a look for them after her pregnancy news broke.

"My hips are too wide for this," Sophie admitted. "They never went back where they should have after I had the boys."

Gabby covered her giggle with one hand.

Sophie held the dress at arm's length, turning it to and fro to make the dress sparkle. "I guess Shane isn't an option as a model. His hips are too wide, as well."

"And his ego is too big." Laurel laughed. "Even if he did fit, *which he never could*—" his shoulders were also too broad "—he'd never agree to be photographed in it."

"I'll do it." Gabby's words were as tentative as her touch on a rhinestone.

Sophie and Laurel exchanged glances. Laurel shook her head.

"Oh, honey." Sophie brushed Gabby's soft red hair from her shoulders. "You're too young for this dress." Sophie was right. It had a severely plunging neckline and the back was nearly nonexistent.

"But I can look older." Gabby wasn't easily deterred. "With my hair up and some makeup."

"Your father wouldn't approve." This, Laurel knew, was a fact.

Mitch didn't approve of Laurel's silver leggings, much less a silver-accented evening gown.

"Please. I don't have a chance like this… ever." There was longing in her eyes, along with a bit of desperation. "Dad will never see the picture."

Sophie held the dress up to Gabby's shoulders. "It's great with her coloring."

Gabby's smile was radiant.

"This is wrong," Laurel said, trying to be responsible and keep the peace with both Mitch and Ashley. But the dress was one of the few things she'd created with pure joy. And joy was written all over Gabby's face.

"Laurel, you deserve credit for this beautiful creation." Sophie carried the gown back into the bathroom. "This will be a little message to remind Ashley who made this luscious thing. Okay, Gabby, you're on. It'll be our little secret."

"I can't believe I'm going to wear Ashley Monroe's famous dress." The girl ran eagerly into the bathroom.

Sophie took Gabby by the arms. "Honey, read my lips. It's Laurel's dress."

"I can't believe I'm going to wear *Laurel's* famous dress." Gabby squealed, but not at full volume. She knew this wasn't a Dad-approved activity.

"I think I'm going to be sick," Laurel said, only half meaning it. Not that Sophie or Gabby were paying attention to her anyway. "Mitch is going to be furious. Look at her, Sophie. She's just a kid."

Sophie was undeterred. "If we do her makeup and hair…"

"Don't," Laurel said in a stern voice. Not that her tone mattered. She was ignored.

"I know how to do that." Gabby reassured Sophie. "Can I borrow your makeup, Laurel?"

"Yes," Sophie said at the same time Laurel said, "No."

"Give me a few minutes and I'll look college age," Gabby said as if the older women would find this admirable. "I've been practicing. I have a cute little nose, but when I wear eyeliner my mom said it looks elegant."

"Indeed." Sophie slipped Laurel a sly glance. "Gabby is just what we need."

"I've got a bad feeling about this, ladies." Laurel tried to sound like a disgruntled traffic cop.

"Relax." Sophie looked as excited as Gabby. "It'll just be us girls and a dress."

Gabby nodded enthusiastically.

The girl's love for the gown ate away at Laurel's objections. It was a fabulous dress, meant to be seen. Laurel sighed, beginning to bend. "And you won't get ideas in your head?"

"I won't disappoint you," Gabby said, more to Sophie than Laurel. She knew who to work in the room.

The bathroom door closed.

Sophie grabbed the pile of clean towels. "I'm going to get my phone. I'll be right back."

The bedroom door closed, leaving Laurel

alone with a memory involving another dress, another argument about who should wear it.

"That's my dress!" Five-year-old Laurel had tugged on the skirt of the blue ball gown Ashley wore.

Not only had it been a birthday gift from the Monroe grandparents, but this dress was also Cinderella's ball gown. Princess seams. A tulle petticoat. A sheer overlay with sparkly swirls that looked like they'd been made with the swoop of a magic wand.

And the dress was blue, not pink. By its nonpinkness alone, the dress was Laurel's.

"I'm sorry, sissy. Mom said I could wear it." Pink-loving Ashley had smiled the delicate smile grown-ups seemed enamored with and tried to turn away. "Don't I look pretty?"

"Listen to me!" Laurel wailed, crushing the stiff fabric in her fingers. *"That's! My! Dress!"*

"Laurel, your sister needs it more than you do." Mom had intervened, working to pry Laurel's fingers from the dress. "Ashley's auditioning for a princess role tomorrow. Princesses always have many dresses to wear. And if she gets the part, she'll need you and your big heart more than ever."

Laurel didn't mind Ashley getting her heart; it was her dress she didn't want to share.

But the tulle had slipped through Laurel's fingers, seam stitches snapping.

Freed, Ashley had turned so fast she'd nearly fallen.

Laurel had caught her, the same way she always did.

"I love you, sissy," Ashley said, wrapping her arms around her.

And Laurel had hugged her back, the same way she always did.

Laurel's hands clenched in her lap.

They might have been identical, but Ashley's sweet voice sounded like joyful bells, and she danced with the grace of a ballerina. She'd been born for the cradling beam of celebrity.

And Laurel had been born to stand in her shadow and help her get there.

MITCH LOOKED UP from researching historic landmark qualifications in Idaho and realized the inn was too quiet. "Gabby?"

It wasn't like his teenage daughter to be silent. She hummed while she cleaned. She pounded the keyboard ferociously when she did her homework. She banged pots and pans when she was in the kitchen.

The door separating their apartment from the inn's common room was slightly ajar. He got up from the kitchen table and pushed it open wider. "Gabby?"

In his wheelchair in front of the muted television, Zeke roused from a doze. "I'm fine." He blinked. Frowned. Cleared his throat. "Were you asking?"

"No, but I'm glad to hear you're doing okay."

The inn's front door opened.

Mitch took a couple steps that way. "Where have you…"

Gabby didn't come into the foyer. It was Shane, smiling like a prosecutor after a hard-won conviction.

"Where have you been?" That line had been meant for Gabby.

Shane's smile curled into a mischievous grin. He shrugged out of his lightweight jacket and rubbed his arms. "Is that chili I smell?"

Mitch nodded.

"It must be Tuesday." Shane chuckled.

Zeke laughed, too. "It is, indeed."

"What's so funny?" Mitch didn't appreciate missing out on the joke.

"All anyone has to do is check in with you or Ivy to know what day of the week it is." Shane climbed the stairs. "In your case, Monday, lasagna. Tuesday, chili. Wednesday, spaghetti."

"Thursday, leftovers." Zeke hadn't smiled so naturally since he'd checked in. "Friday, fish. Saturday, tuna casserole."

"Sunday, pot roast," Shane called.

"Sue me," Mitch taunted. "I'm organized. I run an inn." And cooking had never been a chore he was fond of.

"The inn practically runs itself," Shane said before shutting his door at the top of the stairs.

Mitch turned on Zeke. "Are you complaining about my cooking?" Food was part of the recuperating cowboy's room and board. "Because I'm sure Ivy would love to feed you."

Ivy, who heated up frozen french fries and chicken nuggets and promoted them as the Friday Night Special. At least Mitch cooked from scratch.

"No, sir." But a smile hovered at the corner of Zeke's mouth.

Animated voices and laughter drifted to Mitch from one of the guest rooms upstairs. Belatedly, he remembered he'd sent Gabby to deliver extra towels to Sophie's room. His daughter had probably got to talking and lost track of time, which would've been fine with any guests other than Zeke or the Monroes.

Needing to retrieve her, he climbed the stairs.

"This dress is famous." Gabby's voice drifted down the hallway. "This is so cool."

Mitch gritted his teeth and quickened his steps.

The door to Laurel's room was open, a magazine crumpled on the hall floor across from it. Her back to Mitch, Laurel stepped halfway into the dimly lit hallway. Her hair was piled high and she wore the pink evening gown that sparkled as if it'd been sprinkled with fairy dust. Laurel pivoted, still half-hidden by the wall, and disappeared back inside her room.

"Go slower," Sophie said. "Exaggerate your movements. I need the perfect shot."

Laurel stepped fully into the hallway, one hand on her hip, moving with the grace and confident swagger of a model. Posing as if ready for a photo op on the red carpet.

Mitch's heart dropped to his toes.

That wasn't Laurel! That wasn't even a woman!

It was Gabby, his strawberry blonde, naive, twelve-year-old daughter!

Makeup. Lipstick. Hair piled high. High heels. And a dress that plunged in front *and* in back.

Where was his Barbie-obsessed daughter? The one with the pigtails and braces? He couldn't see her.

Mitch walked down the hall, seemingly in slow motion. But his mind… His mind was in overdrive.

"Gabby." Her name erupted from Mitch on a note of anger.

"Dad?" Gabby barely looked at him before she leaped back into the room, slamming the door behind her.

Whispered exchanges were made. Another door slammed.

Mitch reached Laurel's room and pounded on the five-paneled wooden door so hard it groaned. The inn had been groaning a lot lately. Mitch groaned. He'd been groaning a lot lately, too.

"Come in," Laurel said warmly.

Sophie sat on the bed next to her. "Hey, Mitch."

Gabby was nowhere to be seen, but the bathroom door was closed, and something scurried in there like a trapped mouse.

"Was that my daughter?" Mitch had perfected the art of intimidation in Chicago courtrooms. A hard stare. A firm mouth. A low, accusatory question. Normally, that elicited a desired response—a blurted apology, a stuttered statement of truth.

Sophie didn't crack. "She was curious about

Laurel's dress. She looked beautiful, didn't she?"

Laurel slapped a hand over her eyes. "I told them this was a bad idea."

"You're in contempt." He went all angry judge on her, shaking his finger, lifting his voice. "Don't tell me you had no part in this."

"Dad!" Gabby called, voice brimming with teenage annoyance. "Go downstairs. I'll be there in a minute."

"I'll wait." Mitch crossed his arms over his chest and glowered at Laurel.

Sophie cleared her throat. "I feel I should mention Laurel warned us several times to stop." She gave a little half shrug. "But Gabby and I were caught up in the moment and... just...couldn't."

"I'm sorry," Laurel said, apparently the only female in the vicinity who felt remorseful.

"You knew I wouldn't approve." Mitch turned his gaze toward the window and a blanket of falling snow, searching for calm.

The last thing he wanted was for Gabby to turn out like her mother—fashion obsessed and money hungry—or his father.

He wanted to kick the Monroes out of the inn. But they owned it. It was beginning to feel like they owned him.

Sophie cleared her throat, breaking into

Mitch's thoughts. "Gabby likes to wear dresses, Mitch. And she looks beautiful in them."

"She doesn't need dresses in Second Chance!" This was hiking boots and blue jeans territory. Fishing waders and floppy hat country. They ran an inn made of round logs with wood floors that squeaked, even when covered in durable carpet. "This dress needs to go!"

"Dad." Gabby still hadn't emerged.

"I'm sorry." Laurel stood and placed a hand on Mitch's arm, lightly, gently. Her soothing tone brushed across his anger. "Let me explain."

The need to accept apologies and explanations was strong. Laurel would make promises. She'd reassure him this was a onetime occurrence.

But her red hair, blue eyes and fashion sense were reminiscent of his ex-wife; and promises, like laws, could be broken. His father was proof of that.

He turned away from Laurel. "I'll wait in the hall."

"Dad. You're embarrassing me." Gabby darted past Mitch a few minutes later, feet landing on every squeaky floorboard as she fled downstairs.

"Hey, we need to talk about what went on here." Mitch followed, lengthening his stride to catch up.

But Gabby was ahead. She reached the ground floor and didn't stop running, racing into their apartment and slamming her bedroom door.

"Problem?" Zeke asked, muting the television above the fireplace.

Mitch ignored him and continued into their private quarters, closing the door behind him. Gabby hadn't locked herself in her room. She'd shut herself in the bathroom.

"Gabby, open up." Mitch pounded on the door.

"Leave me alone!" A muffled protest, possibly accented with tears.

Mitch's heart broke in two. "Come on, honey. We need to talk. You can't put this off. I'm not going anywhere."

Her feet shuffled on the linoleum and then she opened the door. *"Dad."*

He didn't think she'd called him Dad as much her entire life as she had in the past few weeks. More than anything Mitch wanted to gather his little girl into his arms, tell her he loved her and know that she'd never change from the sweet darling baby with the toothless grin in the framed photo hanging in the hallway.

But Gabby had her arms locked over her chest and her guilty gaze nailed to the floor. She and that attitude weren't budging.

The hug, the reassurance, it would have to wait for a later date. Hopefully, not years from today. For now, he had to be the father who had the hard conversations. "Gabby, I can't have you dressing up like you're twenty-two when you're twelve."

"It's just a dress." Her face was bright red. All trace of cosmetics gone. "I don't see what the problem is. You had no problem with me playing dress up at Aunt Evelyn's house when I was seven."

"The problem is you're twelve years old." Mitch flailed about for an argument to justify his position. "We only just bought you your first bra last summer and now you want to wear a dress without need of one?"

"*Dad*. Lower your voice! Everyone in the inn probably heard that." Gabby's cheeks flamed red.

Mitch imagined his did the same. They felt hot enough to cook bacon. Of all the arguments he could have made…

"I can't believe we're having this conversation. It was just a dress."

"It wasn't *just* a dress. There was makeup and there was—" his hands circled his head "—hairstyling going on."

There was a knock on the apartment door.

"Excuse me," a feminine voice carried to them.

It was Laurel.

He flung open the door, frowning for all he was worth, ready to tell Laurel to check out, to get out.

"Hey there." Laurel held a small smartphone in a sparkly pink case toward him. "Gabby left her cell phone in my room."

Mitch rejected her offering. "Gabby doesn't have a smartphone."

"Dad." Proving him wrong, Gabby snatched the device.

Mitch felt cold, icy even. He was the crackled frost on the windowpane. The loose, snowy powder being blown off the mountain. He let Gabby use his account to order things she needed online. But he'd never seen a receipt for a cell phone. "Where did you get that?"

Her little chin shot up. "Mom gave it to me for my birthday."

The attitude. The silences. The changes in her personality. They hadn't come from her braces being removed or her envy of Laurel's fashionable wardrobe.

"Please, give it to me." Mitch held out his palm.

"Dad." Gabby clutched the phone over her heart.

Mitch then closed the door on Laurel with the hand that should have held a cell phone. "Is that why you wouldn't let me see your gift when it came?"

She'd unwrapped it in her room. He'd been trying to respect her privacy. And all this time his ex-wife had been going behind his back and encouraging his little girl to lie to him.

He'd felt cold before, but he was boiling now.

"Call your mother." Mitch didn't recognize his own voice. It was cold and detached, and he wasn't proud of it.

This was the hard part about parenting—not being his daughter's friend but being her father. Not going ballistic over her push for independence via unexpected rebellion. Laurel was right about this being a phase. She was right about too much when it came to Gabby. And yet, she'd been wrong to let his daughter wear that dress.

Gabby unlocked the phone and dialed.

"Put it on speaker." His tone had dropped, but he was still half-ashamed that his words were so accusatory. But it wasn't his fault. The fault lay with—

"Hi, sweet thing," Shannon gushed over a background of many voices, laughter and clinking glasses.

"Shannon. It's Mitch." His tone tossed down the gauntlet. "I've just discovered what you gave Gabby for her birthday. This gift is something we should have talked about *before* you bought it."

"Why?" Shannon's voice took on a lethal edge that tried to match Mitch's. Heels clicked on marble; presumably Shannon was walking away from the crowd because the noise dimmed. "All the twelve-year-olds here have cell phones. They text each other all the time."

"She has no one to text, Shannon." All the kids in Second Chance were younger than she was.

"Maybe *I* wanted to text my daughter." A door latched. The sound of the crowd muted. "Maybe *I* wanted some privacy. You know, Mitch, you're always around when I call on the house phone. And because you chose to live in those awful mountains where the power goes out every time you have a thunderstorm, I can't always reach my daughter on the house phone. Gabby is twelve. She needs to be able to talk to another woman about the things she's going through."

"Mom." Eyes squeezed shut, Gabby fell back against the wall.

"Is that Gabby in the background?" Shannon asked.

"Yes. She's here. I have you on speaker."

"Jeez, you could've told me. You always want to make me look like the bad parent."

There was no way Shannon could look like the bad parent to Gabby today. No, that was Mitch.

"Gabby, honey." There was a noticeable change in Shannon's tone of voice. "When your dad gives you your cell phone back—*because you know he's going to take it away just because it was our little secret*—you call me. You call me anytime. We'll talk about changing that custody agreement. You'd like to live with me half the year, wouldn't you?" Before Mitch or Gabby had a chance to respond, Shannon tossed her goodbye. "Love you, girlie!" And hung up.

Share custody? Over my dead body.

Mitch wanted to go to his room, fall on the bed and forget he'd ever been married, which was preferable to throwing away Gabby's cell phone, he supposed. Not that he was going to do either.

Gabby grimaced. "I guess I'll go to my room, where I'll be in time-out until I leave for college." She turned, dragging her feet. "Unless Mom wins that custody battle."

Shannon would ruin Gabby.

He should let his daughter have the last word. She'd gotten the message loud and clear: he didn't approve of her keeping this a secret. But he couldn't. "You can come out for meals, chores and schoolwork if I go with you to the diner."

Gabby choked on a sob and raced to her room, slamming the door behind her.

Mitch shut off the cell phone and shoved it in a desk drawer.

Things were going to be a lot quieter around here for the next few days.

As soon as the crying stopped.

CHAPTER SIX

IT WAS MIDNIGHT and Mitch was pacing down-stairs in the common room.

He had a distinct set of footfalls.

Laurel should know. She'd been listening to him walk the inn at night for several weeks now, often lulled to sleep by his sturdy tread. Tonight guilt acted like a dose of caffeine, keeping her awake.

Granted, things had gotten out of hand. But she'd apologized and…

And Mitch hadn't accepted, the same way her sister, Ashley, hadn't accepted her apol-ogy over the pink dress incident.

Ashley! Ashley! Who designed your dress?

Flashing light bulbs blinded. Popping light bulbs made her ears ring.

Laurel rolled over. Rolled back. Thought about how light her chest felt when everyone around her was happy. Listened to Mitch pace.

Strong. Sure. Steady. His were the steps of a man who knew who he was and how he wanted to live. She envied him that.

Really, he could stay mad at her all he wanted, but Gabby… He and Gabby needed to make up. Maybe if she tried to explain about the dress and what it meant to her…

Laurel sat up gradually, the way she'd learned to sit up since the wallop of morning sickness. Nothing rocked. Her stomach didn't clench. Her head didn't spin. She swung her feet off the bed slowly. All was good.

Take that, morning sickness.

She put on a silky gray robe over her silky menswear-style pajamas and went downstairs.

"You should go back to bed." Mitch's words reached Laurel before her stocking feet touched the ground floor. He sounded as sharp and cold as the wind whipping past the inn's windows.

She hesitated on the bottom step.

"Business isn't pretty." Grandpa Harlan's voice filled her head. "And life isn't always easy. Sometimes you've gotta hug your enemy and sometimes you've gotta punch back."

Mitch stood at the fireplace in blue jeans and a blue knit sweater, back to her, lean body silhouetted by the banked embers. "You don't want to hear what I'm trying *not* to say to you, Miss Laurel."

"Last I heard, a jury doesn't deliberate without hearing both sides of the story, Counselor." Laurel sat on the couch, curling her feet beneath her and draping the brown-and-blue quilt over her legs. She laid the magazine that had documented the whole pink dress mess on the cushion next to her.

Mitch faced her. "What kind of person brings a dress like that to Idaho in winter? I can't demand you get rid of it but…"

"You'll hear me out." Laurel shored up her shoulders and her resolve. "Gabby and the dress… It was my fault. I'm not arguing that. I just… I just wanted you to have my side of the story."

His gaze dared her to back down. "Why?"

"Because I don't want you to be angry at Gabby. Because I don't want to think of you pacing the floors and unable to sleep." Because she'd liked the way he'd looked at her when morning sickness sidelined her and he hadn't looked at her that way since. Because if she could get through to him about the dress there was hope that she could get through to Ashley and her mother about Wyatt. "Please. Sit."

He didn't. But he didn't leave, either.

Laurel hesitated. That scowl… Until today, she'd given him no reason to dislike her other than the fact she was one of Harlan Monroe's heirs. She wouldn't even be here if it wasn't for Grandpa Harlan. Something unlocked inside her head, fitted pieces together. Suddenly, she understood Mitch and why they couldn't reach common ground. "My grandfather gave you a once-in-a-lifetime deal."

"Oh, let's not go there." His scowl deepened.

She leaned forward. "I wouldn't go there if you didn't look at everything I do and everything you think I am through a fear-tinted lens." She purposely softened her tone. "You're afraid."

The embers crackled, flamed briefly, all before Mitch's expression turned wary, but he said nothing.

"You think my generation of Monroes is entitled, that we've been given every opportunity to succeed." All true. "My grandfather didn't leave me money. He hit a reset button, had my dad fire me and left me a share in Second Chance." She let her gaze roam the common room. The antique bed warmer on the wall Sophie was so fond of. The thick log walls scarred from a hundred-year-plus history. The big wood mantel above a fireplace large enough for Andrew and Alexander to stand in. They hadn't inherited a cash cow. "I have savings. We all do, but Grandpa Harlan is forcing us all to start over."

Her stomach churned. Baby didn't like drama any more than she did. Her gaze landed back on Mitch, on determined shoulders, stern features and dark eyes that reflected concern. "But you forget my grandfather gave *you* every opportunity to succeed, as well. A large check and a small lease. His death is a reset button for you, too. And now you're scared that things will change, that Shane will take this all away when your lease runs out. That your daughter will wear dresses and like boys and—"

"That's enough." Mitch ran a hand over his hair. "This is supposed to be about your dress and your side of the story."

"It's about Second Chance and family and a dress you'd like to see gone. A dress I can't let go of." Laurel grimaced, thinking of another dress, a blue princess dress, toddler size. She drew a deep breath and tapped the magazine next to her, tapped the photo of the pink dress. "That's me. Not my sister."

He leaned closer to peer at the picture and headline but said nothing.

Perhaps, like the rest of the world, he couldn't distinguish Laurel from Ashley.

The thought pressed on her chest, testing her composure.

The dress. This was about Ashley and the dress.

"You have to be tough to make it in Hollywood." Laurel searched for words, but there was no sugarcoating the truth. "And Ashley... She's always been in tune with the emotions of others, fragile." It was why she was able to draw from a deep emotional well in a performance. "When she was sixteen, she fell for a singer in a popular boy band. She didn't know he was taking pills to handle the stress of the spotlight. When she found out and broke up with him, he overdosed. Ashley couldn't drag herself out of bed for a week. She was replaced on a film."

Mom had been livid but unable to shout her daughter back to work.

"It wasn't your fault," Laurel had told Ashley.

"It was. He'd be alive if I pretended his addiction didn't matter. If I acted..."

"If you *enabled*," Laurel had corrected.

"How will I know what a guy's hiding? How can I trust anyone?" Ashley's voice was a thin, taut thread about to snap.

"I'll vet every man for you," Laurel had promised, forcing the words past the fear clogging her throat. Fear that her sensitive sister wouldn't be able to handle the stress of Hollywood.

Laurel's gaze found Mitch's. "With help, she

put herself back together again, determined to focus on her career and steer clear of emotional entanglements, but—"

"Is there a point in here somewhere?"

"Yes. You can't survive in Hollywood without being seen at least occasionally out with someone, preferably powerful someones, but Ashley won't go." Laurel closed the magazine, which resulted in Wyatt Halford, the sexiest man alive, staring up at her from the cover. She turned the magazine over. "So because she and I are identical twins, and I would do anything to protect her, I pretend to be famous sometimes."

I pretend Laurel doesn't exist.

Mitch's closed-off expression turned cynical. "How could that be? Ashley must have assistants. An agent. People who'd know her and leak the story."

Laurel shook her head. "My mother is both Ashley's agent and her assistant. I wore that dress the week before we came to Second Chance." Privately, she'd been thrilled with the reaction of the crowd. It'd been the first time anything she'd made had been embraced publicly. "I wasn't feeling quite right, because, you know, morning sickness." Her awkward laugh, so unlike Ashley's, couldn't reach through his closed-off demeanor. "And when someone shouted the question—*who designed your dress?*—the truth came tumbling out. *Me.*"

In that moment, like the night with Wyatt, she'd been seen. She'd received accolades for her talent.

Mitch frowned. "You shouldn't be telling me this."

"Why not? I know you appreciate candid conversation." And her days as Ashley's double were over. "Later, when I showed up at my mother's house, Mom was furious. She reminded me about Ashley's carefully crafted reputation—which didn't include a fashion brand." Because the plan was for child star Ashley to be taken as a serious actress, not another celebrity dabbling in fashion. "When Ashley didn't say anything—" which had hurt more than Mom's harsh words "—I left, still wearing the evening gown. I didn't want that dress to stand between my relationship with Ashley, but I couldn't leave it behind. That dress…"

"You shouldn't be telling *anyone* this," Mitch amended, sounding like a lawyer advising his client.

Did he think she was going public with her past?

"I'm not telling you this because I want you to leak it to the press, *Counselor.*" She thought a bit of attorney-client privilege was in order, implied though it might be. "I'm telling you this so you understand why I can't just ship the dress somewhere else. It stays until I go."

He took a step back and crossed his arms.

"Not everything in life is cut-and-dried or right and wrong. Because of Grandpa Harlan's will—" Ashley had lost a role on a Monroe Studios film "—and because of my actions in Hollywood—" sleeping with Wyatt "—I have to go back and support Ashley. And I promise I'll take the dress with me when I leave." Just as soon as she had the medical all clear to travel.

His expression was still as hard as the rock on the fireplace.

Laurel reminded herself she could spill her guts all over the floor and Mitch still might not care.

"You're afraid, too," he accused in the same voice he'd used to point out she was bored earlier.

"Yes." Why deny it? "I'm afraid my relationship with my sister will be changed forever. I'm afraid I screwed up my one chance to be a fashion designer. But that doesn't mean we'll have more Second Chance fashion shows."

He made that grumpy noise, accented by disbelieving brows.

"Gabby was curious. She volunteered. And for the record, I protested the entire time. At least, until Gabby walked out of the bathroom and did the dress justice."

"But you did her hair and makeup." The jaded attorney trying to poke holes in Laurel's testimony.

"No. She didn't." Gabby appeared behind the check-in desk wearing a faded pink flannel nightgown. "I did."

"Impossible." Mitch scoffed. "You're just a kid."

"Dad, I keep telling you…" The teen rolled her big brown eyes. "You can learn how to do anything on the internet." She scurried back inside the apartment and closed the door.

"Or with a cell phone…" Mitch's butt landed on the arm of the couch. He stared at the closed door, looking shell-shocked. "She grew up so fast."

"Or maybe she's been growing up all along." Laurel stood, heading for the stairs. "And you didn't see it coming."

"We may both have our fears, but that doesn't mean I forgive you, Miss Laurel," Mitch called after her.

So much for world peace.

"I can't control whether you forgive me or not, Counselor. I can only ask that you look at things from my perspective. Because like it or not, you have to deal with the Monroes. Wouldn't it be easier if we all got along?"

He didn't answer her.

"HEY, MITCH." ZEKE bumped his wheelchair through the door and into the common room after Laurel went up to bed. "Want some company?"

Mitch stopped pacing, stopped thinking about fear and promises bent close to breaking, about Laurel and her grandfather, and turned.

Laurel had made some good points about the leg up that Harlan Monroe had given Mitch and others in Second Chance. And there had been tears in her eyes when she'd talked about how fragile her sister was. But that didn't change the fact that Gabby needed grounded people around her. Now more than ever.

Zeke brought his wheelchair to a stop a few feet away from Mitch. "You've got some thin walls in here...*Counselor*."

"Don't tell me you heard all that." Mitch's conversation with Laurel. The second revelation of the day about Gabby. The secret life of Ashley Monroe. He rubbed his face with both hands. He clung to the hope that Laurel would leave as soon as the doctor allowed her to. "Why is no one in bed?" The morning was coming far too soon.

Zeke rubbed his hands over his leg brace. "Since you woke me up, is there anything you feel you need to get off your chest?"

Mitch stared into the bright red embers in the fireplace.

Zeke undid the Velcro straps on his leg brace, shifted and refastened them. "I'm not gonna lie. Ashley Monroe is my celebrity crush. When I first met Laurel, I could barely speak. And now my mind is blown." Zeke's eyes widened. "I was having dinner at the Clarks' a year ago when that movie award show was on. And Ashley Monroe was on the red carpet, except…" The cowboy lowered his voice. "It might have been Laurel."

Mitch fixed Zeke with a hard stare.

"I'm just saying…" Zeke held up his hands in mock surrender. "I feel a little conned."

"Which is exactly why you can't tell anyone." Mitch shook his head. "They do look exactly the same, except—"

"Laurel's got a soulful look in her eyes," Zeke finished for him.

"As if she's been hurt." Mitch nodded. "And her laugh…"

Zeke chuckled. "Like a drunken donkey."

"I wouldn't go that far." But Mitch smiled,

not that it lasted for long. "Gabby's going through a lot right now and I need good role models around here."

"Deep down, you know Laurel's a good person."

Mitch agreed, but he wasn't going to admit it, not when the dress debacle was so new.

"Besides..." Zeke adjusted his leg brace again, slipping his fingers beneath the stiff sides to scratch. "Don't they own this place?" At Mitch's nod, he added, "Kind of makes it hard to kick her out."

Well, there was that.

"You know," Zeke said slowly. "I had a friend who was a little wild during her teenage years. Rebellious. Boy crazy. Why one time—"

"Gabby is *not* wild." How Mitch prayed that was true. "She's twelve and pushing for a little independence is all."

Zeke shrugged. "Whatever you say."

They watched the dying flames in silence. Zeke scratching. Mitch uncomfortable in his own skin.

Try as he might, Mitch couldn't help but think all his troubles traced back to one man. "Did you ever meet Harlan Monroe?"

The cowboy shook his head. "That was before I came to Second Chance."

"Family was important to him. And he made it sound as if everything would be all right if I accepted his offer and stayed in town." They'd had long discussions about life and family sitting on the back porch, drinking beer and watching the local herd of elk graze in the meadow on the other side of the Salmon River.

He'd found Laurel out on that same porch a few days after she'd arrived.

She'd stared at the snowy meadow, tears in her eyes. "I bet this was one of Grandpa's favorite places."

True. What she didn't know—what he couldn't tell her because he'd signed that stupid confidentiality agreement—was that Harlan had told Mitch about himself and his grandchildren. Including Laurel.

"You can't escape being a twin," Harlan had said once as the sky turned purple during a summer sunset. "But you can cast your own shadow. Now, my granddaughter Laurel… She's a twin and she doesn't realize she has a big shadow of her own."

Laurel was living in her sister's shadow. Was that why her eyes were sometimes sorrowful? Or was it because her design career had crashed and burned? The magazine headline had stated Ashley Monroe had made her dress, but Laurel claimed it was her work.

There was more drama between Laurel and her family than she let on.

Mitch ran a hand through his hair. He had his own problems to deal with thanks to one rich old man. "Harlan Monroe was something else."

"Uh, Mitch. From what I hear tell about old Mr. Monroe and his relationship with folks in town—which is not much, but the Clarks at the Bucking Bull did mention something about a legal gag order…" Zeke drew a breath. "Should you be telling me about the man?"

There were two low stone ledges for sitting on either side of the cooking fireplace.

Mitch sat down on one. "It's no secret the dearly departed Harlan Monroe was a savvy businessman." There were things Mitch knew about Harlan Monroe, things he hadn't been told, things he'd looked up on the internet as if he were Gabby doing a report. Harlan Monroe had been a ruthless businessman. Had his buyout offer given Mitch the short end of the stick?

"Hey, uh…" Zeke fiddled with his leg brace again. "I need to ask you a favor."

"I'm not in the mood for granting favors." For being nice. For being a hospitable innkeeper. "It's late and we should both be asleep." Mitch stood, grabbed a fireplace poker and spread the coals thin.

Zeke shifted in his chair. "Hear me out. *Please.*"

It was the urgent way the cowboy said *please* that caught Mitch's full attention.

Zeke's face was pinched, and he wasn't smiling. "Everything in my brace itches. My knee, my ankle, my toes." Zeke raised his gaze to Mitch's. "I can't remove my brace completely or bend my knee at all—trust me, it's excruciatingly painful. I need a pen or a ruler to scratch without moving my leg around."

Mitch went to the check-in desk for a pencil.

"Except…" Zeke sounded pained. "You're not going to like this, but I can't reach the undersides of my toes."

Mitch turned to look at Zeke. "What are you asking?"

"I need you to scratch the sole of my foot." He made his request in a voice barely above a whisper.

The head shake was a natural, masculine, knee-jerk reaction. "Sorry, Zeke. No can do."

Zeke couldn't hold Mitch's sturdy stare. It was clear he felt as bad about asking as Mitch felt about being asked. "Have pity on me, man. At this point if you handed me a bent toilet brush I'd use it on my toes if I could."

Mitch paused, studying the tension on Zeke's face. "You're that desperate?"

"I'm that desperate," Zeke confirmed with a nod.

Mitch glanced toward the staircase and then toward his apartment door. "When I first bought this inn, I never imagined I'd be asked to scratch a guest's toes." Mitch retrieved a new pencil from the check-in desk. "Don't tell anyone about this."

If Shane knew, he'd have a field day.

"My lips are sealed," Zeke said.

Mitch held the pencil at arm's length as if Zeke's digits might bite. "Just... Promise me this. Don't ask me for a sponge bath."

Zeke managed to look both horrified and relieved. "Never."

"WHAT'S WITH THE do-not-disturb sign?" Sophie asked when Laurel granted her entry the next morning. She wore a comfy pair of gray sweats and a preppy yellow-and-gray-striped sweater.

"My dress and I are avoiding Mitch." Laurel was propped upright in bed, knitting. She wore jeggings and a celery-green, off-the-shoulder tunic with iridescent pearl beads at the neckline. "He still thinks I'm a bad influence on Gabby." She rarely came across someone she couldn't win over with a smile, some kindness and common sense. But that man…

"I can't wait to hear what he thinks of me, the instigator of the event." Sophie flounced on the bed, making her glasses go askew. She straightened them. "I guess you apologized again and he didn't accept? You can't force everyone to get along the way you tried to when we were kids."

"I wasn't so successful one year. Do you remember how angry Grandpa Harlan was at us over the toppled Christmas tree?" Laurel shook her head.

"Was that the year of the Victorian choir? When Grandma Estelle was dying?" At her nod, Sophie patted Laurel's leg. "You'll win Mitch over. I'm off to get coffee before the boys get out of the shower." Sophie moved toward the door, opened it and nearly toppled into Shane.

He frowned. "What's with the do-not-disturb sign?"

"It's defective." Sophie poked her brother in the chest. "Because everyone seems to be disturbing Laurel."

"Except Mitch," Laurel murmured, although it was too early for him to come by to clean.

"Speaking of Mitch…" Shane ushered his

sister back into the room and closed the door behind them. "I need a favor from you two."

Sophie pushed up her glasses with one hand and propped her other hand on her hip. "I have a bad history with you and favors, brother dear."

"Likewise," Laurel said.

With his usual panache, Shane ignored them. He had thick skin and a smile slicker than a shady salesman. "I know I promised to drive you both to Laurel's doctor's appointment tomorrow, but I need to stay here."

"Fine. I'll drive her," Sophie grumped, hand still on her hip.

Shane's smile hardened into place. "I'd rather have Mitch drive." At their open-mouthed silence, he added, "I need him out of town."

"Mitch will never agree to that." Laurel unraveled a row of uneven stitches Odette would never approve of. "He doesn't like me."

"His loss," Sophie murmured.

"I'll take care of Mitch," Shane promised. "But it would be an easier sell if Sophie and the boys weren't part of the transportation deal."

Laurel and Sophie exchanged looks.

"Why?" Laurel was the first to ask. "You've been disappearing every day for weeks on

Mitch's snowmobile and haven't told us anything."

"He's got a woman somewhere," Sophie mumbled. "He's always got a woman somewhere."

"Wrong. Cousin Holden is the ladies' man." He tried to look sincere, but this was Shane, master of the Machiavellian. "As for what I'm doing, I'd rather not say."

"Whatever," Sophie huffed in apparent disbelief. "What's in it for us?"

"Yeah, what's in it for us?" Laurel nodded, although she wasn't convinced Shane could get Mitch to drive her two doors down to the Bent Nickel Diner, much less sixty miles away to the doctor.

"I'll watch the twins so you two can rummage to your heart's content in the trading post and the mercantile for a day." He nodded toward Laurel. "As long as Laurel gets the medical go-ahead to do so."

"You never babysit, *Uncle* Shane." Sophie narrowed her eyes at her twin. "And we could be in there for hours."

"You can take all day," Shane promised.

"Agree. Quickly." Sophie turned to Laurel so fast her short brown hair swung in the air. "Agree. Before my brother changes his mind."

"Not so fast." Now it was Laurel's turn to

give Shane a narrow-eyed stare. "What's in it for me?"

"You're catching on to the game." Shane nodded his approval. He walked to the bathroom door and pointed inside. "I'll back you up when you're ready to confront Ashley about that pink dress."

"There will be no confrontation with Ashley." She hoped. Laurel waved his offer aside.

"A yet-to-be-named favor?"

"Better." Laurel could hardly contain herself. A favor from Shane was golden. He didn't do anything by half measures.

"Good enough for a deal?" Shane extended his hand to Sophie.

"Good enough for a deal," Sophie confirmed. She opened the door and held up the do-not-disturb sign. "Should we take this down?"

Laurel shook her head. "Let's wait and see if Shane can pull this off first."

"Oh, I won't disappoint. But I'm going to broker this tomorrow morning at the last possible minute. Wouldn't want Mitch to back out."

"My brother, the king of the Hail Mary." Sophie scoffed.

"Just call me the king." Shane preened, a

look he could pull off with his overly confident attitude no matter what he wore.

Sophie scoffed again and then cocked her head. "Do you hear that?" She hurried down the hall toward her room—in the opposite direction of the stairs and caffeine.

Shane left, too, but headed toward the stairs.

"Baby." Laurel rubbed her tummy. "Let's practice our speech." The one about Wyatt that she had to give her family. Because once she had the all clear to travel, she was coming clean.

Sad, though, to think one handsome, ornery innkeeper would be happy to see her go.

CHAPTER SEVEN

"Dad." Gabby trotted beside Mitch on the way to the Bent Nickel the morning after her grounding. "You can't be serious. I've apologized about the phone, *and* I took responsibility for the hair and makeup."

She wanted her phone back.

"Overruled," Mitch said. It hadn't even been twenty-four hours. He adjusted his grip on the logs he was carrying to contribute to the Bent Nickel's woodstove.

"Well, at least let me sit with Laurel to do my knitting later." She switched tactics. "I learn a lot from her."

That was just the thing. She learned all the wrong things. "Overruled."

"Well, that's not fair."

They walked along the path he'd cleared earlier with the snowblower, passing the general store. Mack waved from behind the checkout counter.

"As your father, I reserve the right to limit the time you spend with the Monroes." Meaning

Laurel. She'd made some good points last night, but he wasn't ready to reach out to shake her hand and declare a truce. Not unless it meant she'd leave.

"And now you're just being stubborn." Gabby hefted her neon-yellow backpack higher on her shoulder. "You let me hang out with Roy as much as I want, and he nearly started a forest fire when we went camping last summer!"

Mitch didn't have to look at his daughter to know she was rolling her eyes. She used that roll-your-eyes tone of voice he was coming to hate.

"Dad, this thing you have against the Monroes is getting old. What Laurel said last night—"

"The only thing getting old is me." He wished Gabby hadn't heard everything Laurel had said. He was cold. The wind chafed his face. And he felt as if his daughter was slipping out of his protective embrace. Balancing the wood, he opened the door to the Bent Nickel, determined to keep trying.

"Dad." Eye roll. Shoulder drop. Attitude. "You have to accept the fact that I'm growing up." Gabby skipped to the rear of the diner with the other kids.

"No, I don't," Mitch said under his breath.

He deposited the logs on the stack by the woodstove and moved toward the community coffeepot, stuffing a couple bucks inside the jar. It was going to be a several-cups kind of day.

"What's shaking?" Roy got up from his chair near the woodstove and slapped Mitch on the back. Lucky for Mitch, the old man was wiry or that might have hurt. Roy lowered his voice. "Meaning what's the Monroe situation?"

"Same as yesterday."

But it wasn't the same as yesterday because he'd learned too much about Laurel. She was hurting. She tried to make light of the rift in her family, but he could see in the lines framing Laurel's blue eyes that it pained her. And that pain made him soften.

Mitch sat at the counter near Ivy, close enough to hear Gabby talk to her friends. Roy claimed the stool next to him.

Mitch studied his daughter, who didn't seem as broken up about things today as she'd been yesterday. Her face wasn't pale. In fact…

Was that makeup on her face?

Holy smokes. It was.

"Unbelievable." He caught Gabby's eye and swiped his hand over his own brown orbs. "Seriously?"

"Dad." Ginormous eye roll.

Had Shannon sent cosmetics, too? Or was that something else Gabby had ordered online?

His daughter huffed. She puffed. And then she blew down any chance she had of being seen as a mature young adult. "When can I get my phone back?"

From behind the lunch counter, Ivy gasped, horrified. "You gave her a cell phone?"

The kids stared at Gabby in awe.

"I didn't." That earned him a sympathetic glance from Ivy.

Ivy understood exes and their inappropriate gifts all too well. Just last Christmas, her ex-husband had sent a video game console to her young boys with a set of video games rated for older teens.

The door opened and Shane came in. "Good morning," he called out as if he was Second Chance's favorite son.

Mitch wanted to roll his eyes, especially when several residents greeted Shane warmly in return. He grabbed some coffee and sat in his regular booth by the front windows.

Dori Douglas entered the diner next. She was seventy if she was a day and didn't come out much in the deep winter months. She cast her gaze around before heading toward Shane's booth.

"What's that all about?" Mitch asked Ivy, tilting his head toward Dori.

Frowning, Ivy took a rare moment to stand still and stare.

Roy had spun his stool around when Dori came in. He spun back and pointed his thumb toward the odd couple. "Do you see what I see?"

"No." Mitch glanced at Dori and Shane. There wasn't anything wrong with Dori eating with someone, except she was here with a certain Monroe. And according to Harlan, Shane was a dynamo who could accomplish anything he put his mind to.

What had he put his mind to?

Maybe Mitch should worry. "What do you see?"

"Oh, my." Ivy's slim brows bent toward each other. "Shane is making friends. Is that a good thing? For us, I mean."

Roy nodded. "I'll take it as a sign. Shane wouldn't sell out his friends."

Mitch wasn't so sure, but kept that thought to himself.

Roy bent over his mug and whispered to Mitch, "Where are you on your surprise for those Monroes?"

Mitch had told the handyman about his plans yesterday afternoon. He answered in a whisper of his own. "I found out how to file for historical significance. I requested more information and hope to hear back today."

"Shane won't see this coming." Roy spun his stool back and forth, a quarter turn each way.

Odette entered the diner. She, too, surveyed the occupants before heading straight for Gabby. "I've come to check your work."

"Uhhh…" Gabby closed her laptop. "It's at home."

"And…" Odette's bushy brows lowered.

Gabby's shoulders slumped. "I'm not as far as I should be."

"I told you this was your last chance." Odette didn't wait for Gabby to say how far she was on her knitting. She turned on her snow-booted heel and stomped off. "Bring me what you've got later."

"I bet Laurel is further along on her knitting than I am," Gabby mumbled.

Mitch caught her attention. "Aren't you here to do schoolwork?"

His question earned him another eye roll.

A LIGHT KNOCK on Laurel's door preceded the door opening, which wasn't unusual. Everyone seemed to barge right into Laurel's room.

It was a good thing she was always dressed.

This time her visitor was Odette. Same bright red snow pants, same three-layered style above the waist—pink turtleneck, gray V-neck sweater, chunky black sweater over it all. "What's with the do-not-disturb sign?"

"It was a test." No one had passed.

The old woman hung the sign on the interior doorknob. "I came to look at your stitches."

"I have a lot of stitches for you to see." She'd gotten several feet of narrow scarf done, more than her end result since she'd unraveled row upon row of uneven stitches. "I used up more than one ball of yarn." Laurel laid her work in progress across the bed.

Bending over, Odette inspected Laurel's teal stitches between her thumb and forefinger, every inch. She straightened and frowned. "You're productive, I'll give you that." She took three balls of fuzzy coppery yarn and thick metal knitting needles from a jacket pocket. "Try this." She turned to go.

"Did I do something wrong?" Laurel held up her teal scarf like a sacrificial offering. "You want me to abandon this? What about quilting?"

"You didn't stitch with patience." Odette slipped out the door.

Laurel followed her into the hall. "So there's nothing wrong with my scarf? It just missed patience?" Sadly, there was no hiding Laurel's impatient disappointment with her would-be mentor. She hadn't realized how important Odette's approval was to her.

Odette scurried off around the corner and down the stairs.

"Come back and see us sometime," Zeke said from below. "Maybe stay a little longer."

The front door slammed.

"We don't bite!" Zeke called after her.

Laurel came slowly down the stairs still carrying her eight-foot-long teal scarf.

"What was all the hubbub about?" The ginger-haired cowboy adjusted the wheelchair so that he could face her squarely, the leg in the brace propped straight out in front of him. "Odette was like the wind, blowing in and blowing back out." He rolled toward her. "Hey, are you okay?"

"I was hoping she'd give me quilting lessons." Laurel sank onto the couch. She wrapped the scarf around her hand like a thick blue bandage.

"You don't seem okay."

"Odette didn't like my stitches." Laurel fell back on the cushions and stared into the large fireplace across from her. It was full of cold ashes. "And I don't know how to do them any better."

Zeke positioned his elbows on the wheel-chair's armrests. "Can I tell you a story?"

"Why not? I seem to have time on my hands."

The cowboy wiggled his bare toes. "Like Odette, my dad was a bit of a perfectionist. Which would have been fine if he was also a people person. But he wasn't much for people or talking, and he tended to find imperfection in me or what I'd done when I thought things were *good enough*." He put these last two words in air quotes.

She had a feeling she knew where his story was going.

"Now, I'm thinking you may be from Hollywood and unfamiliar with the way things work in a small town." Zeke's voice was kind, stitched with a thread of cheerfulness that invited Laurel to lighten up. "Most of us are social, especially in the winter months." He glanced toward the door. "Now Odette and her ilk, she's different. She's more like my dad, if you get my meaning."

"I do." Laurel dug her fingers into the soft yarn. "You're saying no matter what I do I won't be good enough for her." Laurel's heart sank. It was like her situation with the pink dress and her family. It was like the situation with Mitch and Gabby. "What do you do when you can't win?"

Zeke stared across the room as if he was looking at something more interesting than the check-in desk. "Well, I created a new set of rules for myself."

CHAPTER EIGHT

DAY TWO WITHOUT Gabby in possession of her cell phone dawned clear outside.

The storms were inside the Lodgepole Inn.

Mitch squinted at the computer screen behind the check-in desk, reading the fine print regarding submission for historic status for the third time. He didn't want to mess things up.

The lodge was quiet this morning. Gabby was at the diner doing schoolwork. After telling anyone who'd listen about his loyal, talented cutting horse, Zeke had returned to his room, smile strained. The Monroes were upstairs, only the occasional creak in the floorboards indicating they were awake. That *she* was awake.

He hadn't seen Laurel since their conversation two nights ago. He stayed in his apartment with the door closed around the times she usually came down for tea or passed through on her way to the diner for meals. He didn't know if her eyes were filled with laughter or hurt.

All good.

But that meant he was stuck in the same prison cell as one unhappy teenage girl.

Not so good.

He'd hit his limit with dramatic sighs and door slams. So as soon as he heard Laurel get her morning tea from the kitchenette at the bottom of the stairs, the check-in desk was it. And it was where he stayed when Gabby left for the diner where she was scheduled to take a math test.

"What are you looking at, Kincaid?" The familiar male voice dropped from the stairs above him.

Mitch startled, clicked the computer window closed and swung around to face Shane. "You've either been taking sneak-around-the-house lessons from my daughter or vampires do exist."

Shane smiled, moving closer, placing his loafered feet on spots only Gabby had learned didn't creak and groan. "Your daughter tells me you're going to Ketchum this morning. I was thinking..." Shane put his arm around Mitch's shoulder as if they'd belonged to the same fraternity in college. "I was supposed to take Laurel to the doctor today, but something's come up and I need to stay."

Right. Mitch smelled deception, as distinct as dead skunk on a hot highway.

"What could you possibly have on your agenda that would keep you in Second Chance?" Mitch asked. The forecast called for sun, and the county snowplows had already been by to clear the highway passes.

"I've got a meeting." Still smiling, Shane hovered on the stairs.

"A phone meeting?" Because no one came to Second Chance in February for a face-to-face. There was too much risk of being snowed in.

"You want to listen in, Kincaid?" Shane always pushed Mitch's buttons.

Mitch clenched his jaw. "You're telling me you have a job interview?"

The smile drained from Shane's expression.

It drained right down the stairs on silent feet and jumped into Mitch's veins.

Now Mitch was the one smiling. Harlan would be thrilled.

Or not.

There was something insincere about Shane's expression. He liked being straight with people about as much as a rattler. There was definitely something else going on here.

Mitch's smile hardened. "I hear the airport hotel in Boise is hiring."

"You want me gone, don't you?" Shane looked down his nose at Mitch.

"Absolutely." On so many levels.

"Take Laurel to the doctor for me." Shane ascended the stairs without so much as a creak of wood. "Her appointment is at one." He didn't wait for Mitch's reply.

Could Shane really have a job interview? If it was true… If Shane got a job and left… The pressure to protect Gabby's innocence, Harlan's wishes, and Second Chance would be lifted. If Shane left, it might mean he and the Monroes would respect the status quo—one-year leases, perhaps even a stipend for a town doctor and handyman.

And if Laurel didn't go to the doctor, she couldn't be cleared to travel. If she was cleared to travel, she was heading back to Hollywood to protect that famous sister of hers, taking the red carpet–worthy dress with her.

Mitch locked his computer and stood. Darn right he had to drive Laurel to her appointment.

Except…

Mitch froze.

He and Laurel. He and Laurel and Gabby.

The drive to Ketchum was at least an hour each way. And he'd promised Gabby a trip to the bookstore. They'd be stuck in his SUV. Laurel and Gabby chattering away. Mitch with his jaw clenched.

But she's grounded.

He could use that as an excuse. She'd argue and roll her eyes, but he'd hold firm. Mitch grabbed his jacket and hurried two doors down to the Bent Nickel.

Roy greeted him when he arrived, following Mitch to the woodstove. "Anybody packing up at the inn?"

"No." Mitch spotted Gabby in the back.

Roy sighed and shook his head. "That's a shame."

Mitch nodded. It was a shame. But maybe Shane would get a new job today. Maybe he'd leave tomorrow. "I'm going down the mountain. Anyone need anything?" Mitch had no time for coffee. He stuffed a couple bucks in the coffee jar anyway.

"You can get most anything delivered nowadays." Odette sat at the counter. Her gaze tried to penetrate Mitch's. "Everything except *doctors*. If you haven't noticed, we need one here in town." The spry old woman slid off the bar stool and headed for the door, scowling at the lot of them as she shoved her arms in her thick green jacket. "Do you know I haven't seen a doctor in weeks?"

Roy took that as his cue. "How goes the search for a new doc?"

"Don't ask," Mitch mumbled. His inbox was woefully empty of inquiries.

"Why are you headed down the mountain?" Ivy called from the kitchen.

"Don't ask." Mitch turned to the back corner of the diner.

Eli Garland presided over several tables shoved together. He ran the homeschool program, and instead of meeting with kids for only an hour or two a week, the teacher made himself available most weekday mornings at the diner. There were a lot of kids in attendance today since the roads had been plowed. They were mostly silent, working on tablets or laptops, scribbling on lined paper or coloring in workbooks.

Gabby sat in a corner, head bent behind her laptop screen. "Hey, Dad," she said when she noticed Mitch. "I know I said I'd come right back after my test, but Mr. Garland reviewed my notes on my history paper and now I'm knee-deep in it." She glanced up at Mitch with attention-glazed eyes, which was preferable to the contemptuous way she'd looked at him in the past forty-eight hours. "Would you mind if I stayed here?"

Gabby wore a blue knit cap with white puppies knit in the brim. Her hair hung in two simple braids. No makeup had been applied. No eye rolls executed.

There's my girl.

"School is priority one." Relief flooded him. "I'm going down the mountain. I'll be back by dinner. When you're done here—"

"I'll go straight to my room." Her gaze returned to her computer screen.

Mitch turned and headed toward that door.

That was easy, he told himself as he walked back to the inn, feeling unsettled once more.

In his experience, things that came too easily—like unbelievable real estate deals and one-dollar leases—never turned out well.

THE ONLY ACTING role Laurel had mastered was the impersonation of her sister.

And now Shane wanted her to cover for him with Mitch.

Feeling like an imposter about to be caught, Laurel descended the creaky staircase of the Lodgepole Inn, feet strapped in her new snow boots, arms encased in a new thick jacket. Overheated, she balked midway down.

"Feeling okay?" Mitch stood at the check-in desk. He wore blue jeans, a gray polo, a heavy blue jacket and a concerned expression.

"I'm feeling…" *Like a liar.* Panic had her

swaying on the step. She clutched the handrail. "Where's Shane?"

"Didn't he tell you?" The concern in his eyes disappeared, replaced by a shadow of suspicion. Mitch grabbed a set of car keys. "I'm driving you to your doctor's appointment."

Only if she let him. Laurel remained in the middle of the stairs.

The inn was quiet. Sophie and the boys were upstairs, as planned. Shane was elsewhere, as planned. Had Zeke been around, he'd have been talking. He wasn't around, either. Was he in on it, too?

Mitch wasn't meeting her gaze. Was he still upset about Gabby and the dress? Or did he know Shane was manipulating him?

Probably both.

This was an important day for Laurel. Doctor's appointment. Lab work. Sonogram. And if things went well, she'd have no excuse not to call her family, not to go home.

The world tilted. Today of all days, Laurel wanted to avoid Shane-induced drama with Mitch. She gripped the handrail and proceeded down the stairs. "I can drive myself." If Shane had left the keys inside his Hummer.

With a sigh, Mitch gently took hold of her elbow as she passed the check-in desk. "How much experience do you have driving on the snow and ice?"

"None." She shouldered her black leather hobo bag. "I'm used to gridlock traffic, not snow."

There was a flash of kindness in his eyes, causing a twinge of guilt in her belly. "Really. I'm happy to drive you."

The banter. The teasing. The empathy.

Baby noticed it all.

"Does anyone resist those kind eyes, Counselor?" she mumbled, feeling her resolve crumble.

"No," Mitch said with a bewildered half smile. His confusion didn't slow him down. He opened the door and ushered Laurel to the porch. "Life would be easier if people would just do what I wanted them to."

That was a statement best left to argue on another day. This one was beautiful.

The winter weather in Second Chance was fairly predictable—temperatures around freezing, gusty wind and snow. The wind was always frigid and rushed down the mountain as if trying to steal her breath. When it was snowing, the sky was a gunmetal gray. When it wasn't snowing, the sky was blue and the clouds were big and fluffy and seemed almost close enough to touch.

It wasn't snowing today. The sun glittered off snow-covered mountains and tall, snow-dusted pines. It'd been snowing so long she couldn't remember the last time she'd seen such a clear blue sky.

Laurel stumbled coming down the steps and stopped gawking at the world around her and watched her footing. She needed to watch her footing with Mitch, too. That didn't stop her from asking, "Why did you move to Second Chance?"

Mitch was ahead of her. He stopped walking and turned to consider Laurel's question or perhaps to consider if he wanted to broach such a personal topic with her. His breath came out in visible puffs. His dark hair contrasted against the eight-foot snowbank behind him, which glittered in the sunlight as if frosted with diamonds.

"I was disillusioned with the legal profession," he admitted, his words carefully chosen, reluctance in the deliberate cadence of delivery. "And my…marriage."

She wasn't going anywhere near the M-word or disillusionment at work, but curiosity got the better of her. "Are you originally from Idaho? Had you been here before?"

He shook his head. "I'm from Chicago. And I…" His dark gaze pierced hers, searching for something, although she wasn't sure what it could be. After a moment, he continued, "I'd had a bad day. I went into this coffee shop downtown, an out-of-the-way dive." His story picked up momentum. "And I couldn't bring myself to look at a newspaper headline or what was trending in the news. So to keep my mind off… To keep my mind *occupied*, I picked up one of those real estate pamphlets and there—on page two—was the Lodgepole Inn." He glanced fondly over his shoulder at the log structure. "Looking much like the way it does today, except it was for sale."

Laurel was surprised he'd shared so much, and hoped he'd keep going. "How old was Gabby when you moved here?"

"Six months. She's never known any place but Second Chance." His lips sealed closed, a sure sign he thought he'd said too much.

Laurel shoved her hands deeper in her jacket pockets, warmed by the personal information he'd revealed. "We better get moving if I'm going to show up for my appointment on time."

He nodded and led her to a forest green SUV parked nearby. Someone had instilled manners in him. He opened the passenger door for her and plunked a water bottle in the center console. "You need to stay hydrated."

"Baby is grateful." Although that sounded ungrateful. She waited to say more until he sat behind the wheel next to her. "If I drink too much water, I'll need a pit stop."

"Welcome to your new reality." Mitch backed the SUV out and headed down the highway, taking the road that branched south. "You've got to think about Baby now."

Did he realize he'd used the name she'd given the little one growing inside her? "Trust me. I've been thinking of little else since I found out I was pregnant."

"Of course. My bad." Mitch slowed as they approached a turn. "You've been wondering how to up your protein intake, eat more greens and stay hydrated."

"Sarcasm." Laurel shook her head. "That would seem to indicate you haven't forgiven me the dress-modeling incident, Counselor." Shoot, she hadn't meant to bring that up.

"I'd forgotten how important keeping the peace is for you, Miss Laurel." He slid her a considering look and an almost smile. "What's my forgiveness worth?"

Excitement fluttered in her chest as if he was flirting with her, which she knew could not possibly be true. "I hadn't realized such a thing was for sale." Really, the man was full of surprises.

"The price of my forgiveness is honesty."

Laurel's fingers tingled with apprehension. But it could have been because she'd looked right as they rounded the bend and couldn't see the ground.

Baby doesn't like heights.

"I think I was honest with you the other night," she said absently.

"And I'd appreciate that same honesty moving forward."

"Sure." Softball-size snowballs tumbled to the road from the ridge above them. Laurel was suddenly glad she hadn't attempted to drive alone. "Are we in any avalanche danger?"

"I'd never say never. The mountains are unpredictable."

Laurel gripped the door handle with one hand and pressed her stomach with the other.

Mitch marked her look of horror with a shake of his head. "What? I thought we were being honest."

"I think I'd prefer you lie to me." She sucked in air, feeling familiar heat originate in her belly, burn through her chest and flame into her ears. "Or I might be sick."

She might be sick anyway.

"Drink some water and talk to me." He handed her the water bottle.

"About what?" She sucked down several gulps of water.

"Tell me about your boyfriend."

"Uh… No boyfriend."

Mitch made a disapproving noise deep in his throat. The noise of a father of a young girl who didn't want her to make the same mistakes Laurel had.

She wasn't going to expand on the fact that this was an unplanned oops. Or how complicated her impending oops was. "Women—*and men*—raise kids by themselves all the time. Take you. Exhibit A."

"But the father knows about Baby, right?" Occasional kind eyes aside, Mitch was too perceptive, too dogged in his pursuit of information.

"He'll know soon." She forced herself to sound committed to the fact.

They reached the top of one mountain and began their descent. Laurel's cell phone began to ping with messages.

From Mom.

Come home. Ashley's publicist thinks it's the perfect time to go out with Wyatt a second time before he starts his next film. We haven't had much good buzz about Ashley since New Year's Eve.

When Laurel had gone out with Wyatt. From Ashley.

We need to talk.

Is Ashley okay? Does she need me?
Laurel would've once dropped everything to call her twin. Today she sent her a simple text.

I'm not ready to talk.

Laurel shoved the phone back in her purse. "Bad news?"
Her phone pinged again. And again. Her mother must have noticed she'd read her message. She was probably sending all kinds of arguments about why Laurel should hightail it home.
Ping. Ping. Ping-ping.
Mom was an incredibly fast texter.
"Who is that?" Mitch asked. "Someone has a lot to say."
"It's my mom." Panic had Laurel chugging breath like a freight train trying to pull too many cars up a steep hill. "Once my mom gets involved with Baby... She'll take everything out of my hands." Laurel pressed her palm against her stomach. She didn't want her mother to orchestrate her pregnancy.

"Are you okay?" Mitch asked.

"No. I…I…I need some time…" The world rose up in a white haze and closed in around her. "No one's going to give me space. Everyone's going to be upset and there is nothing…" She gulped. "*Nothing* I can do about it."

Mitch glanced at Laurel and slowed to a stop—right there in the middle of the narrow highway!

Laurel's heart raced. Her lungs were playing like an accordion accompanying a speedy yodeler. Her head felt light. "Ignore me. I chirp when I stress."

"You need to slow down," he said.

Not literally. Not to a stop.

"What are you doing?" Laurel choked out, glancing over the thin snowbank that separated them from a cliff. Growing up in California, you learned not to stop on the highway. Ever. "Someone's going to—" *pant-pant* "—come down this hill—" *gasp-gasp* "—and hit us." Her last words rode out of her mouth on a whine of air. She had more than her safety to think of. She had Baby to think of. "I should never have let Shane talk me into this."

Mitch undid his seat belt, turned in his seat.

"Relax and fill your lungs with air. Baby needs oxygen."

He was right, of course. But… "Baby needs a safer place to stop. Drive, please."

"Not until Baby gets air. That's why I'm telling you to breathe, honey. I can't do it for you."

Mitch was being nice. Baby liked nice. Baby liked nice a lot.

Laurel bent and put her head between her knees. Mitch was being nice to her, his voice gentle. She'd bet his gaze would be filled with kindness, just as it had been when she'd first arrived in Second Chance. Tense pregnant women—she'd read on a blog—were susceptible to kind men. They took advantage of said men's kindness, laid their heads on said men's strong shoulders and let their guards down.

Laurel's eyes filled with tears and she sucked back a gasp, trying not to let her guard down. "Being pregnant is hard." And scary, since she was going it alone. "Pregnancy is harder than knitting with patience and precision."

Mitch rubbed her back and said nothing, possibly because she wasn't making sense.

The wind rocked the SUV.

Laurel held her breath and clenched her prickling hands.

"Breathe. Don't panic."

"I. Never. Panic." She was the one who

people called when they panicked. "How can…you be…so calm? And why aren't we moving?" She was a woman on a ledge, dangling on a precipice when she knew at any moment this sham of a peaceful life would crumble and she'd tumble over the edge.

Sorry, Baby.

"We just came over the summit." Mitch's hands moved back to his side of the SUV. "The air is thin up here. That can make people feel light-headed and numb."

There was a reason for her body to feel this way?

Laurel drew a deep breath, grasping on to the logical explanation, seeking balance, trying not to sound like she—the sturdy Monroe—was crumbling inside while her head was between her knees. "Does the… Does the altitude make people do foolish things?"

"Yes." That sounded like a bedroom *yes*.

Laurel sat up slowly. She looked into his eyes—*his kind, kind eyes*—and then for no reason whatsoever—*except for the altitude thing*—her gaze dropped to his mouth—*his kind, kissable mouth*.

Laurel gasped and closed her eyes, willing herself to be anywhere but here, alone, with a man she wanted to kiss.

The wind shuddered past, rattling the SUV in a way that sounded like a chuckle.

"Can you just drive?"

Mitch chuckled, much like the wind-rattled SUV.

"There's nothing funny about *this*, Counselor." Laurel cracked her eyes open and peeked at him.

He stared back, knowing exactly what she meant by *this* if the rueful smile was any indication. *This*. Their attraction.

"How do you think I feel about it, Miss Laurel?" Oh, the intensity of his gaze.

Her heart pounded. "I know you're not blaming Baby and my increasing hormones the way I am." Laurel closed her eyes again. "But from your perspective? You have an impressionable young daughter and I'm pregnant with no man waiting in the wings to step up and make an honest woman out of me. Not that I'm a floozy." *Was that still a word?* "I made an error in judgment, that's all. But if I were in your shoes, I wouldn't want me around as a role model, either." That hurt more to say out loud than she'd thought it would. "But honestly, that pink dress did not lead to my downfall."

"That pink dress was made for seduction. That picture of you…"

"I'll take that as a compliment." And she'd try not to take anything else from it. Like a kiss. "And that's the end of discussion about *this*."

Mitch sighed heavily, which was nice since he probably had more arguments why their attraction could never be acted upon.

"We should go." Laurel glanced over her shoulder to see if there were any cars coming down the hill.

The road was still empty.

"Very few people use this highway during the peak of winter." There was a different timbre to his voice now. Less the Kind Mitch and more Mitch, the Hater of Monroes. "You'll appreciate the sparse traffic when you drive away from Second Chance in a day or so."

He'd pivoted to a new topic with ease. They probably trained lawyers to do that.

He snapped on his seat belt. "I can drive you to the airport whenever you're ready."

He couldn't wait to get rid of her. That stung. "In no time, you'll be back where you belong."

"But nothing will be the same. I'll go back to being invisible. And my dreams…" Tears gathered in her eyes. She turned her head toward the window and tried to ignore how her stomach did somersaults.

"You're going to land on your feet," Mitch said, once more using his kind voice.

Laurel wiped away her tears. "Every day the world chews up people's dreams and spits them out." That was what Grandpa Harlan used to say. "Some people aren't strong enough to bounce back from that."

"You're stronger than you know," Mitch said gruffly, putting the SUV in Drive. "If I can see it, it must be true."

Her stomach stopped flip-flopping.

Laurel hugged his words to her chest, if only because they made Baby feel more secure.

CHAPTER NINE

"WE'RE HERE." MITCH'S deep voice and the slight jolt of the SUV as it came to a stop roused Laurel.

She blinked and rubbed her cold cheek. She'd been resting it against the window.

He'd stopped in front of a wide, shoveled walkway leading to the medical building.

Laurel stayed buckled up, staring at the building's tinted windows that revealed nothing about what was inside or what awaited her.

Since she'd discovered she was pregnant, worry about the fallout of her news and logistics about how she was going to make things work had been her chief concerns. But now...

"Laurel?" Mitch prompted.

Her hand gripped the door latch, but she didn't pull it free. "I'm going to be a mom."

"Yes."

"But..." Laurel dragged her gaze around to Mitch. "I've never changed a diaper in my life."

"That doesn't alter the fact that you're pregnant."

Laurel choked on a breath.

His mouth worked as if it couldn't decide upon a gear—neutral or a driving grin. He settled on a neutral smile, one that reassured.

"Don't worry. I took parenting classes when my wife was pregnant with Gabby. We learned how to change diapers and burp babies. The hospital required us to do it."

"I don't want to let Baby down." She watched a pregnant woman emerge from the clinic, accompanied by an older woman, possibly her loving, supportive mother. Some of the high-elevation numbness returned. "Nobody important knows I'm pregnant."

"I take exception to that remark."

"You know what I mean." She looked at Mitch again, him and his cynically quirking brows. "My parents. My siblings."

"And the father," Mitch said as if she needed reminding.

"Him, too." The heat was blasting through the vents, but Laurel was still chilled. Her toes ached with cold. "I'll tell them today." Starting with Ashley.

"You're procrastinating, Miss Laurel." Sighing, Mitch found a parking spot. "You can't run away from pregnancy. You're going in."

Panic threatened to swallow her up again. She'd promised Cousin Sophie she'd tell her family after she saw the doctor. But then again, she'd promised her sister, Ashley, she'd only be gone a few days and it'd turned into four weeks. "But—"

He reached over the console and took Laurel's shoulders, turning her to face him. "All your life you've been caring for your sister and putting her needs first."

Laurel nodded.

"When you become a parent, you put your child's needs first." His fingers pressed on her shoulders as if trying to make his words sink into her very core. She wanted him to pull her closer. She wanted to sink into his strong chest and make that strength hers. "You put them above all others. Often above your own needs and dreams. But if a dream is important you have to chase it, if only to show your child that dreams matter."

Mitch was a well-educated, smart man. And yet, he ran an inn in the middle of nowhere. With sudden insight, Laurel knew why. He'd chosen to make his daughter his priority.

"Did you always know you wanted to be a lawyer?" Had he given up a lifelong dream for Gabby?

"No." Mitch laughed mirthlessly. "My father was a cop. I was raised to honor the law and speak the truth. To believe in things like rainbows and dreams. Only it turned out my father wasn't quite so honorable. He was dirty, lying about everything. Who he was. What he valued." Mitch stared deep into Laurel's eyes. "When they locked him away, I was sixteen. I promised him…" He grimaced. "I promised him I'd become a prosecutor. I promised him I'd do what he should have done."

"You wanted to make things right in the world after yours had been upended."

His brow furrowed. "Only, somewhere along the line I became a defense attorney." He sounded disappointed in himself.

"I hear the money's better," Laurel said softly, trying to lighten his spirits.

Mitch nodded. "But the lies… They get bigger. And I discovered I can't fight to right a lie."

The cold from outside penetrated Laurel's chest. The Twin Switch was essentially a lie. He'd never understand her predicament.

"I miss practicing law. Sometimes." His grip on her shoulders eased. His gaze turned distant. "At its best, I used to help people get their lives back on track. I used to think I was making a difference in my little corner of the world. But…"

He'd been hurt, too. *Disillusioned*, he'd said earlier. It was there in his voice and the vulnerable look in his eyes.

"But you have Gabby."

He smiled, coming back to her. "There is that."

She'd seen Mitch smile before. Kind smiles. Polite smiles. Rueful smiles. But never a smile like this. A smile of pure, unapologetic joy. That smile. It reached into her chest like a heart-to-heart hug. It said everything was going to be all right.

"I don't regret anything I gave up," he said. "My choices made a difference in Gabby's life and laid a foundation for the woman she's going to become. My daughter is going to go out and make a difference in the lives of others. And that's an extension of me. That is, if…" His hands fell away abruptly as if he realized he'd been holding on to Laurel and shouldn't have been. "Come on. I'll walk you in."

If…

If he could stay in Second Chance.

He got out and came around to open her door, during which time Laurel realized she was warm from head to toe and Baby wasn't lurching.

Mitch didn't know it, but he'd just made a

difference in another life—Laurel's. He'd rejected their attraction. He'd reject her if he knew the truth about Wyatt. But he'd made her feel better about parenthood and the choices ahead of her.

I can do this.

She just might have to repeat that statement a hundred or so more times before she believed it completely.

Laurel let Mitch help her out of the car and held on to his arm as they traversed the icy parking lot. He'd probably walk her up to the doors and leave her.

The outer doors slid open and Mitch didn't leave.

The inner doors slid open and Mitch didn't leave, but he did pause.

It felt like every pair of eyes in the waiting room turned their way. Some even lowered their gossip magazines to look at them.

Laurel had forgotten she shared a famous face with her sister. Out of habit, she drew her red hair forward and turned, pretending to study a photograph of the majestic Sawtooth Mountains hanging on the wall.

Mitch frowned slightly but didn't return to his SUV. Instead, he marched Laurel across the lobby to the receptionist.

"Oh, I know who you are." The receptionist

gushed the way Ashley's fans did when they recognized her. "Welcome, welcome. Such a surprise."

She thinks I'm Ashley.

What would pregnancy rumors do to her sister's career?

Laurel took a step away from disaster.

Mitch placed a gentle hand at the base of Laurel's back, keeping her steady. "Baby first," he murmured.

He was right.

That didn't erase the urge to flee, but it made her ignore the impulse.

The receptionist shuffled papers. "You're the surprise referral from Dr. Bishop. I can't remember the last time we had a patient from Second Chance. We were all surprised when he called us. We'll need this paperwork filled out and get you back to see the doctor lickety-split."

She hadn't been recognized?

Relieved to be anonymous, Laurel let Mitch lead her to a seat near the windows and set pen to paper. The mundane task of filling in her address and health history set her mind at ease. It helped that Mitch sat next to her, his arm draped over her chair back.

All too soon, a nurse emerged from a door and called, "Laurel?"

Laurel tried to get to her feet, but her knees buckled, and she sat down hard.

"I've got you," Mitch said. And he did. He helped her to her feet and over to the nurse.

"Follow me," the nurse said.

And they did.

It all happened so fast.

And then Laurel was sitting in an exam room with Mitch.

SHANE WAS OUT the door and down the steps of the Lodgepole Inn before the white truck's engine shut off.

He stood near the driver's-side door, feeling as if he'd just received a long awaited, much longed-for delivery—a real estate consultant.

Talking to town residents hadn't given Shane what he needed to make a presentation to the family. He'd put Flip's recommendation to talk to Gertie Clark on hold for just that reason. What Shane needed in order to give his family and the town a plan for what happened next were facts and projections.

"You must be Glen Keugler." Shane thrust out his hand.

"Yes." Glen was a slight, elderly man with a hunch to his shoulders that didn't straighten upon standing. "And you must be Shane Monroe. Glad to meet you." He took in the vista that was Second Chance's main drag. "Interesting town. Been on this road several times. Can't say I've ever stopped. You say you're considering developing some land?"

"Maybe. Everything's up for discussion. That's why you're here." Shane needed an unbiased assessment of Second Chance—in its current state, in some quaint iteration of itself as a preferred stop on a highway, and as some type of redevelopment project. He glanced over his shoulder toward the diner. "Your firm specializes in a unique form of market analysis."

At the Bent Nickel, Roy pressed his nose against the glass, turning to say something to whichever residents were inside.

Glen nodded. "Our economic models are based on information from similar communities across the country."

"Let's walk down here." Shane led Glen away from the diner.

"My team of consultants has a depth of commercial experience." Glen's gaze swept his surroundings with a calculating eye. "It's unlikely anyone would protest if you wanted to build a resort this far out."

"That's interesting." Encouraging if he'd been Cousin Holden, who was adamant they challenge the will and Grandpa Harlan's state of mind or sell the town as soon as possible. And Shane? He was still collecting facts to make an informed decision, trying not to admit that the small town was growing on him, frustrating as his situation was.

"On the other hand, old towns like this have valuable tourist potential with the right guidance." Glen surveyed the main drag once more. "I see many darkened storefronts."

"Snowbirds and failed businesses."

"I looked over the property records you sent me, though," Glen said, his voice carrying farther than Shane liked. "If you decide to parcel the land into ranchettes or a resort, you'll need to be prepared to answer questions if anyone does look your way—naturalists, environmentalists, preservationists. Second Chance borders national lands, so I can't guarantee who will want to be involved."

Shane cast a glance over his shoulder. No one was following them. Good. "What kind of questions?" Glen made it sound like there were a lot of hoops to jump through.

"It could be anything." Glen slowed. "The extent of intended development. Ecological impact. Historical significance or as yet unpassed preservation plans. Even something as seemingly mundane as discrepancies in property specifics." The older man stopped walking and turned to face the town proper. "For example, you told me a cabin was missing from the town survey."

"My cousin Ella discovered it was gone." Shane didn't want to linger in town. He wouldn't put it past Roy or Ivy to join them. He continued walking toward the fork in the road and the buildings beyond it. "I think my grandfather moved it to Philadelphia."

Glen followed, still at a slow clip. "But we need an explanation."

"Why?" Shane's foot slipped on the icy road. He caught himself before he fell. He'd resisted buying snow boots. He'd been raised to live the leader look. Image was important. Corporate leaders didn't dress like they lived on a mountain, even when they were temporarily living on a mountain. But unlike his grocery delivery recipients, his attire earned him no points with Glen.

"You haven't been here long, have you?" The older man pointed to Shane's leather loafers.

"Trust me. I've been here too long." Shane missed the bright lights and nonstop action of Las Vegas. He missed hot days and warm nights, short sleeves and bathing suits. Especially women in bathing suits. All the women here were either bundled up like snowmen or old enough to be his grandmother.

"Let's run the hypothetical." Glen stopped to study the old steepled church across the highway. "Let's say the missing cabin was Abraham Lincoln's."

"Which it most definitely is not." Thank heavens, because this was complicated enough already.

Shane's phone buzzed with a text message. It had to be Holden. No one else texted him anymore.

Glen chuckled. "For the sake of argument, let's say it was Lincoln's cabin and it had vanished. How would you, as owner of the town, answer questions when the government asks?" Glen turned his gaze to Shane, white brows lowering. "Because if anyone decides they want to stop you from developing the land or tearing down these wonderfully pre-served old buildings, all it takes is just one discrepancy for a judge to sign a cease and desist order."

"I'll track down a paper trail." Shane walked the center line of the highway. "I called you for a reason, Glen. I called you because your web-site promised recommendations about unusual properties." To nurture the existing businesses or to cut their losses and run. Those were the answers Shane sought.

"My recommendations take time." Glen gave Shane a knowing smile. "And cost money."

Shane moved a chess piece in his head and smiled back. He might not have a regular paycheck at the moment, but he had savings and investments. "Name your price."

"YOU WILL NOT stay here during the exam." Laurel tried to sound firm, but her tone wavered, and she clung to Mitch's hand.

He let her.

She was scared. While the nurse had taken Laurel's vitals, she'd asked three times if things were normal. While a lab tech had taken her blood, she'd asked twice about the tests they'd run.

She'd stared at the ceiling and told Mitch, "Baby doesn't like needles."

He didn't have the heart to tell her pregnant women got stuck with all different kinds of needles. Things were about to get real.

"Mitch." She squeezed his hand. "Did you hear me?"

He nodded. "The last thing either of us wants is for me to be present during your physical exam."

The door opened and a woman in a lab

coat rushed in. She had shoulder-length blond hair that seemed tousled by the wind, black-rimmed glasses and a slightly distracted air about her as she flipped through a file. "Mrs... *Monroe*." Her gaze flicked in the direction of Mitch. "And Mr. Monroe." She shook their hands quickly, still talking, leaving no opening for correcting assumptions about who Mitch was. "I'm Dr. Carlisle. I've got a few questions before the exam."

She had more than a few questions, and she probed Laurel carefully on her answers.

Finally, she closed her file. "Okay, Mrs. Monroe. I'd like you to change into a robe and then the nurse and I will return for your exam. Mr. Monroe can wait outside until I'm through and then we'll bring him back to discuss things."

Mitch didn't have to be told twice. He high-tailed it toward the door and would've kept on going if not for the nurse ordering him to sit in a nearby chair.

"First baby?" she asked. Her scrubs were decorated with laughing cartoon rabbits.

"No."

"First baby with your wife?" She nodded toward the room where Laurel was undressing.

"Uh...yes." At this point, why should he explain they weren't a couple? That didn't mean he was going to stay around to hear the doctor's prognosis. Laurel deserved some privacy. He'd slip out to the lobby as soon as the nurse turned away.

"When I take you back in, hold her hand again," the nurse said in a voice that accepted no argument. "She needs you."

She needs you.

Three words and Mitch couldn't get out of the chair. Laurel had acknowledged the chemistry between them when they'd stopped on the summit. He could acknowledge it again. Here. Where she couldn't see. And continue to do nothing about it. But she could use his help. Even a stranger could spot that.

He scrubbed a hand over his jaw, trying to decide what was best for the both of them.

At a nearby counter Dr. Carlisle yawned as she signed everything her staff put in front of her. When she finished she came to stand near Mitch, checking her cell phone.

"Your staff is efficient," Mitch noted.

"Almost too efficient." The doctor rubbed her eyes. "Your wife is my twentieth patient today."

"That's a lot of patients." And the day wasn't over.

"I love the miracle and beauty of pregnancy, but sometimes I long for a return to a general practice." She pinched the bridge of her nose. "I had a hard time choosing a specialty."

"If you're speaking about a change of career in more than passing, I could help you with that," Mitch said, not one to miss an opportunity. "I'm the mayor of Second Chance and we're looking for a new town doctor. We offer a generous retainer, plus a slow pace. Most mornings you'd get to sleep in. And the views are spectacular."

"Don't give her any ideas." The nurse with the cartoon bunny scrubs reappeared, wheeling what looked like a sonogram machine. She knocked on Laurel's door.

At Laurel's word, the doctor, nurse and machine disappeared into Laurel's room. It was the perfect opportunity to make his exit.

And he would have if not for the haunted look in Laurel's eyes when they'd pulled up. And the noticeably absent *hardy-har-har* of her laughter during the trip down. And the way she'd clung to his hand in the exam room.

She needs you.

Mitch sighed.

The regular beat of the sonogram machine drifted beneath the doorway. Laughter erupted, including a familiar *hardy-har-har*. Laurel was fine. He wouldn't be needed after all.

Mitch stood, intending to wait for her in the lobby.

Before he'd taken one step, the door was flung open and the nurse dragged him into the dimly lit room. "This, you have to see." She closed the door behind him, grabbed his arm and positioned him bedside, near enough to take Laurel's hand again.

Which he did.

Laurel smiled up at him as if they'd been holding hands and sharing secrets for years.

"Well, Mr. Monroe," Dr. Carlisle said grandly. "According to your wife, you've been through a lot the past few weeks. But it seems as if you've passed a hurdle. She's feeling better and the babies are healthy."

"Babies?" Mitch squinted at the sonogram screen. Sure enough, there were two beings outlined there. Big heads. Fragile-looking arms. Hearts beating in tandem.

Two babies.

His knees felt weak.

Two babies who might not have a daddy.

His gut clenched.

"We're predicting baby girls." Dr. Carlisle moved the sonogram wand. "But it's early."

Twin girls.

Something in his chest softened. The same

something that softened sometimes toward Laurel.

Mitch remembered the long nights walking Gabby up and down the hall while he crooned "Itsy Bitsy Spider." The long days when Gabby didn't nap and was fussy. He remembered his baby girl's first smile. Her first words. Her first steps. Her first eye roll.

If Laurel didn't tell the father, some schlub was going to miss out on a lot of great times with Laurel's babies.

"I suspected twins, but…" Laurel glanced apologetically toward Mitch as if he was indeed her husband. "Multiples run in my family. Does this mean more bed rest?"

The doctor handed the sonogram wand to the nurse and then wiped the clear jelly from Laurel's bare belly. "As long as you take care of yourself and listen to your body, you can do almost everything you normally do."

Mitch cleared his throat. "Can she fly?"

"Yes. For the next few months."

Disappointment stabbed him in the gut, which was ridiculous. He wanted Laurel to leave.

Dr. Carlisle drew the paper drape over Laurel's legs higher and then the hospital gown lower over her stomach. "Nowadays, we encourage pregnant women to live normal lives.

That said, at your elevation no aerobic exercise beyond walking. Certainly, no high-impact activity or heavy lifting." The doctor flipped on the room's light but lingered. "Has anyone ever pointed out the resemblance you have to that actress who played a princess in a television movie recently? I'm sure you know who I'm thinking of. The woman with the red hair."

Laurel's mouth formed a little O.

"She gets that all the time." Mitch came to Laurel's rescue. "But my wife's nose is bigger, and her teeth are crooked."

Laurel stared at Mitch as if he'd lost his mind.

He had. Or he wouldn't be in an exam room with her, saddened by her upcoming departure.

"And I had such high hopes for you." The nurse shook her head.

"Hey," Mitch said. "My wife may not be glamorous or famous, but she's beautiful and she's mine." In that moment Mitch believed it. His comment had put a fire in Laurel's eyes, one aimed at him. "Look how she glows."

Laurel pressed her lips together and turned her stare toward the ceiling, but her cheeks blossomed with color.

"Nice recovery, Mr. Monroe." Dr. Carlisle turned to leave.

"We're all nice up in Second Chance." Mitch couldn't resist one more plug. "Come up for a visit on your next day off and you'll see."

"I sleep on my day off," Dr. Carlisle said briskly. "But thanks for the offer."

CHAPTER TEN

"I APPRECIATE YOU playing chauffeur," Laurel said when Mitch pulled into his narrow garage in Second Chance. And holding her hand during her office visit. Not that she was going to bring that up. "I would've been a nervous wreck driving on that road." Or sitting in the exam room alone.

They hadn't spoken much on the ride back. Laurel had a bag of information at her feet and a ball of anxiety near those babies she was carrying.

What did she know about motherhood? She'd had years to perfect a sewing stitch, who knew how long to master knitting, but only a few months to learn how to be a good mom. To twins!

"It wasn't like I was tricked into driving." Mitch, the man who'd been her rock all day, sounded as if he was teasing her.

"There was that," she said weakly. "I'm sorry about Shane."

He waved her apology aside. "And then there's the issue of dressing up my daughter."

"I *know* I apologized for that." Multiple times.

Mitch nodded. "Which leads us to the end of the road." He pressed the remote to close the garage door, plunging them into near darkness. The snow covered half the windows on either side.

"The end of the road?"

"You got your medical clearance." He turned to face her. "You're leaving Second Chance."

The ball in Laurel's stomach dropped. "Yes." She had to go back to Hollywood.

"The roads will remain open the next few days." He rested his head against the glass, casting his face in shadow. "You have time to help Sophie look for that da Vinci she's hoping for in the trading post and time to be honest with yourself."

She was honest with herself, all right. He had no idea the number of truths she kept inside.

"Laurel, the truth is you didn't call anyone to gush over your happy news," he said simply, surprising her. "And now you're going to drag yourself upstairs as if this pregnancy is the end of the world because you're worried about every little thing in everyone else's life."

She scoffed. "I wasn't—"

"Oh, you were. Don't forget who you're talking to." He tapped his chest. "You've got your *husband* here."

She smirked, but the fact remained. He was right. "I *was* going to mope around my room. But not forever. People won't like me much when the truth comes out about my pregnancy." And that included the conservative single dad sitting next to her.

Mitch tsk-tsked. "You need to set aside the family drama you're dealing with and think about how you'd feel if things were different. What if you had a caring dad for your baby?"

Laurel's breath hitched.

Him, the babies whispered. *We want him.*

"What if you had a better relationship with your mother and sister? In an ideal world, wouldn't you be ecstatic to know you were going to be a mom?" Mitch didn't sugarcoat her situation. He simply challenged Laurel to set everything other than the babies aside.

And then he took her hand and waited.

Truth pressed down on Laurel, on her shoulders and her tear ducts. "Yes, I'm happy." Yes, that gave her a twinge of guilt for her responsibilities back in Hollywood. "But I'm also a realist. What am I going to do for money when my savings run out? Where am I going to go? I'm not sure I could get another job as a costume designer in Hollywood, but even if I did the cost of living is huge and the hours are brutal."

"You'll figure it out. The same way you figured out that pink dress." He squeezed her hand, barely smiling. "Go inside and make some calls. Have the hard discussions. And then find the joy your babies deserve. Find that joy and hold on tight."

Mitch Kincaid was unlike other men she'd met. He didn't have a charming facade. He didn't have eyes that lit with calculation the moment she walked into a room. He didn't rely on smooth words and expensive automobiles to impress. He just showed up, said his piece and then left you to it.

Silence wrapped around them. Silence drew them close. Although neither one of them had moved.

Silence waited patiently. Expectantly. And yet without demands.

If Laurel chose not to speak, there'd be no judgment. No disappointment.

There would just be Mitch and his strong hand circling hers.

And in that hush, something warm circled her chest. Something safe and comforting and unfamiliar.

"It sounds like you've always put Ashley first, ahead of what you want and need. It's time to be Laurel Monroe, to embrace being a mother, to be proud of what you've done so far and to take the time to dream about what you want in the future."

The babies swooned, making the world tilt.

I could lean on those sturdy shoulders.

"You missed your calling, Counselor. You should have been a support nurse for pregnant women." Laurel leaned across the console and kissed his cheek, drawing back when she wouldn't have minded moving her lips to his. "Not that you'd see many pregnant women in need of advice living in an oversize log cabin." He might want her gone, but at least they'd found common ground.

Mitch smiled. "I like the inn. It has history and character and substance."

Like him.

She should get inside. She had calls to make. And yet she lingered. "I can't say the inn is perfect. It has closet rods that are several inches too short."

"No one's perfect." That smile. It was contagious. It didn't make fun—how could it with those kind eyes?

No. That smile said, *Life doesn't always go as planned, but it can still be a good thing.*

It said, *There's more to life than careers and name making.*

It said, *I see you, Laurel Monroe. You're a good person.*

That smile. It made her feel…special.

But that smile. It'd disappear the moment he learned the truth about her.

LAUREL MONROE WAS a surprise.

That, in itself, was surprising.

Mitch prided himself on being a good judge of character. He'd misjudged Laurel.

Despite her high-heeled boots, shiny black leggings and thin, sparkly sweaters, she wasn't a style chaser, more concerned with appearances than substance. She wasn't a spoiled little rich girl. If he looked beyond her outward features he'd find an intelligent, interesting, vulnerable woman. He wanted to take her to dinner and talk until the wee hours of the morning. He wanted to hold her in his arms, learn more of her secrets and perhaps share some deep, soul-baring kisses.

If only she wasn't a Monroe. Because he couldn't tell her anything. He'd signed a legally binding document. He'd given Harlan his word.

He followed Laurel toward the inn, walking at a much slower pace, letting the frigid wind cool him down. She'd received the medical all clear to leave town. There would be no more intimate discussions. No more riding together in companionable silence. No more feather-light kisses pressed to his cheek.

"Mitch!" Roy darted out of the Bent Nickel, scarecrow limbs pumping in his haste to reach him. "Hey! Hey, Mitch!"

"What's up, Roy?" Mitch asked, watching Laurel disappear inside the inn.

"We got big trouble." Panting, Roy pressed a hand to his breastbone as if he had heart-burn. He needed to stay away from Ivy's chili. "It's Shane. He had a Realtor up here today. Or maybe an appraiser." He waved a hand be-tween them. "Somebody was here."

Mitch's blood pressure spiked. Somehow, he kept from howling. In addition to not hearing so well, Roy didn't see too well, either. De-tails. Mitch needed details. "Which was it? A Realtor or an appraiser?"

Roy shrugged. "He parked over there on the other side of Shane's Humdinger."

Mitch glared at the offending Hummer. "Did anyone ask his name? Or get his card?"

"I was inside the diner and couldn't see what the sign said on his truck. Ivy was upstairs with her kids and by the time she came back down he was gone." Roy shoved his hands into his jacket pockets. "What does it mean?"

Mitch was afraid to guess. But he knew where the answers were—with Shane. "It's okay, Roy. I'll take care of this."

Mitch marched to the inn, feet crunching the thin layer of snow on the ground.

"You," he said when he found Shane in the common room talking to Laurel and Zeke. He pinned the cowboy with a significant look as he tossed his jacket aside. "This could get ugly. No one's going to fault you if you retreat to your room."

"Free entertainment?" Zeke grinned, repositioning his wheelchair. "I'm not going anywhere."

Shane sat in the corner of the couch nearest Zeke, looking the part of the sinister corporate man in his khakis and expensive leather shoes. His gaze hardened, but he said nothing.

Mitch came to stand opposite him, back to the hearth and a small fire that did little to warm him. "You succeeded in getting me out of town. And now you can tell me why."

A smile flirted on Shane's lips. "Kincaid, you lack finesse."

Mitch's hands fisted. "I'm not asking you to talk about whatever grand master plan you have regarding Second Chance." Although that would be nice. "I'm asking you, the owner of this town, to tell me, the mayor of this town, who you met with today. I was under the impression you couldn't drive your cousin to her doctor's appointment because you had a job interview."

"Let's try to keep things civil." Laurel moved to stand next to Mitch.

"I take full responsibility for misleading you." Shane was serious, for once. "But Kincaid, lighten up. You see conspiracy in everything."

"And you don't see the value of transparency and teamwork." Anger spit out of Mitch in short, sharp syllables. "You think you alone can decide what's good for this town? You couldn't run this inn, much less Second Chance. It'd be a ghost town under your watch."

"Is that a dare?" Shane's gaze narrowed. "Would you like to place a bet?"

"Shane." Laurel stepped between the two men. "You can't keep everyone in the dark the way Grandpa Harlan did."

"Hear, hear." Zeke applauded.

Shane frowned at each of them in turn. "Let me handle this my way."

"No." Laurel put her hands on her hips, her

tone as fiery as her hair. "As part owner of this town, I demand to know what you're up to."

"Start with telling everyone who you met with today," Zeke clarified, proving he'd witnessed Shane with someone. Not surprising since his regular spot in the common room put him on the south side of Shane's Hummer, opposite the diner. "Or I will. He had a big sign painted on his truck door."

Shane's chin came up. "Stay out of this, cowboy."

Just when Mitch was ready to jump back in the fray, Laurel beat him to it. "I call in my favor, Shane."

What?

"Laurel." Shane's frown deepened.

Mitch's temples pounded. "Am I such a big threat to you? Are you afraid I might throw a wrench in your plans?"

"Stop. Both of you." Laurel held up a hand. "You promised me a favor, Shane. Don't break your word and upset my babies."

"Babies?" Sophie and her twins practically tumbled into the room from the stairs. "Oh, my gosh. Aunt Laurel is having twins, boys!" She and her kids ran over to surround Laurel. "Wait until Ashley hears about this."

"Hang on, Sophie." Laurel gently disentangled herself from the group hug. "I'm trying to claim my favor from Shane."

"Don't waste your favor on him," Shane cautioned, pointing at Mitch. "Kincaid won't believe a word I say."

Mitch smirked. He was right about that.

"But I'll believe you," Laurel said firmly, taking hold of Mitch's hand.

Righting her red glasses, Sophie noticed the hand-holding and grinned from ear to ear.

"I'm so glad I didn't leave." Zeke leaned forward in his wheelchair. "The acoustics are horrible in my room."

Shane jabbed a thumb in the cowboy's direction. "Does he have to hear, too?"

"Yes," said Mitch.

"Yes," said Laurel.

"Heck, yeah," said Zeke.

The twins giggled, hopping around like bunnies on a warm spring day.

Shane rubbed his forehead and looked to his sister.

"I'll go with the crowd and say yes." Sophie hadn't stop grinning. "Not that I have any idea what's going on."

"Unbelievable." Shane shook his head. "There's a reason good managers hold their cards close to their chest. Too many cooks spoil the soup."

"Dish out your soup, brother dear." Sophie lifted one of her boys to her hip. "Without any more mixed metaphors."

Sophie's other son, the one with the cowlick, lifted his hands, requesting to be picked up, too. Laurel picked him up instead, releasing Mitch's hand to do so.

Immediately, Mitch's hand felt empty.

I'm going to miss her when she leaves.

Mitch pressed his palm to his thigh, holding on to Laurel's warmth and support, hoping she had someone to lean on when her twins arrived.

"Is Uncle Shane in trouble?" asked the boy in Sophie's arms. Mitch thought he might be Andrew.

"Not if he tells the truth." Sophie gave her brother a significant look. "Because that's what good boys and responsible adults do."

Both boys stared at their uncle expectantly.

"Okay, okay." Shane gave in. "I hired a real estate consultant. That's my big secret. Are you happy?"

Unhappy, Mitch groaned. "Does this mean you're selling?"

"I'm one vote in twelve, Kincaid." Shane smirked. "I can't answer that question."

Mitch kept forgetting about that. To him,

Shane was the face of his predicament. More Monroes? He gritted his teeth.

"So what's this consultant for if not to sell the town?" Zeke's normally good-natured smile had vanished.

Shane spared his sister a pained look before answering. "*This guy* specializes in evaluating small towns like Second Chance with the purpose of making recommendations for investors and—"

"Investors?" Zeke groaned. "Now I'm not happy. Next thing you know, there'll be a big-box store selling cases of toilet paper where the church used to be."

"You didn't let me finish." Shane stared at Sophie. "You see what happens when you relinquish control? No one lets you finish."

Mitch's temples felt like they were being battered with hockey pucks. "Do you have more to say?"

"Yes!" Shane shouted, bringing Gabby from the apartment and making his nephews cover their ears. "He's not a listing agent. He presents alternatives based on the town's character, its resources, its potential to be something more or to remain something..."

"Less," Mitch finished for him. "You were going to say *less*. I take offense to that."

"I was going to say more. As in, *more*

charming." Shane pushed his dark, wavy hair off his forehead. "If I could just finish."

"Let's hear him out." Laurel snuggled her nephew closer in her arms and glanced up at Mitch.

It was on the tip of Mitch's tongue to say no, that he'd heard enough bad news for one day, but there were her big blue eyes and—

Shane continued, "What you all seem to forget is that we're in this together. I can't speak for my siblings or my cousins, but I have no desire to evict people and no desire to tear down the town where my grandfather was born. What if I destroy the cabin he grew up in?" Shane ran one hand around the back of his neck. "I take offense to the town's attitude toward me. I'm not the enemy."

"He's not," the boy in Laurel's arms said. "He's Uncle Shane and we love him."

"That's right," seconded the boy in Sophie's arms.

In the ensuing silence, Mitch sank to the hearth seat, not knowing what to believe.

"This is a surprising change of events," Zeke said, looking as shell-shocked as Mitch felt. "Is Shane a good guy now? Black hat exchanged for white?"

"Save us the cowboy humor," Shane grumbled, his face still flushed.

Laurel set the boy she held on the floor and then hugged her cousin. She was always the first Monroe to try to mend fences.

"What's that for?" Shane held himself stiffly.

Laurel patted his shoulder. "Because you surprised me and I'm proud of you."

"I'm just trying to do what's right without everyone getting in my way." Shane pointed at Mitch. "In the hospitality industry that's called efficiency. And yes, I could run this inn all by myself, and the town, too."

"If he could just learn to shut up and quit while he's ahead." Zeke tsk-tsked, earning another frown from Shane.

But the cowboy's words unlocked one of Mitch's memories.

"You lawyers…" Harlan Monroe had shifted in his chair on the back deck of the inn and grinned. "You try to be so clinical, pretending you have no heart. But good lawyers are good because they care, they risk, they hurt." He gestured with his beer bottle to Mitch. "Which case got to you?"

Mitch had sat silent, clutching his beer bottle as if it were the lock on his past.

"That many, huh?" Harlan sobered. "Well, I suppose being taciturn keeps all that disappointment inside. Unlike my grandson Shane.

Now, he's a man who doesn't know when to shut up. The gift of gab makes him darn good working with people, though. Darn good. If you can stomach all those words."

Mitch got back to his feet. "I'll take that bet, Shane."

"To run the inn?" Shane laughed.

"To run *the town*." Mitch felt a smile coming on. This man had the power to change the town for the better or to destroy it. His opinion mattered to the rest of the Monroes or they wouldn't have put him in charge. "You can be an honorary town councilman, like your grandfather was."

There was a moment of silence as that knowledge sank in.

"Like my grandfather was," Shane echoed. "If I do this, will you trust me to make the right recommendations for the town's future?"

No one spoke.

Everyone waited for Mitch's response, including Gabby.

"If your actions prove to be sincere, then yes," Mitch said, for both Shane's benefit and his daughter's. "I'll trust you." His gaze drifted to Laurel's.

Her eyes were shining with approval.

Selfishly, he wanted her to stay. Despite her

grandfather's wishes. Despite her dreams. Despite her need to watch over her twin sister.

Because when Laurel had his back, Mitch could face anything.

But now he wondered...

Who watched out for Laurel?

"HERE GOES NOTHING." After helping broker a truce between Mitch and Shane, Laurel knew it was time to make things right with her family.

With her door closed and the do-not-disturb sign hanging on the doorknob, Laurel sent a video chat request to her mother and sister.

On the bed next to her, Sophie squeezed her hand. "I'll be right here."

"Mom. Ashley." They showed up in the same frame on her mother's line, white kitchen cabinets in the background. Laurel swallowed thickly and tried to keep a smile on her face.

I'm pregnant. Joy, I should be feeling joy.

Laurel held the phone in front of her face. "I...have some...wonderful news."

Gah! She sounded like a caught fish gasping on a dry dock.

"Are you coming home tomorrow?" Ashley's smile didn't quite reach her eyes. She looked hopefully fragile as if she'd been on the receiving end of their mother's sharp comments once too often recently.

"You're coming home?" Mom moved in front of Ashley. "That's wonderful news. We have so much to do."

"Mom. Listen." Laurel's mouth was drier than Palm Springs in August. "I'm—"

"I can't think of anything better than having you home," Mom said in her I'm-so-sweet voice.

"I can," Sophie murmured, elbowing Laurel.

Mom kept on talking, a trait Dad once confessed had led to their divorce. "Let me tell you what I've worked out regarding our pink dress."

Our pink dress? Even the babies shuddered.

Laurel pressed on. "Can I share my news first?"

Mom talked over her. "There's a New York designer interested in buying our fashion line."

"She's talking about your dress," Sophie fumed, losing whisper volume. "Give me that phone."

Laurel stood, facing Sophie so her mother and sister couldn't see she wasn't alone. "But—"

"Hear me out," Mom said, irritation rounding her vowels. "There's good money in it for you, too."

"Too?" Sophie pushed her glasses higher. "How much of *your* dress is *your* money?" Clearly, Shane wasn't the only one with business sense in that branch of the family.

"This designer wants an entire line of red-carpet gowns." Mom's smile was brittle, but then again it often was. "Ten. Twelve. More if possible. We've discovered a new revenue stream."

Sell, sell, sell, Laurel's worried, single-parent brain chanted. Raising kids took money and she was unemployed, living off her savings.

"Don't you dare agree," Sophie said, coming to her feet and reaching for the phone.

Laurel backed away. That number of dresses meant serious money. And being a red-carpet fashion designer was her dream. "Who's interested?"

Mom walked through her living room, leaving Ashley behind. "Xuri Wu." She gushed as if she'd designed the pink dress. "She is so avant-garde."

Xuri Wu wants to work with me?

Laurel gulped. Xuri designed cutting-edge fashion. That was heady, impossible, dream-come-true stuff.

"She's dominating the red carpet, Laurel." Mom's excitement came through her voice with more clarity than her suddenly blurring image on the small screen as she passed by a bright window.

"I know that." But a reality check was sinking in.

Xuri used bold floral designs and sharp lines. Her style was everything Laurel's wasn't. Xuri was worldly, confident, risk taking. Xuri Wu would laugh if she knew Laurel was knitting.

Laurel had been silent too long.

Mom sensed an opportunity to close the deal. "So you'll do it?"

"No!" Sophie whispered, shaking her head so vehemently her red glasses slid down her nose.

Laurel frowned. Torn. Mitch said her children should come first.

Not at the expense of who you are.

"I need to think about it." Laurel glanced at the coppery scarf she'd begun knitting with chunky needles. It was hard to believe someone wanted her to design for their fashion house when Odette had rejected her knitting endeavors.

"At least ask to see the contract." Sophie flopped back on the bed.

Smart. "And I need to see the contract,"

Laurel added, practically slurring her words together in her haste to get them out.

"Contracts are my area of expertise." Mom morphed into The Momager. "We can't put them off much longer because of your Idaho hiatus. Don't be an artiste when you haven't got anything to back you up."

"I have the dress," Laurel said meekly, adding in a mumbled, "and some partially completed scarves." Speaking of which, here was the perfect bridge to the reason for her call. "By the way, Mom, I'm—"

"And what about Wyatt?" Mom switched gears faster than a race-car driver. "Ashley can't go out with him a second time. We have no idea what you two talked about on that first date. You have to come back and do it."

Oh, what a disaster.

"There will be no second date with Wyatt." Laurel placed a hand on her belly. "Dump him. Tell him there was no chemistry. Tell him—"

"That's not for you to decide." There was no sweetness from her mother anymore. "Get on the next plane. Ashley needs press. Since your father terminated her contract on that film, we need to rebuild."

"I'm *not* giving up my dress to you. I'm *not* dating Wyatt Halford. And I'm *not* coming home tomorrow because—"

"I can't talk to you like this." Mom broke the connection.

"—I'm pregnant!"

But her mother hadn't heard.

CHAPTER ELEVEN

"SOPHIE, LET'S GO find your da Vinci. The babies and I need fresh air." Door open, Laurel sat on her bed, lacing her snow boots. She called to Sophie down the hall.

She needed to stretch her legs. Mitch might have paced downstairs last night, but Laurel had tossed and turned until she'd given up and knit while Mitch got his steps in. She couldn't shake the gut-punching feeling that she was letting Ashley down. But what could she do differently? Neither her mother nor Ashley were answering their phones, which was no more than Laurel deserved after two weeks of her own cellular silence.

I should go home and face them.

Regret squeezed her heart. She didn't want to leave the peace of Second Chance for what was sure to be a media circus in Hollywood.

Thunderous small feet ran down the hallway. Laurel stood, bracing herself for impact, but the twins raced past her room.

"Bye, Aunt Laurel!" They crashed into a

wall at the other end of the hall soon after, giggling and pounding on wood. "Wake up, Uncle Shane! Wake up! Wake up!" Their voices were so similar, Laurel couldn't distinguish one from the other. "Open up, Uncle Shane! We love you!"

Pound-pound-pound!

"I'm gonna milk this for all it's worth." Sophie stood in the doorway and grinned. "A full day without my boys. What a gift!"

A door unlatched.

"Look!" Shane cried. "It's my most excellent nephews! Let's go find some trouble."

Sophie's eyes widened. She stepped into the hall. "Not too much trouble, Shane."

"There's never too much trouble." Shane laughed, but it sounded more like a villainous cackle. "Come on, boys. Show me how you hop like a bunny down these stairs."

Laurel wrapped the teal scarf she'd made around her neck multiple times. She'd gotten a little carried away with the length.

"Maybe long scarves will be a trend this year." Sophie pushed her glasses back into position. "Like overly long sleeves used to be."

"Unlikely." Laurel grabbed her coat and a grin. Her situation hadn't improved since yesterday, but she still had her babies and her joy. "But I like it."

They went downstairs. Shane was leaning against a wall, drinking a cup of coffee while the twins tumbled in circles around Zeke's wheelchair, deftly avoiding his propped-up broken leg.

"I'm under siege. Cannonballs everywhere." Zeke's smile seemed to grow when he looked at Sophie, who pretended not to notice.

And wasn't that interesting...

Shane's phone buzzed. He checked the display and chuckled. "Here's a question from Cousin Holden. He's asking when Laurel is returning to California for Aunt Gee."

"My mom called Holden?" Anger flushed Laurel's veins. "And he texted you?"

"You know how much your mother loves Cousin Holden." Shane shrugged. "What do you want me to say?"

Laurel hesitated, feeling as brittle as an overcooked cookie, on the brink of crumbling.

"You should follow your heart," Sophie said sagely, looking at her boys with love in her eyes. "And if you aren't sure which direction that is, you should stay here."

"Think of your future," Shane said with a rare dose of seriousness. "Go home and take care of those babies. Aunt Gee will come around. I can decide what to do with this town."

"Like I'm chopped liver," Sophie mumbled.

"You can take off, too, sister dear." Shane's tone turned smarmy. "You aren't serving on the town council."

"Oh," Sophie huffed. "Don't try to turn the mess you made yesterday into something it's not."

"That's right." Mitch appeared at the check-in desk. "You're *sitting in* as an honorary, *temporary* member." He wore a thick blue jacket and knit cap, a sure sign he was headed outside. He cradled multiple pairs of snowshoes, which he'd offered to loan to Laurel and Sophie. "Oddly enough, I find myself agreeing with Shane on one note." His dark gaze landed on Laurel. "Laurel should go home."

Laurel's heart twisted in her chest. All Mitch's words of encouragement. All the times she'd felt seen… She'd thought after they'd banded together against Shane that Mitch would stop trying to get rid of her.

What did it matter? As soon as the truth was out, Mitch wouldn't look at her the same way. He valued truth and integrity. The circumstances of how she became pregnant were proof she couldn't meet his high standards.

She held her head high, refusing to let him see how much his words hurt. "Home? I don't know where that is anymore." Since Laurel had had to vacate the condominium she'd lived in before she came, the one owned by the Monroe Holding Company. "Maybe this is my home now. I mean, not this inn, but Second Chance." She glanced at Shane. "Isn't there an unoccupied cabin I can move to? Me and my dress, that is."

Everyone fell silent. Even Alexander and Andrew stopped counting spokes to stare at her.

"Why is everyone looking at me?" Oh, the irony. Now wasn't the time to miss being an overlooked shadow. "Sophie said I should stay until I knew where my heart lay." Laurel tried not to look at Mitch. She really did. But…

It was those babies, plain and simple. They looked at Mitch with longing.

And Mitch? There were mixed messages in those dark eyes.

Laurel's chin notched higher.

Gabby entered the room. "Dad, can I have my phone?"

"No." Mitch didn't turn to face his daughter. He kept staring at Laurel, an indecipherable look on his face.

Gabby didn't give up. "Dad, *when* can I have my phone?"

"When I can trust you again." But Mitch said it while he scanned Laurel's attire—a thin blue boatneck sweater and leggings made out of gray sweatshirt material. "Laurel should go home. Today."

Laurel's hands knotted into fists and those fists landed on her hips. "Because my wardrobe is a bad influence on Gabby? Didn't you just tell me yesterday that I needed to be happy about my pregnancy? Did you ever stop and wonder if maybe I'd be unhappy if I went back to Hollywood?"

For once, Gabby didn't speak. She watched their exchange with interest.

But she wasn't the only one interested in their argument. Everyone was watching.

"Let's set aside your happiness for a moment and think about your daughters'." Mitch set the snowshoes on the planked floor by the door. "What's best for your babies might not include hiking through the snow at six thousand feet."

Laurel frowned. She'd expected a fight about her stylishly bad influence on his daughter, not a safety lecture.

Shane gestured toward Mitch with his coffee cup. "He's got a point."

Sophie snorted. "Neither one of you has been pregnant, so what would you guys know about it? I mean, just look at her." Sophie gestured at Laurel. "She's in her prime and so healthy. I bet she could climb any mountain out there, right?"

Zeke didn't take his eyes from Sophie. "Right," he breathed.

"Oh, boy," Shane mumbled. His words unlocked the freeze on the twins.

Alexander ran to Shane, grabbing his legs. "Let's find trouble."

Andrew followed. "Lots and lots of trouble."

Shane barely kept his coffee from spilling.

"There's a town council meeting in an hour," Mitch said without relinquishing his intense regard of Laurel. "Plenty of time to sled or build a snow fort outside."

"Boys, we're being dismissed." Shane saluted and began bundling the twins in their jackets. "Which is good, because this isn't our fight. I'll tell Holden you're staying here for now, Laurel."

"How about tell Holden we need her here?" Sophie helped her kids into their boots. "I know I do."

Facing Mitch, Laurel widened her stance, like a boxer preparing for a long round. "I'm not giving up on my dreams by choosing to stay." It would be impossible to pursue her career as soon as her news broke. "I'm going across the street, not climbing Kilimanjaro. I know when you first met me I was weak with morning sickness, but I'm okay now."

"When I say you should go back to California, I only have your best interests at heart." Something hard in his gaze softened. "Those dreams of yours will be harder to reach from Idaho."

Try impossible.

"Oh, wow. This is awkward." Gabby smiled, looking anything but uncomfortable. "Privacy boundary breached. My dad has the hots for a guest."

Laurel's cheeks had never heated so fast. Shane snagged Andrew's jacket zipper halfway up, and Sophie fell over trying to put Alexander's boot on.

"Gabby," Mitch cautioned.

The teen refused to acknowledge his warning. "How did this happen? A few days ago, you didn't even like her." Tossing her strawberry blond hair, Gabby gave Laurel a sweeter than sweet smile. "No offense, Laurel."

"None taken," she choked out.

"Gabby!" Mitch said louder, turning to face his beloved ray of sunshine.

"Dad." The girl crossed her arms over her chest and arched her brows. "You can buy my silence. Any old time."

"With your cell phone," Mitch guessed.

"I'm going to hire that girl someday." Shane hustled the twins outside. "She'll make a great negotiator."

"If she survives her teenage years," Zeke added, half under his breath.

Sophie mumbled something about needing to impart safety rules and followed Shane and the twins out the door.

"I will not be blackmailed." Mitch raised his voice higher than his hunched shoulders. "A cell phone requires maturity."

"I can be mature." Gabby was yelling now, too.

Laurel was reminded of the shouts of her parents, her mother berating Ashley when she didn't land a job, her father chastising her older brother when he didn't make the basketball team. She hated confrontation, but she couldn't move. Not her feet anyway. The only thing she could move was her lips. "Stop this."

They didn't hear her.

"I'm growing up fast," Gabby announced. "Everyone says so. Everyone but you!"

"You're growing up *too* fast," Mitch retorted. "Which some might take to mean you're too big for your britches!"

"Please stop." The walls closed in on Laurel.

"I'm going to look up what that phrase means later." Gabby frowned. "Along with themes for spring weddings because you do want to marry Laurel *before* the babies come, don't you?"

"Gabby!"

"That's enough!" Laurel shouted, stepping between them. "Be quiet. Both of you. You're upsetting my girls." She laid a hand on her belly.

Gabby smiled like a satisfied cat, and Mitch continued to scowl at his daughter, but they'd stopped hollering at least.

"Let's begin the conversation again," Laurel said in a calm voice. "This time using your indoor voices. Mitch, I think I can decide what dreams to pursue and what dreams to put on the back burner in order to be a good mother." Although she appreciated his consideration. Too much. "And thank you for offering to loan me snowshoes. I could use *a little* exercise and Sophie could use the company." She pinned Gabby with her gaze. "And you, girlfriend. When you've done something wrong and get caught, like running a red light or smuggling contraband—" meaning her cell phone "—you have to serve the time. Which means your father needs to establish an end date for your infraction."

"When she turns eighteen," Mitch murmured.

"Dad!"

These two...

"Remember my babies. Please." Laurel held up her hands and turned to Mitch. "Counselor, your suggested, reasonable length of punishment is..."

Mitch chewed on Laurel's peacekeeping proposition to the limits of Gabby's patience—who, by the way, hadn't faired any better with her knitting with Odette than Laurel had. "A month."

"Two weeks," Gabby countered.

"Two weeks on the condition you disable all social media apps upon repossession." Mitch answered so quickly he must have been considering his terms last night while he paced.

"Deal." Gabby smiled, a real one this time. She ran over to her father and hugged him. "I love you, Dad."

"I love you, too, honey," Mitch said gruffly, patting her awkwardly.

"Ahh..." Zeke sniffed as if he was touched by the father and daughter hug, although from his smile Laurel knew that wasn't the case. "Who needs TV when I've got drama at the inn?"

Gabby's cheeks blossomed with color, but she didn't run away. She took Laurel's hands.

"You know I'm okay with you and my dad, right?"

"Umm…" Laurel wanted to disappear. "Thanks, but we're just friends." The look Mitch gave Laurel just then made her heart pound. Was she wrong about the friend thing?

"I'm off to do schoolwork." Gabby smiled and skipped into her room.

Laurel cleared her throat.

Mitch's gaze was intense. A flutter grew inside her chest, urging her to lean into Mitch's embrace. They'd agreed not to talk about the attraction between them, but apparently that didn't mean they wouldn't be aware of it.

Friends? It didn't feel like it.

"I'm going to escort you across the street to your destination." Mitch disappeared into his apartment. "You'll need poles, too."

"You don't have to do this."

"I do," he called back. "Sometimes snowshoes take a while to get used to."

"I'm sure we'll be fine." Ella had conquered the skill when she was here.

Mitch gave Laurel a small, yet determined smile. "But I have the keys to those buildings. If I… If you let me accompany you, I'll shovel the snow and unlock the doors."

"That's an offer a single lady can't refuse," Sophie said, having stepped inside. She turned so only Laurel could see her, and mouthed, *He's a keeper.*

Sophie misunderstood. Mitch was indeed a keeper.

He just didn't want to keep her.

"SNOWSHOEING IS LIKE ICE-SKATING," Laurel said, snowshoeing behind Mitch.

"Snowshoeing is *nothing* like ice-skating, Laurel." Sophie brought up the rear. "It's more like walking on water."

The sun glittered off the snow bright enough to blind Mitch, had he not been wearing sunglasses. He walked sideways up the mountain in his snowshoes, stomping down snow so the women could safely follow. The slow pace allowed him to dwell too much in his head.

Laurel's announcement that she wasn't leaving town weighed on him.

Red-carpet dress designers didn't live in small, remote towns. Harlan had spoken proudly of Laurel's gentle nature and creative talent. And babies... Babies needed readily available medical care. He still had no responses to his ad for a town doctor. She couldn't stay. It wasn't safe and she wouldn't be happy.

"When I say snowshoeing is like iceskating," Laurel sounded like something had worn thin—her patience or her stamina, "I meant I don't like either one."

Sophie laughed, the sound an echo of her children's laughter as they raced down Sled Hill with Shane.

Mitch stopped climbing and turned, searching Laurel's face to see how she was holding up. Her cheeks were rosy. Her blue eyes bright. She looked fine. She looked happier than she'd been ever since she'd arrived in Second Chance.

Laurel caught Mitch staring and waved him off. "I'm chirping, Counselor, not giving up."

Chirping. It was a term Harlan used to use when he was venting about something.

With the beginnings of a smile, Mitch began to tell Laurel as much. Until he realized he couldn't share that. If he was going to uphold the nondisclosure agreement, he'd have to watch everything he said.

Mood dampened, Mitch resumed his climb, noting Roy heading toward them.

"Given the Lee family founded this town and were related to Grandpa Harlan…" Sophie gulped in air. "We should come naturally to snowshoeing."

"Says the woman who hasn't worked out in years," Laurel teased.

"Don't judge." Sophie didn't sound as if she

minded being baited. "You'll see how hard it is to parent twins *and* exercise soon enough."

A part of Mitch wanted to smile, to enjoy their banter. But he had to put some distance between them and honor his promise, even if it seemed Harlan wasn't able to honor his.

"Morning." Roy had reached the mercantile. "I bet you could use a hand." He had a shovel strapped to his back, same as Mitch.

Mitch wasn't going to refuse. Several feet of sloping snow blocked each door. "If you dig out the mercantile, I'll dig out the trading post."

"It's beautiful up here," Laurel said. "Cold. But beautiful."

"I have two words for you." Mitch stopped long enough to look back at Laurel, smiling despite his best intentions to remain detached. "Snow pants. Make that three. Sensible snow pants."

Sophie was wearing them. Laurel was not. If she fell in the snow, she'd get wet and be chilled to the bone.

"Here's the thing about snow pants." Laurel sounded like she was winding up for a lecture. "No clean lines. No silhouetted shape. There's nothing aesthetically pleasing about them."

"It pleases me to be warm." Mitch returned to the business of clearing snow, which only served to overheat him in his snow pants.

Finally, Mitch cleared the snow away from the trading post door, dug a key out of his pocket and opened the lock.

"You might want to step back in case any 'varmits' come scurrying out." Roy had reached them, leaving a compacted trail from one building to the next. "Be careful, ladies. And don't forget to have Mitch unlock the mercantile." Spry as a man thirty years his junior, Roy headed downhill, taking the path Mitch had made earlier.

Laurel reached Mitch's side, or as close as she could with her snowshoes on. "Why are the doors kept locked?"

Sophie grabbed a corner log for balance as she joined them. "Is this like Area 51? Top secret and classified stuff for Second Chance?"

"The door stays locked in winter to keep animals out. And locked in summer to keep the curious out. There are no secrets here." Mitch felt bad saying that. There were secrets in Second Chance aplenty, but they were kept by residents, not in any cabin. He opened the door and steadied the women while they removed their snowshoes.

"It's dark." Sophie stepped inside first, her voice thin and uncertain.

"The snow is blocking the small windows." Mitch wedged the door open to allow as much natural light inside as possible, not to mention a clear path to escape if anything bigger than a mouse had somehow gotten inside. He dug in his backpack and handed them each a flashlight.

"Here's to finding a da Vinci!" Sophie ventured inside.

"You came prepared." Laurel looked at him the way she had in his SUV right before she'd kissed his cheek.

Mitch's heart beat a little faster, even as his head cautioned him to consider all moves carefully. "I've been inside before."

"And you didn't want to shovel all that snow for nothing." Laurel hesitated on the porch with him, mischief lighting her eyes. "Sophie wouldn't go in if she couldn't see."

Mitch got lost in the depth of her blue gaze. "About what Gabby said…"

Laurel leaned in closer. "About you having the hots for me?" Her eyes sparkled. A guarded sparkle, but a shine nonetheless.

He nodded, mouth suddenly dry.

"Look at this! Laurel, you need to get in here."

Neither Laurel nor Mitch budged.

"We already knew we had a thing," Laurel allowed in a whisper. "I don't think it's progressed to the hot stage. I don't even think pregnant women can be hot."

Except for her leggings, Laurel was bundled up like a permanent Second Chance resident—hat, gloves, serviceable jacket and snow boots. The teal scarf she'd knit was wrapped around her neck like thick ribbons of frosting on a cupcake. Her blue eyes were bright, her cheeks had a rosy glow and she'd announced her intention to stay in town.

Who cared if she hadn't embraced the concept of snow pants?

But she's supposed to leave, a quiet voice in his head reminded him. A voice that sounded like Harlan's.

Mitch set aside legal considerations, promises made to old friends, and smiled at the beauty before him. "You don't think this thing has progressed? You don't think pregnant women are hot? Why, Miss Laurel, you thought wrong." He succumbed to an inclination he'd had for weeks. He bent and kissed Laurel. It was a relatively chaste kiss, but it managed to jolt his system like too many shots of espresso.

Laurel gasped dramatically and drew back. "What was that for?"

If taken at face value, her words might have given him pause, perhaps establishing a regret or two. But Mitch factored in her slightly breathless tone of voice, the dazed look in her eyes and the upward tilt of her lips.

He smiled and breathed the fresh mountain air, feeling as spunky and mischievous as Gabby had earlier. "That was just to see if we have the hots or not. That kiss could have been a dud."

Oh, not likely.

She lowered her lashes. "It wasn't much of a kiss to judge."

Mitch drew her close, bent down and kissed her again. This time when he released Laurel, her breath was as ragged as his.

"I can make a judgment now." With effort, Mitch set her aside. He had responsibilities— a town meeting, a teenage daughter, the latter of which was probably somewhere watching. He'd made promises. In that moment Mitch didn't care. "It's the hots. Definitely the hots."

"I'll say, Counselor." Cheeks aflame, Laurel turned on her flashlight and entered the trading post. "I'll say."

CHAPTER TWELVE

LAUREL STOOD INSIDE the doorway of the trading post, watching Mitch make his way carefully the twenty feet back to the road.

From here the town of Second Chance looked like a postcard she'd once received from a friend who'd visited Aspen. Snow-covered trees, rooftops and mountains. Pristine and perfect. Her heart felt light. The cares that came with her pregnancy lessened.

Mitch kissed me.

Joy, the unabashed joy she'd felt when she'd seen her babies on the sonogram screen, coursed through her veins.

Mitch kissed me.

It felt as if the babies were fluttering with joy, as well.

In the afterglow of their kiss, Laurel refused to think about the truths that had to be told, the ones that would douse the light in Mitch's eyes when he looked at her.

"Gabby's right. Mitch has the hots for you."

Laurel turned and faced her cousin with a

big smile and confirmed, "Mitch has the hots for me."

They both laughed.

Sophie grabbed her hand and drew her inside. "Don't be freaked out. This place is awesome. But it's packed tighter than a fridge at the holidays."

She was right. There were narrow paths through the stacks of stuff. Not an inch had been overlooked, not even the walls had escaped.

"Um." Laurel's gaze roved around the large building, finding no oil paintings by da Vinci, although there was a black velvet clown painting on the wall. "These are your treasures? Grandpa Harlan's treasures?"

"There's a treasure right here. Look at this handmade pottery." Sophie tugged Laurel across the dusty planked flooring to a bureau with what looked like unfinished pottery on top. "They look rustic like that because they were made by people with a passion for artistic expression but who were often self-taught." Sophie was an art nerd.

Laurel was just realizing her idea of art was an oil painting or a marble sculpture. Not stuff like this. She picked up one of the pieces. "Is this a pitcher?" It was. The ceramic was shaped and painted as a man's face, his nose was the spout. "Are you sure these are valuable?"

"Well, they're valuable to me and art historians. I'll have to research the mark on the bottom to see who made these." Sophie hugged herself and looked around the dim, musty room with a wide smile. "This is fabulous."

"Okay?" Laurel didn't try to hide her doubt. This was creepier than some of the prop rooms at Monroe Studios. Colder, too.

"He entrusted this to me."

"Who?"

"Grandpa Harlan. He entrusted these things to me the same way he had entrusted his art collection to me."

Had Sophie's eyes not filled with tears, Laurel might have argued that any one of the Monroe grandchildren could have entered the trading post and called dibs.

Not that she thought there was anyone but Sophie who'd be interested in...

"What's that?" Laurel pointed across the room. But she knew. It was the antique dress form Cousin Ella had told her about last month. At least, she hoped that was what it was. It looked like a short ghost.

Laurel picked her way past barrels and between cardboard boxes that were bulging and threatening to fall apart. Past signs from gasoline stations whose companies had long gone out of business. Past an old bicycle and cobwebs as thick as thread.

Finally, she reached the dress form, pulling off the thin drape. The base was made of iron. The torso covered in padded canvas. It was about four feet tall and made for a woman with the shape of Mae West.

Laurel laughed. "Oh, wow. I feel inadequate." Although that part of her had been expanding, too.

"Aha." Sophie reached her, shining the flashlight briefly in Laurel's eyes. "I bet the expression on your face mirrors the expression on my face when I found all that pottery." Sophie picked up an old cast-iron toy fire truck sitting on top of a cardboard box. The paint was faded. The wheels were bent. It looked much loved. "I wonder if this was Grandpa Harlan's toy when he was a boy."

Laurel's heart melted. "Do you think all this belonged to him? Or to his family?" Was this part of their history?

Sophie shrugged. "When we arrived, Mitch said we owned whatever was inside the buildings." Sophie picked up a wire crate filled with empty milk bottles. "I feel like an archaeologist who's just been let into the heart of a pyramid, one that's never been opened before. Do

I need to document things here? Do I need to sort them by decade?" The art curator was alive and well.

"That depends, I suppose, on what we should do with all this." Laurel turned the dress form around, exposing the laces in the back that helped keep its shape. She was afraid to touch them lest they break. "I'd like to keep this."

"I'd like to keep it all," Sophie breathed.

Something scuttled on the floor a few feet away. They both jumped.

"Correction." Sophie looked around nervously. "I'd like to keep it all in a place with bright lights and a big kitty."

"WHAT'S HE DOING HERE?" Roy's bushy white brows drew down at the sight of Shane entering the Bent Nickel. He pushed up the sleeves of his blue coveralls.

"Shane's an honorary town councilman." In the afterglow of Laurel's kiss, Mitch had forgotten this was going to be a prickly meeting and that he hadn't warned the rest of the town council. "I've invited him to represent the Monroes. We're opening the channels of communication."

Sophie's twins were bunny hopping across

the floor toward the counter, trying to land only on the white squares of linoleum.

"Two hot chocolates for my rabbits, please." Shane smiled at Ivy as if he hadn't heard Roy's accusatory question. "And I'll be getting some coffee." He withdrew two ten-dollar bills from his wallet, gave one to Ivy and stuffed the other in the empty community coffee jar. He lifted his nephews onto stools at the counter before pouring his own cup of coffee. "What's on the town council agenda today?"

"How to get rid of Monroes," Roy grumbled.

There was a gasp. And it didn't come from Ivy or Shane.

Ivy's son Nick stood at the end of the counter in his standard morning uniform of *Star Wars* pajamas and brown bear slippers. "Are you boys here to play with me?" He toned down his enthusiasm a notch. "Or to go to school? Because Mr. Eli said you could come, but it's early and he's not here and RJ never wants to play with me." RJ being Nick's older brother.

"Hot chocolate first," Ivy said, pouring hot water into mugs she'd filled with powdered hot chocolate. She stirred the twins' cups, topping them with ample whipped cream. "Nick, go upstairs, brush your hair and teeth, get on clothes—no shorts now—and bring down your toy soldiers."

"You know, there are rules we have to abide by with Monroes like him." Roy pointed a finger pistol at Shane. "One of which is Not Welcome Here."

"You know, we need new rules if we're going to get along and thrive." Mitch patted the white Formica tabletop nearest him. "Let's meet here today." They usually congregated at the counter, but that was going to be populated by kids. He went over to get himself a second cup of coffee. Dealing with Roy and Shane at the same time was going to take extra caffeine.

"New rules," Roy mumbled. He dutifully sat at the table, scraping the chrome chair legs across the linoleum floor. "If we needed new rules, we wouldn't have the old rules."

"Can I ask…" Shane sat across from Roy. "Were any of you elected? Or are these positions that you volunteered to fill? Not that I'm judging," he added quickly, but with sarcastic overtones.

Mitch sighed, thinking of Laurel and her desire for peace. He sat next to Shane.

No one answered the honorary, temporary town council member.

Ivy drifted over to the table, hesitating before taking a seat. She didn't usually sit during their meetings. She usually wiped down counters, refilled salt and pepper shakers, napkin holders and the like. "Welcome, Shane. And since we're speaking of rules, we have some here at the Bent Nickel. You know about contributions for coffee." She gestured toward the woodstove at the front of the diner. "Everyone also chips in a log or two each visit to keep the place heated."

"Such a friendly community," Shane said in an uncommonly conciliatory tone. "I'll bring some of my friend Mitch's wood next time."

Mitch closed his eyes briefly. What were the chances Laurel would kiss him again if he kicked Shane out of the meeting?

Slim to none.

Not that he should be kissing Laurel at all. It felt like a conflict of interest… When he wasn't kissing her.

"And let me just say…" Ivy shook her finger at Shane. "Your grandfather loved this town the way it is."

Mitch swallowed too quickly, sending coffee down the wrong pipe.

Shane pounded his back, none too gently.

"And Harlan hoped you'd agree." Ivy was on one of her rants. "He hoped—"

"Ivy." Roy looked aghast. She was about to break the confidentiality agreement.

"That you'd help us stay the course."

"Ivy," Mitch gasped, shrugging Shane's backslapping off.

"He hoped by setting you free from his company and his purse strings that you'd make a name for yourself separate from his." Her words echoed in the near-empty diner like a protester's last rallying cry. She blinked, coming off her proverbial pedestal. "I wasn't supposed to tell you that."

"You think?" Roy asked, hands fluttering.

Ivy frowned. "But I don't regret it. Even if Harlan's lawyer shows up and…"

Oh, she regretted it now. Her gaze roamed the diner as if she was seeing it for the last time. Her eyes filled with tears.

Shane cleared his throat. "Grandpa's lawyers won't hear anything from me." A statement that launched Ivy out of her seat and into Shane's arms, an ungainly move.

Mack entered the diner, late as usual. "What's going on?"

"Newsflash." Looking uncomfortable, Shane set Ivy back on her feet. "We're all on the same team." He waved a hand, indicating the two women should sit.

Nick burst back into the dining room, looking as if he'd forgotten to brush his hair in his haste to collect an armful of green plastic soldiers. "Come on, guys, we're going to have fun."

The twins climbed carefully off their stools

and carried their whipped cream–less hot chocolates with two hands.

"In case Mitch hasn't told all of you about the *consultant* I met with yesterday," Shane said briskly. "I'm paying someone to explore options for the town's future. I hope to choose one both the Monroes and the residents find palatable.

"So before you go painting me as the bad guy, let's all join hands and sing 'Kumbaya,' which is why Mitch invited me to join your coven."

"Not funny." Mitch frowned. Neither was the resemblance he suddenly saw between Shane and Harlan. The same nose. The same sarcasm. And he supposed he'd have to add the same heart, given what Shane had said yesterday.

"I have questions." At the head of the table, Ivy leaned forward, expression stern, and tapped the Formica with her finger. "About your intentions for the town's infrastructure."

"Yeah." Frowning, Roy shifted in his seat, shifting his white bushy brows just as much. "Like, will I still have a job keeping up vacant cabins come spring? Are you gonna build a luxury hotel? Or some of those cookie-cutter McMansions everybody talks about?"

"Are we bringing back a doctor?" Ivy's firm demeanor cracked, opening to worry. "Is the

Bent Nickel still going to be the hub for home-schooling? Will we still have slow winters? That's important to us."

"Um…" Shane turned to Mitch. "I hadn't thought about any of that."

"That's because you've been thinking big picture." Mitch let annoyance creep into his tone. "We're worried about a smaller canvas. Businesses and families need to know if the leases are going to continue or if you want us to buy you out. Do we need to save every penny? Make contingency plans? These are things that keep us up all night."

Shane sat up straight, looked at them each in turn. And what a look…

He didn't smirk. He didn't look down his nose. For once, bless him, for once, Shane looked at the residents of Second Chance with respect and seriousness. "These are all valid, important questions. But let me ask you. If you were in my shoes, what would you think is fair? What would you do?"

No one answered.

At least, not at first.

"I'M GOING NEXT DOOR." Dust and grime clung to Laurel's jacket and gloves. But she had a small pile of items—an antique sewing kit, a vintage wooden inlaid darning egg, trolley garters still in the package, dress patterns from the forties. "Do you want to come and check out the mercantile?"

Sophie was digging through a box on the floor that held car insignias wrapped in yellowed 1930s newspaper clippings. She didn't look up. "I'll stay here a little bit longer. You know, I don't trust Shane to be able to watch the boys all day. But I haven't been disappointed with anything I've found yet."

Leaving her treasures behind, Laurel went outside and strapped on her snowshoes. Out of habit, she patted her pockets for her cell phone until she remembered she'd left it in her room.

Movement at the diner caught her eye. Inside, Mitch sat with Shane at a table.

Mitch. He made her happy. And he seemed to be happy that she was staying. Admittedly, he hadn't been happy at first. But he'd gotten happy after kissing her. And now he was sitting with Shane, presumably not fighting.

Life was good.

Leaving her poles behind, Laurel smiled as she walked along the path that Roy had made to get to the mercantile.

The trading post had been built with logs. The mercantile had been constructed later and was made of brick. Mitch had opened the door before he left, and she hoped all the critters had taken an opportunity to go outside and enjoy the sunshine. She removed her snow-shoes and went inside.

"Oh." Here was joy.

Whereas the trading post had been packed, the mercantile looked to have been cleared out recently. There were shelves on one wall and a glass case with bolts of cotton stacked inside. And the main area was clear. There was enough room for a couple to dance on the clean wood floors or for a customer to pivot to and fro as she caught her reflection in the mirror, trying on a one-of-a-kind Laurel creation.

Sunlight streamed through windows and illuminated a painting on an easel—a small pond surrounded by deep red roses. The face of the grinning moon reflected off the water. It was whimsical and caught her imagination.

"What are you doing in here?"

Laurel whirled, unsettling the babies. She reached out to steady herself on the glass case. "I'm… I'm…"

"Trespassing." An old woman stood in the doorway. Her green knit cap was pulled low over her head. Her bulky jacket draped to her knees. White, fur-trimmed snow boots came midcalf. The woman's face was pale with soft wrinkles, and her limp grayish-brown hair hung on her shoulders. "Who are you?"

Laurel swallowed. "I'm Laurel Monroe?"

She snorted. "You're not sure who you are?"

"No. I am." Laurel got a grip. "I'm Laurel Monroe. Who are you?"

Low gray brows dropped lower. The woman looked Laurel up and down. In a few smooth moves, she was out of her snowshoes and inside the mercantile. "Perhaps you don't know that this place is mine."

"You lease it?" Laurel took a step back. "No one told me this building was being used." There were many vacant buildings, homes and cabins in town, some leased by snowbirds, some that Grandpa Harlan had purchased and never leased.

The woman shook her head, emitting a sound of frustration. She still hadn't told Laurel who she was.

"I'm sorry, you have me at a disadvantage. I don't know your name."

The woman laughed. "Everyone knows me, just like everyone knows Odette." She gave Laurel a sly look. "I know who you are now. You've been knitting."

"Yes." Laurel held out the ends of her teal scarf. "I'm very patient." Except she wasn't feeling patient with this woman who refused to divulge her name.

Her laugh turned hard-edged. *"Patient?"*

She tossed her hands. "That Odette. I wouldn't have told you to be patient. I would've told you to create with passion-fueled speed, which is the way Odette makes quilts. Not that she'd reveal that to you."

Laurel didn't like this woman picking on Odette. "Who are you?"

"My name is Flip. And you're trespassing." She was pushy. Oh, so pushy.

Laurel decided to push back. "You did hear me say my last name is Monroe?"

Flip walked around the easel and admired the painting. "I've been using this as an art studio." She picked up the canvas from the easel and walked out the door. "I'll give you a dollar if I must."

Laurel followed her. "You want to rent this place?" She hoped not. It was darling.

Without letting go of the painting, Flip put her snowshoes back on and left. She moved easily and with only one pole, using the trail Roy had made.

"Hey!"

Without turning, Flip raised her hand in the air and made a dismissive gesture.

"What's going on?" Sophie stood on the porch of the trading post. "Who was that?"

Laurel marched across the tamped-down snow to rejoin Sophie. "I'm not sure. I don't know what kind of bee got in her bonnet, but she was angry."

"Hey, um…" Sophie waved her hands in the air. "Shouldn't you put your snowshoes back on?"

No sooner had Sophie pointed out her mistake, than Laurel sank in the snow up to one knee. She listed and then tumbled downhill.

Leaving her stomach at the top.

"ODETTE NEEDS A DOCTOR." It was the first time since Shane had come to Second Chance that Ivy didn't turn her nose up when she looked at him.

"Is she sick?" Shane had knocked on her door one day and she'd told him to go away without opening up. "Is she terminally ill?"

"No." Roy was still studying Shane as if he wasn't sure he wouldn't bite. "But Odette likes to make sure."

Shane rubbed his forehead. "I'm not following." He'd been trying to keep up with everything the town council was saying, trying to see their point of view even when they'd been unable to see his concern for the bottom line.

"Odette gets anxious when she can't talk to a doctor every day or so." Ivy stood and caught her son's eye. "Nick. Don't shoot people."

"Ah, Mom." Nick slouched across the table

where he and Sophie's twins played. "I'm a soldier. I have to shoot somebody."

"It's okay," Andrew said solemnly. "He was just shooting us."

Alexander nodded, scratching his cowlick. "We're playing."

"No shooting." Shane was with Ivy on this one.

"Nick, you know the rules," Ivy said in a firm voice. "Toys can shoot other toys, but not people." Ivy gathered her thick brown hair, mumbling something about gifts from her ex-husband Shane didn't quite catch. "Where was I?"

"Odette." Mitch had turned his chair sideways. He stared out the window toward the trading post and mercantile where Sophie and Laurel were scrounging through what Shane imagined was junk.

Shane had peered into enough vacant cabins and storefronts to know the town was filled with it.

Ivy sat back down. "When Odette gets anxious, she doesn't knit or sew. And when she doesn't knit or sew, she comes into the diner and…"

"Let's just say," Roy picked up where Ivy left off, "it's in the best interest of town harmony to hire us a doctor ASAP."

"I'm not sure that qualifies as an emergency need for a doctor." Shane had been in town a month and the worst medical need he'd witnessed was Zeke's accident, which—admittedly—had been nasty and could have been life-threatening if not for a doctor in town. But that was one event.

"It's a priority." Mitch leaned forward, eyes narrowing as he stared out the window. "I've posted for a doctor and asked around."

"Do we have any candidates?" How hard could it be to hire a doctor?

"I talked to Laurel's doctor about the position." Mitch's words slowed. "She seemed promising, but no one is ever seriously interested in practicing here until they see the view from the doctor's cabin."

"That's a million-dollar view." Roy's chest swelled. "Got one of my own right next door."

And he paid next to nothing for it.

Shane rubbed his forehead. "You have a candidate in mind, Mitch?" Trust Mitch to be unable to close a deal. "Let's get her up here."

"How?" Mitch stood, still focused on whatever was happening outside. "She's working overtime at the clinic with only one day off a week."

"We wine and dine her and show her that view." Shane knew the view they were talking about. He'd stood on the doctor's front porch and stared at smooth blankets of snow that extended from the other side of the Salmon River to the Sawtooth Mountains. That view tended to put the problems a man had in perspective. "Leave the planning to me."

Mitch left it, all right. He bolted out the door without his jacket.

"It wasn't that bad of an idea," Shane called after him.

Roy turned in his seat. "What the heck?" He grabbed Mitch's jacket and his own, and motored toward the door at a slower pace. "Did one of them Monroe girls just tumble down a snowbank?"

"Sophie?" Shane's blood ran cold. "Laurel?"

Ivy turned to Shane, as smug as she'd ever been with him. "Do you see now why we need a doctor?"

CHAPTER THIRTEEN

"ARE YOU OKAY?" Mitch skidded to his knees in the snow and gathered Laurel into his arms. His heart was pounding, his hands shook and he was cold, inside and out. "Laurel, are you okay?"

Laurel nestled against him, and his arms had never felt so full. "I don't like ice-skating, snowshoes or body sledding."

"That's a joke, isn't it? You didn't hit your head on the way down, did you?" Mitch ran his fingers beneath the multiple loops of knit scarf. "Do you hurt anywhere?"

"When my heart stops racing, I'll let you know." Her eyes were shut tight.

"Oh, my gosh, Laurel." Sophie had descended the hill at a much slower pace, walking in her snowshoes. "You about gave me a heart attack."

"Do you want me to call an ambulance?" Roy draped Mitch's jacket over his shoulders, not that it warmed him at all.

"No ambulance." Laurel opened her eyes.

They weren't dilated. "I'm just a klutz, but I'm okay."

"Are you sure?" Mitch asked, drawing her closer still. Fear eating his insides. "The babies…"

"I feel like someone put me on the spin cycle in the dryer." Laurel stared up at Mitch and tried to smile. "I don't think I need medical care." She levered herself out of Mitch's arms and stood on her own two feet. "Although a hot shower would be nice." She was dusted in snow from head to toe and her bright red hair was in disarray.

Sophie brushed off the snow and tried to fix her hair a little, at least until Laurel told her it was fine.

"I'm okay. Really." She laughed a little, and then laughed harder, that *hardy-har-har*. Her cheeks turned pink. "I'm so embarrassed. Did everyone see me fall?"

"Probably only me and Sophie." Mitch helped her across the highway and back to the inn.

"I missed the whole thing." Roy trailed behind them with Sophie, sounding remorseful.

"If you've seen snow plunge down a mountain, it probably looked similar, just with more color." At least Laurel's sense of humor was still intact.

Still, Mitch didn't want to remember how she'd tumbled and how his heart had gone along with her. She could have hurt herself on a bush or a fallen log. There were some on the slope. They climbed the inn's steps slowly. Mitch threw open the door, surprising Gabby, who stood behind the check-in desk staring down at her phone, the same phone that should have been in the drawer in their kitchen.

Gabby jumped, spun and bounced off the apartment's door frame. She stumbled back and fell on her butt. The phone skittered away.

"She wasn't expecting you," Zeke called out from his position on the sidelines by the fireplace, leg propped parallel to the floor.

Mitch escorted Laurel to the couch and then hurried to help his daughter to her feet. Gabby's nose was bleeding and she was wheezing like a punctured tire.

"Da-ad..."

"I've got you." Mitch tilted her head back and pinched her nose. "I've got you." He led her into the bathroom in their apartment, trying to temper his competing emotions. Which was hard, considering he'd gone from the cold adrenaline rush of fear after seeing Laurel fall to the sudden hot rush of anger at discovering his daughter defying him once more.

"I'm sorry," Gabby said, minus the lisp. She hadn't put in her retainer this morning.

Strike two.

"Sit." He wet a washcloth and put it gently over her nose. "Pinch."

Gabby was crying, snuffling as she breathed through her mouth. She knew what she'd done was wrong. She shoved her retainer in. "I wad taking a pik-dure of mydelf for Mom." The retainer only made her nose-pinched speech worse. "She called da house and wanted to dee what I look like withoud my blaces."

A test, he was sure, set up by Shannon to see who Gabby would obey.

"I wasn't the perfect child, either." Laurel spoke from inside their kitchen.

"You shouldn't be up." Mitch went to Laurel and guided her into a seat at the kitchen table. "You might have a concussion."

"I didn't hit my head. Besides, I've been watching Alexander and Andrew's technique of the cannonball move. I tucked and rolled. Sometimes it felt like I was flying." Her lower lip trembled. She wasn't as unaffected as she'd have him believe.

Gabby shrieked from the bathroom. "Daddy! I bloke my nose." She ran into the kitchen. "I bloke id. I bloke id. I lofed my nose. My cute liddle nose. Id's huge!"

234 SNOWED IN WITH THE SINGLE DAD

Blood dripped onto the linoleum and her T-shirt from her bulbous nose.

Mitch returned to his daughter's emergency and guided Gabby's hand with the cloth back to her nose. "Pinch, pinch. Pinch it until it stops bleeding." He settled her into a chair next to Laurel. "Once the bleeding stops we'll get you an ice pack, Gabby. And then I'll call the medical advice hotline for you and Dr. Carlisle for Laurel."

"See?" Roy was in the kitchen, too. He looked back over his shoulder at Shane, who hovered behind him. "We need a town doctor."

With one hand on a shoulder of each of his nephews, Shane appeared worried. Sophie stood near the door, removing her jacket. She seemed worried, too.

"I'll be fine," Laurel repeated firmly. "We'll both be fine."

"Nod me." Gabby wheezed. "Look ad my nose!" She removed the washcloth, letting blood flow.

"Gabby, please." Mitch again put the wash-cloth on Gabby's nose.

"I'll call the doctor," Shane said in a take-charge tone. "You keep things calm in there."

Half an hour later, Dr. Carlisle was satisfied with Laurel's condition—no abdominal pain, no cramping, no dilated eyes. Apparently, falls during the first half of pregnancy weren't as serious as falls in the last trimester. And the medical clinic offered advice for Gabby's care that wasn't much beyond tilting her head up, pinching her nose and then making sure she could breathe through each nostril.

"Someone will need to stay with you the next few days," Mitch said to Laurel. "If you feel dizzy or queasy, if your ears ring or your head hurts, you need to speak up immediately. You heard the doctor." Shane had put her on speaker. "She said you could have a concussion even if you don't have a bump on your head."

Wide-eyed, Laurel nodded.

"What about me?" Gabby stared up at Mitch with eyes that were red rimmed and puffy. Her nose had stopped bleeding and she was speaking clearer now that the tears had stopped. "How do you know my nose isn't broken?"

"Because the only thing broken in this house—" Mitch finally let his simmering anger and worry bubble over. He used his foot to slide Gabby's cell phone from beneath the table "—is this phone." He plucked it up, removed the battery and stowed it in the safe in the pantry cupboard. When the safe clicked closed, he felt like he could breathe again .

That was when Gabby really started to cry.

"WHAT ARE YOU gonna do?" Roy demanded of Shane as Mitch helped Laurel upstairs. "We need a doctor in town."

Shane nodded, watching Sophie and the twins follow his cousin up the stairs.

"Did you see all that blood?" Alexander dragged his feet.

"It was awesome," Andrew said, passing him on the stairs. "Wasn't it?"

"Yeah," Alexander agreed.

"Boys," Sophie scolded from a few steps above them. "It's not nice to find blood awesome." She sounded as anxious as Shane felt.

What if one of the boys had ridden their sled past the barrier on Sled Hill and onto the ice? What if they'd hit their head or fallen through? What if Laurel developed a concussion? Or began to miscarry? The road to the nearest hospital was long and often closed. Worry turned into icy fear. How was he supposed to protect his family?

Mitch was right.

Shane had been thinking too broadly. He'd lost sight of the important everyday details.

"Shane." Roy shook his shoulder. "What are you gonna do?"

Shane acknowledged the concern, but was still at a loss as to a quick solution. "Mitch said he's already advertised for a doctor. What else can I do? Kidnap someone?"

Roy chewed on those words as if Shane had been serious. "You know…that idea's not half-bad."

Zeke chuckled.

Shane gave the cowboy a hard look.

Zeke shrugged. "The entertainment never ends around here. I should have broken my leg and moved in sooner."

Roy's eyes gleamed. "We can do this."

"Must be some way I can help." Zeke grinned. "I fully support any plan to bring a doctor to town."

"Don't encourage him." Wanting to reinforce he wasn't interested in the wild scheme, Shane checked his cell phone, despite not hearing any new messages come in. Not even from Holden.

"Hear me out, Mr. Highfalutin Monroe." Every white whisker on Roy's face bristled. "It's like Mitch said. Every doctor we've had has been reluctant to take the job until they see that view. We just need to invite this doc of Laurel's up here—"

"On one of her days off, which will also need to correspond with the mountain passes being clear." Shane shook his head. "Impossible."

"You could ask her out to dinner." Zeke tapped his leg brace as if reminding Shane how his life had been saved by a doctor in town. "If you bring her on a Friday, Ivy's special includes french fries."

"You're scaring me now." Shane backed toward the door. "You two almost sound serious."

"Her cross-cut fries are the best," Roy said eagerly. "What do you say?"

Shane's phone buzzed with a text, saving him from answering.

Holden.

What do you want me to do about Aunt Genevieve?

Laurel needed monitoring for several days. Much as his aunt was a pain in the butt, she was Laurel's mother. Aunt Genevieve's attitude would change once she learned her daughter was pregnant. He hoped.

Shane texted back.

Bring her here.

Why not kill two birds with one stone? Get Holden to see there were real people here, people Grandpa Harlan had cared for. People who were their responsibility to care for. They were Monroe tenants after all.

"What do you say, Shane?" Roy demanded sharply. "Are you with us?"

"Yeah," Zeke seconded. "Will you ask this doctor to dinner?"

"Gentlemen, I'm going to think on that."

Because there were dates, which could end badly—no harm, no foul—and because there was kidnapping under the guise of a date, which could end with someone in prison.

"I CAN'T SLEEP down here." Laurel snuggled deeper into the corner of the couch and adjusted the blue-and-brown quilt up to her neck.

Mitch had insisted Laurel sleep downstairs, where people could take turns watching both injured patients—Laurel on the couch, Gabby in a sleeping bag with extra pillows on the floor. Laurel had changed into her silky menswear pajamas because Mitch had insisted she be comfortable.

Comfortable?

There was no way she could relax with Mitch watching her every breath. Besides, if there was something wrong with her, if they did have to rush her to the hospital or the doctor, she shouldn't be wearing pajamas. She should be dressed.

Comfortable?

Laurel had too much to worry about. "I can only sleep upstairs." An exaggeration, since she'd dozed during Shane's watch.

"If you'd like to go to sleep, stop talking," Mitch said in a rumbly whisper from the other side of the couch. It was midnight, the time he usually paced. By rights, he should look worn-out and haggard. Instead, he looked rested and handsome.

"Jeez, you're so tense. Shoulders to your ears. Legs tucked to your chest. And your voice... I didn't help, I'm sure, when I lost my cool with Gabby earlier."

It was true. She became apprehensive when tension grew and voices rose. Laurel tried to shrug, but there wasn't a huge difference between her shoulders and her ears. "It's who you are. My mother has a bark, too. But yours is more about protecting what you love..." While her mother's was merely territorial.

His gaze sharpened, an attorney looking for proof. Or perhaps a father looking for reassurance, because his gaze drifted to Gabby, and he said, "You think I went too far? Confiscating her phone with no return date in sight?"

"No." She caught his hand, caught his eye. "In this case, I think the punishment fits the crime."

"Then what's bothering you?" His fingers curled around hers.

"I'm going to be a mother and I can't seem to hold my ground." To put herself first. To put her babies first. To stand firm on her principles. "Unless that ground is thousands of miles away and I'm snowed in. This is the longest I've held out against my mother's wishes."

"Once your babies are here you'll have their backs, the way you've had Ashley's." His eyes took on that kind look she liked so much. "And you'll develop a bark of your own. But, Laurel, who's got your back?"

She didn't have to look far for an answer. It was there in his dark eyes—him. Mitch Kincaid, former defense attorney.

"Go to sleep, Laurel. Don't worry." But there was nothing restful in his gaze. It energized. It magnetized. It crystallized the attraction between them until it was an almost-tangible thing.

"I can't sleep with you looking at me," she grumbled, feeling restless and unsettled once more. It had nothing to do with how Mitch stared at her. Nothing to do with how much she'd enjoyed his kiss.

"You didn't have a problem with me looking at you this morning at the trading post." He'd recognized nothing, all right. As an attorney, he was probably trained to identify nothing and know it meant something.

Laurel huffed her answering smile out of existence, hoping the babies wouldn't get any ideas. "Now I'm really not going to be able to go to sleep. It's getting hot in here. I should go upstairs."

"Hotness." He chuckled, the sound fading slowly into a sigh. "All kidding aside, I won't be able to get any rest if I can't check on you."

The babies heaved a heartfelt sigh, getting ideas about couches and kissing.

"I guess that means we'll have to talk about something else." Something besides hotness and watching her back. Laurel cast about her brain for a topic. Pacing was out, as was anything to do with Gabby, dresses or Hollywood. "How did your town council meeting go today?"

He took his own sweet time answering. "Shane surprised me. He always comes across as something of a…"

"Jerk," she finished for him, not upset in the slightest. "The word you're looking for to describe my cousin is *jerk*. Although I prefer *intense*. But I assure you his heart is in the right place." Just like Mitch's. "Shane has always been in competition with the world, but especially with our oldest cousin, Holden." Holden was a Wall Street financial guru who'd always considered himself better than others. "There was this one time I thought Shane had Holden beat." She warmed to her story, tension easing as she recalled the bittersweet memory. "It was Christmas, and we were all trying to find the perfect gift for Grandmother Estelle, because she had cancer."

"She was wife number four?"

"Yes." How did Mitch know that?

"And what happened this fateful Christmas?" Head tilted back against the cushions, eyes half-closed, he took a break from staring at her to study the fire.

For the moment Laurel could breathe easier.

"My brother Jonah started it all by writing a play we performed on Christmas Eve." His was the most heartfelt gift and hadn't involved a parental credit card. "Meanwhile, Cousin Holden hired a Victorian choir to sing. Cousin Bentley got wind of the choir and hired a Santa Claus and a horse-pulled sleigh. And Shane, not to be outdone, hired an organ grinder with a live monkey."

"Clever," Mitch said flatly.

"Yes, because Grandma Estelle used to call us her barrel of monkeys, and Grandpa Harlan used to say we were his favorite circus act." There was something wrong with

Mitch's reaction to her story. Was she reading him right? Or was she getting a concussion? "Grandma Estelle was thrilled with everyone's gift, but the monkey was clearly her favorite. She laughed and laughed. And then her poodle chased the monkey up the Christmas tree, which toppled into the fireplace and nearly burned the house down."

"And Harlan was upset." Not a question.

"Fuming." Laurel nodded, wondering what bothered her about Mitch's responses to her story. "He told us we'd ruined his Christmas. He disappeared for hours." Laurel had imagined he'd gone to his country club to have a drink with his buddies and complain about his spoiled, unruly grandchildren. "Meanwhile, everyone was pointing fingers at everyone else. It took a while for tempers to ease." And Laurel hadn't been the only one trying to smooth ruffled feathers. "In the end, we all apologized, and Christmas went on, but Holden doesn't let Shane live it down."

"And of course, you always tried to keep the peace between the two."

She nodded.

"But that was the last time you saw your grandmother." Mitch spoke with such certainty.

It gave Laurel pause. In fact, all his comments had the feel of affirmation, not reaction. "You've heard this story before. From my grandfather." She pushed herself up higher against the cushions. "Why didn't you tell me?"

Mitch rolled a shoulder in a half shrug. "You know why."

The confidentiality agreement.

Laurel wanted to find his copy and rip it to shreds. "But I was telling you a story you knew, and you didn't say anything." She gathered her knees in the circle of her arms. "What else have I told you that you've heard before?"

"Laurel." He reached across the cushions and found her foot beneath the quilt. "You know there are things I can't tell you."

"Secrets about my grandfather's past? Or confirmation that you know mine?" Intellectually, she recognized he'd given his word and sworn an oath. Emotionally, it pressed on her chest and held her to the couch cushions. Why? Because she wanted to love this man and to do so she needed no secrets between them. There were too many secrets in her life already.

"You and I, we value the truth and a promise." He followed the sweep of her ankle to her knee. "We develop relationships based on trust and reliability. And I…" His hand fell away.

"I can't always give you the truth right now, the whole truth and nothing but... And that's no way to begin a relationship."

He'd held her hand while they watched her babies on a sonogram screen. He'd talked her through a panic attack. He'd kissed her on a crisp, snowy slope. He'd as much as promised he'd have her back.

And now he wanted to draw a line? Set up boundaries?

"The relationship boat has sailed," she said. His voice had been imprinted on her brain. His touch on her soul. His heart... "We began something with you knowing this... And your prejudice against my family... And your abhorrence of my clothes... And..."

He kissed me anyway.

And she'd let him, although she knew when he found out the truth about her past pretending and scheming he'd no longer look at her the way he was now. It wasn't just a stupid piece of paper standing between them anymore. It was her lying, and the truth was just waiting to tumble out and for her to be judged and found wanting.

"We can be friends." His voice enticed with a compromise. One that couldn't last once the truth was out.

She couldn't sit with him any longer. Laurel

got to her feet, edging past his sleeping daughter to stand out of reach. "I may be reluctant to hold my ground when others' feelings and well-beings are at stake, but at least I'm honest with myself about who I am and how I feel." Her words felt hollow. All too often she'd pretended to be someone else, stuffing her feelings deep inside.

Laurel rushed toward the stairs, pausing on the bottom step. "And do you know what the irony is? I've been marveling that you see me. Me. Not Ashley. But when we first met, you were just like the rest of the world. You judged me by how I looked, by the facade, the once-wealthy Monroe who wears leggings in the mountains instead of snow pants. Did it ever occur to you that I can't fit in pants that don't have elastic waistbands?" That she was sensitive about her expanding waistline and her body? Even if she knew she shouldn't be?

He said nothing, but he looked shocked.

"I'm having twins. I'm going to be as big as a whale in a few months. Allow me the right to pick and choose what I wear." To follow her instincts and her heart. To work hard to make amends when the details of her pregnancy became worldwide news. She left him, hurrying up the stairs in case Mitch decided to stop her.

He didn't.

Laurel's feet felt heavy. He wasn't coming after her.

Laurel's heart felt heavy. He wasn't falling in love with her. He didn't think he should while Grandpa Harlan's nondisclosure agreement was in place.

She made it to her room and collapsed on her bed, falling asleep on a damp pillow, waking only when someone opened the door to her room. "If you value your life, Mitch, you'll go away." She pulled the quilt over her head.

"Harsh words for a woman who claims to have patience." Odette stomped across the room toward the bed, legs rustling—no doubt—because she wore sensible snow pants. "Did you make this? I found it downstairs."

Laurel rolled over and sat up. Odette was holding the copper scarf Laurel had been working on yesterday.

She must have left it in the common room. "Yes, that's mine and it's beautiful." Yes, that was mutiny in Laurel's voice. The combination of disappointment in Mitch and lack of sleep made her cranky. "I took some silver thread I had and wrapped it around the yarn. Go ahead. Tell me I suck."

Odette stared at her hard enough to drill holes. "So certain."

"Yes, I've enjoyed learning a new skill, but

I'm ready to move on." From knitting and Mitch. And speaking of moving on, she tossed off the covers and glanced into the bathroom, stopping when she saw what was there.

Or rather what wasn't there.

"Where's my dress?" The pink gown wasn't hanging on the shower curtain rod.

Laurel did a quick survey of the main room and a surprised, if scowling, Odette. And then she darted back into the bathroom and pulled the shower curtain aside to make sure the dress hadn't fallen in the bathtub. It hadn't. "Thank heavens." But… "Where's my dress?"

A door opened.

"You mean this one?"

Laurel poked her head out of the bathroom.

Odette took the pink dress from the closet and held it up.

"What's it doing in the closet?" Anger skittered across her skin. Mitch had secrets he couldn't share. He didn't want to start a relationship with untold truths between them. And yet he couldn't honor this one thing. She marched to the closet. "I told him…"

The top shelf had been removed and the clothes rod had been raised to near the ceiling, so the pink evening gown's hem wouldn't touch the floor.

Oh, Mitch.

Her heart tried to reattach the halves she hadn't realized were cracked apart.

After her fall, she'd showered and then spent several hours downstairs under the watchful eyes of everyone, reclining on the sofa. Mitch must have taken the opportunity to move the rod.

And of course, he didn't tell me.

"Is this your work?" Odette spread the delicate skirt, studying the rhinestones.

"It is."

The old woman raised sharp gray eyes to Laurel's face. "What on earth do you need me for?"

Laurel looked from the sunflower quilt on the bed, to the coppery knitting, to the dress. "You have an eye for color and composition."

"So do you."

Odette stretched to hang the dress in the closet once more. "This should be in a garment bag."

"I can't…" Laurel's throat threatened to close. "I can't close it up like that." As it was, she was having second thoughts about shutting it in the closet.

Odette stared at Laurel's pajamas. "Did you make those, too?"

"Yes."

She fingered a cuff of Laurel's long sleeve and let out a lengthy sigh. "You don't need me."

"I do," Laurel insisted. "At least let me be the judge. Let me watch you work."

Odette's eyes narrowed. "You'll get tired of me. I have a temper."

"If you haven't noticed—" Laurel crossed her arms over her chest and stared the older woman down "—I'm patient."

After a moment Odette laughed and headed for the door. "I'll see you later this morning."

She was out the door before Laurel remembered to ask about Flip, the woman who'd accosted her at the mercantile. She hurried out into the hall, but Odette was already gone.

CHAPTER FOURTEEN

MITCH POURED HIMSELF a cup of coffee and yawned.

But yawning didn't stop the wondering about what might have been and what might still be. What might have been with Laurel had he not accepted Harlan's buyout offer? What might be if Laurel decided to stay in Second Chance?

"Laurel has a tremendous imagination," Harlan had said. "It can take her places."

Laurel needed a man who could go with her to Hollywood, New York or Milan. She needed a man who wasn't worried that his daughter's head might spin out of orbit from exposure to all that fashion and all those celebrities.

Mitch stared at the town's application for historical significance, his head spinning. The process required learning the town's history. He knew more about the history of the Monroes than that of Second Chance. What good did it do him?

Earlier, he'd heard Odette come in, greeting Zeke. She'd gone upstairs to visit Laurel.

He'd practically told Laurel he'd watch out for her. And then what had he done? Let her out of his sight.

Mitch made sure he was in Odette's path when she came downstairs. "How is she?"

"She's prickly about you." Odette pushed past him without breaking stride. "That's how she is."

Mitch returned to the kitchen table and the small print and narrow empty boxes on the historical application. Would it help if he sent in a copy of the history report Gabby had done on the town last year? If he asked Laurel, she'd say yes and point out how proud his daughter would be to be part of such an effort. If Shane saw Gabby's report, he'd laugh. His high-paid consultant would probably laugh, too.

Mitch shelved the idea.

Gabby shuffled out of her bedroom, wailing like a wounded ghost, *"Dad."* She had dual shiners and her nose was swollen.

"It doesn't look so bad." Just like she'd gone three rounds in a mixed martial arts championship bout and lost.

She wailed again and shut herself in the bathroom.

Laurel would've attempted to make peace.

Mitch took his paperwork to the check-in desk, filling out a box or two. Mostly he stared out the window as the rising sun chased away shadows outside but did nothing to warm or brighten the muddled emotions inside Mitch.

"Roy and I have an idea about the doctor."

Mitch jumped. "Holy ninja." He hadn't heard Shane come down the stairs.

Zeke startled awake in his wheelchair, flinching as if his broken leg hurt. "What'd I miss?"

Shane laughed. "That never gets old."

"I almost fell off my stool." Mitch curled his fingers around the pen. "You've got to stop walking around my home like that."

"No can do." Shane grinned. "It's emotionally satisfying to scare the living daylights out of you."

Of course, Shane wouldn't stop sneaking around. That would be the equivalent of waving a white flag and wearing a pair of jeans and a sweater like a normal dude.

Mitch shook his head. "At least clear your throat or something when you leave your room, so you don't give me a heart attack."

"Speaking of heart attacks and doctors…" Shane reached for his thin jacket hanging by the front door. "When you told me about Laurel's doctor you mentioned she had a day off. We should call and see what that day is."

"First, we should call and see if she'd *like* to meet with us." Shane was always jumping the gun.

"Hopefully, the roads won't be closed for our trip." Shane put his jacket on, not bothering to zip it up. He dared Mother Nature the same way he dared Mitch.

"What trip? Are you leaving?" Hope sprang in Mitch's chest.

"No." Shane waved to Zeke. "We're going to interview that doctor of Laurel's."

"Dr. Carlisle? But…she's not interested in the job!"

"She will be." Shane slapped Mitch on the back. "Your other rooms here are inhabitable, right?"

"Yes." They were dusty, but otherwise ready for guests. Before Mitch could ask who Shane expected to fill them, he was out the door.

Mitch's coffee mug was empty. He carried it into his kitchen.

"Dad." Gabby stood awkwardly near the sink. "I look hideous." Her gaze strayed to the pantry.

He stroked her hair. "I give you a lot of freedom, trusting you'll make good choices.

Somehow, we're going to have to rebuild that trust."

"Okay." Her word was so faint he could barely hear her. "Can you tell Mom? You know, she's going to call when she doesn't get a picture of me with my braces off."

Or a text, or a message from Gabby on social media.

"It's your job to tell your mother." Mitch shook his head. "You can call her from the house phone. When you're wrong, you need to admit it."

Gabby's eyes teared up and her lower lip trembled. "But…"

"Good morning." Laurel stood near the check-in desk, wearing a smile that didn't reach her eyes. Or Mitch, for that matter. "And goodbye. This is a courtesy announcement. I'm feeling fine and going over to Odette's."

"By yourself?" Mitch's temples began to pound. It was too soon for her to venture out on her own. "Wait. I'll go with you."

"No, thanks." She disappeared into the small kitchen alcove, probably to make her morning tea.

Gabby sniffed, reminding Mitch he had to finish one hard conversation before he started another.

"Honey." He took his daughter by the shoulders. "We need to talk about your punishment."

"You have my phone," Gabby said mulishly as if that was punishment enough.

He didn't like that she was still missing the point. "You weren't supposed to have it for two more weeks."

Gabby shuffled her feet.

"You have a choice—sit in the common room, go over to the diner or ask Laurel if you can go with her to Odette's." He was hoping for option three.

"Dad." Gabby gestured toward her face. "Look at me. No way am I going out in public like this."

Mitch shook his head. "Those are your choices."

"Remind me never to cross you, Counselor." Laurel set a tea mug down on the check-in desk and came into the apartment to carefully draw Gabby into her arms. "You can come with me and test the waters with Odette."

Gabby said something that sounded like *thanks*.

Laurel patted her back. "You'll live through this, Gabby. And someday, we'll see your pretty face again, smiling and everything."

Gabby broke free of her embrace and fled to the bathroom. "Nobody's on my side!"

"I feel exactly the same way," Mitch murmured, turning to Laurel.

But she was gone, too.

"Why do I have to come with you?" Gabby sniffed, snowshoeing next to Laurel to Odette's house. She wore orange snow pants, a knit cap pulled down low and a purple jacket zipped up to her neck. None of it hid the damage to her face, especially not in daylight.

The sun was out, and Second Chance looked picture-perfect. It just didn't feel picture-perfect. It felt like a postcard Laurel could only admire, not someplace she belonged, not someplace she'd settle into forever. Mitch would always see Laurel as a Monroe. Legally, he couldn't be anything more to her than a tenant. That gag order her grandfather had imposed made certain of it. If she was going to stay here, it would only be a temporary stop until she decided where to raise her babies.

Trudging beside her, Gabby made a teenage sound of angst that reminded Laurel of eye rolls and claims of *"not fair."*

Laurel sighed. "Your dad gave you a choice, you know. You can go to the diner and see all your school friends, if you'd rather."

Without deviating from their course, Gabby pulled her knit cap lower around her ears. "I haven't even finished my first scarf and you've almost finished two." The retainer lisp was back, making her sound younger.

"Maybe you were behind on your knitting because you were spending too much time on that phone you used to have."

Gabby made a strangled noise in her throat. "You're just like my dad."

"I'll take that as a compliment."

The babies got all snuggly at the mention of Mitch, much the same way Laurel had snuggled into Mitch's arms after her fall. The babies believed in happily-ever-afters. Laurel tried to remember she knew better.

"You know," Laurel said, trying to be helpful, "it's not just an apology that your dad wants to hear. He misses the Gabby I met when I first came to Second Chance. She was awesome, by the way." Fussing with her teal scarf, Laurel climbed the steps to Odette's front door. When she realized Gabby hadn't followed her, she turned.

Gabby's cheeks were pale, a stark contrast to her dark bruises. "I hate my life."

Laurel came back down the steps. "And whose fault is that? You lied to your dad. You disobeyed him. And then you walked yourself right into a wall."

"I don't know what's happening to me."

Gabby's eyes pooled with tears. "I get mean for no reason. And I say things…" She wiped her wet cheeks. "Sometimes, I don't even like myself."

"Look up teenage hormones. You're not alone." Laurel put her arm around Gabby's shoulders and gentled her voice. "The good news is you have nowhere to go but up, my friend." She hoped the same applied to herself.

Gabby sniffed. "I'm still your friend?"

"You are, indeed." Antsy to see Odette at work and more than a bit cold, Laurel moved them up the stairs, silently admitting snow pants had their advantages.

"I thought everyone hated me. Dad is so mad, and you made fun of me this morning." Her words were choked with remorse.

"Your dad takes everything very seriously. And I try to lighten things up." She gazed down at Gabby, at purplish eyes and a bruised nose. "Maybe I teased you too much this time. Do you forgive me?"

"I suppose I have to." Gabby tried to smile. "You're going to marry my dad after all."

Before Laurel could deny it, Odette opened her door without her knit cap on. Her porcupine gray hair stood at attention. "Are you going to lollygag all day or come inside?" She peered at Gabby's face. "Huh. Those bruises are no excuse for slow productivity, so don't even try to use it as one unless you want to hear about the time I had cellulitis on my fingers—the pus-filled kind." She opened the door wider, beckoning them inside. "And I have pictures."

"Please don't ask to see them." Laurel shivered.

"I walked into a wall," Gabby admitted in a small, tear-filled voice.

Odette waved a hand. "I didn't ask." She dragged a kitchen chair beneath the window. "Sit here and get to work on that scarf of yours in the sunlight. I'm sure there are people in town who need it to keep warm."

The teen didn't budge. "There are?"

Odette scoffed. "Don't you ever look beyond the bend in the road?"

"I'm not allowed to go beyond the bend in the road." Gabby's words wound up into a wail.

"There's no crying in the sewing circle." Odette scoffed louder and tossed her hands. "If you need to cry, you'd best skedaddle."

During their exchange, Laurel stood silent, taking in the colors and craftsmanship inside Odette's cabin.

The cabin was open concept and comprised of a large living room, a sewing nook and galley kitchen. Two doors were closed, perhaps leading to a bedroom and bathroom. A framed baby quilt hung on the wall above the fireplace. The crazy quilt had been pieced together with various hand stitches around irregular-shaped blocks of faded fabric. When Sophie had seen it and tried to buy it, Odette hadn't taken it well.

There were knit items everywhere. A standing hat rack was draped in scarves of every color and knit caps—tiny blue baby caps, larger black adult caps, colorful caps with yarn braids and yarn tassels. A cream-colored poncho hung there, as well.

Knitting always takes the shape of its owner.

Odette's knitting was as tightly wound as Odette herself, but it was also whimsical.

Laurel's teal scarf was bland and amateurish. But the chunky coppery scarf... That had Laurel's imprint. A bit of sparkle.

A cross-stitched Christmas stocking hung from a hook in the kitchen instead of a frying pan. There was a pink-and-red friendship quilt stretched out on a frame. Finished quilts of all colors and patterns stacked on deep bookshelves. The colors spoke to Laurel of artistry and passion.

Laurel was envious, but she was also in

heaven. She bet everything in this cabin gave Odette joy.

"We don't have all day for me to repeat myself," Odette huffed, because apparently Laurel hadn't heard her. "I said, come over here." She rattled a chair next to her worktable.

Laurel drifted over, drawn more by the brightly colored fabric stored in a large wicker basket than Odette's words. "What are you making?"

"A baby quilt." Odette sneaked a sly glance at Laurel. "Know anyone having a baby?"

"I know someone having *two* babies," Gabby piped up, sounding more like her chipper self than she had in over a week. "Laurel's having twins."

"Two babies?" Odette clucked. "Then we'll each have to make a quilt."

Laurel's palms were sweaty. She wiped them on her leggings.

"First off, we have to pick out a design." Odette stared at her expectantly.

"I saw a quilt the last time I was here." Laurel glanced around.

"Do you mean the one above the hearth?" The old woman twisted to look at it. "It was your grandfather's." She jerked back around, fingering the red-and-pink fabric on her quilt frame as her cheeks filled with a similar color.

"Ignore me." Because she'd signed the same paperwork Mitch had.

"My lips are sealed," Gabby said pertly.

Odette made a growling noise deep in her chest that had Gabby ducking her head.

Laurel looked at the crazy quilt. There was no order, no pattern, to the pieces. Unpredictable. That was a good metaphor for Grandpa Harlan's life. Although faded, the colors had once been vibrant. Dark browns. Rich burgundies. Deep purples. "That quilt means something to you?"

"It does." Odette finger combed her unruly hair. "I'll tell you about it someday."

"New Year's Day," Laurel said under her breath. The day all the nondisclosure agreements expired.

Odette nodded. "Might kick the bucket before then. I'm old and there's no doctor in town."

Shane would have pursued the conversation further. More than anything, he wanted to unravel Grandpa Harlan's past, unwilling to wait until the end of the year.

Having a different agenda, Laurel cleared her throat. "That wasn't the quilt I was thinking of. It had a flower pattern, but the petals were elongated. The fabrics you chose were teals and—"

"That was a sea glass quilt." Odette rummaged through a pile of finished quilts stacked on a chair. "A traditional sea glass quilt. Nowadays the pastels of sea glass are used in any pattern—a log cabin or a sunflower design—and they call it a sea glass quilt."

"I've never seen sea glass," Gabby said wistfully. "Or the ocean. Or Hollywood."

The adults ignored her.

Odette shook out the quilt Laurel remembered. It had been made for a twin bed and had one very large block in the middle. "You'll want to make the main pattern smaller, with lots of sea glass blocks. Four or six inches square."

Laurel nodded automatically, but said, "No." Because suddenly, she saw the quilt clearly and it sparked something inside of her—an excitement to make her vision a reality. "I want to make one big piece, like yours."

"That would be copying," Odette said, clearly horrified.

Gabby laughed.

"I don't want to copy," Laurel grumbled. "I want to use yours as inspiration. The drama. The largesse."

Gabby laughed again. "Sounds like copying to me."

"Best focus on your own problems, Rocky," Odette cautioned, tapping her nose. "And get those stitches done." The old woman gave Laurel a rare grin. "I can't say I agree with your choice of design—one big piece of sea glass for a small project—but it's your quilt."

"When will you teach me how to quilt?" Gabby squeezed her ball of yarn like a stress ball.

"When you finish that scarf," Odette said sternly.

Gabby gasped and snatched up her knitting needles. "Promise?"

Odette walked over to the girl and offered her finger. They made a pact on a pinky swear. "Now, the teal family..." The old woman hunted through stack after stack of cotton quilt quarters, rolled into manageable sizes. Finally, Odette laid out ten colors. "This should work."

Laurel stared at the collection of fabrics without saying anything, wishing she didn't want to say anything because Odette was the expert here. But she couldn't stand not saying anything. "These two don't go." She pulled two of the fabrics aside. "The patterns on those are too large and the colors too washed out."

"That's exactly why they go." Odette arranged the fabric as if each one was a petal. "Small patterns and bright colors here in the center transitioning to bigger patterns and lighter colors on the outer edge." She raised her brows, daring Laurel to contradict her.

Laurel took that dare. "But the color spectrum goes from teal to a sandy brown. It's not a true ombré."

"It's a traditional sea glass color scheme." Odette's gaze narrowed. "Are you arguing with me?"

"No. We're having a discussion."

"But you said *you*—" Odette pointed at Laurel "—wanted to learn from *me*." She tapped her chest.

"I did. I do."

Odette touched each colored quarter of fabric from the teal down to the sandy brown. "And you said you'd do anything to make a quilt with me."

Did I?

She had.

Laurel studied the discarded fabrics, but reality was she couldn't live with them. Not without a fight. "What I meant was—"

"You wanted me to approve of you making a quilt based off mine, so you'd feel safe doing it. Let me tell you, that pink dress you made was a risk. You didn't use fabric to achieve an ombré effect. You used silver thread and rhinestones."

"I did." Laurel nodded slowly.

"Don't play it safe. Safe is lonely." Odette removed the lightest colors on the worktable. "You don't like sand. Fine. Let's go with something different." She chose two predominantly black prints and laid them where the sand had been so that the center color was teal, moving to softer teal, and then black. "Now, this...this will be a masterpiece."

Black on a baby quilt? Even if it was only an accent? Laurel wasn't so sure.

Odette's door was flung open and Flip entered. She looked around with a sour expression. "What is this? A sewing circle? A quilting bee?" Her gaze stuck on Gabby's face. She knelt in front of the preteen, hands on her knees. "Whoever did this to you will pay, I swear." She stood and fixed Laurel with a hard stare. "Who did this to her?"

Laurel leaned around Flip to catch the bruised preteen's eye. "Gabby?"

"It was self-inflicted." The smallest of small answers. Gabby sniffed as if she might cry. "I'm the one responsible." And then she recaptured some of her spunk because she said, "And I'm on the mend. Just gotta take it one day at a time."

Flip made a noise that conveyed disbelief and impatience all in the same breath. "When my husband was alive—*mind you, he was the sheriff*—he wouldn't have believed you." The collection of fabric they'd been arguing over caught Flip's eye. She stomped over to the worktable and studied their choices.

"We're making a sea glass baby quilt," Odette said.

Flip huffed and rearranged the fat quarters. "They'll never expect this."

She'd arranged the colors in a kaleidoscope of light, dark, light, dark. There was less teal and more black.

"That's an old trick." Odette moved the fabric around again, this time removing half the fabric choices—the black prints. "How about this one? A floral and a geometric pattern of the same size print and teal color palette complemented by a similar color fabric in a larger print on the outer edges."

"Why do what's been done before?" Flip rummaged through the basket of choices with paint-stained hands. She laid out a flowery teal, a flowery brown and a shiny taupe.

It was Odette's turn to huff. "That's so five years ago."

While the two older women tried to one-up each other on a color scheme, Laurel backed up until she stood next to Gabby. "Who is Flip?"

"Odette's sister," Gabby whispered back.

Flip pulled fabric from the bottom of the basket. "This is what you need to do. Black. Deep rose. Vibrant purple. Asparagus green."

The inspiration for Flip's colors was clear—Gabby's bruised face.

Laurel moved closer, taking in the colors and the powerful way they worked together, but also feeling uncomfortable. "It's supposed to be a baby quilt."

"Fine. Be predictable. Go with a fish pattern." Flip picked three different fabrics, set them on the worktable and then marched to the door. "Milky white. Pale lavender. Dusty rose." Her lip curled in disgust. "Softies don't deserve my mercantile." She slammed the door on her way out.

Shades of my mother.

Through the window, Laurel watched Flip march up the hill on a well-worn trail in the snow.

Soft. Understated. The colors Flip had chosen were just that. And a fish quilt was so... expected.

"I hate to admit it." Odette stared at the three colors. "But both color combinations are better than what we chose."

Laurel fingered the crisp, cool fabric with the washed-out colors. Although there was a place for soft, she didn't want to be seen as delicate. "Does Flip help you choose fabrics for every quilt?"

"Yes." Odette looked sheepish as she spread out the washed-out fabric quarters. "Do you still believe you can learn something from me?"

"Yes." There was something here to be gained beyond a handmade baby quilt.

No matter what color or style quilt she made, she'd have to prove to Flip she wasn't a softy.

An image popped into her head.

An image of the brick mercantile filled with color and texture and light, paintings and quilts and knit goods, and two chubby babies sitting on a bold quilt on the floor, playing with noisy rattles.

A boutique filled with beautiful things and artistic expression. Items that would delight people. A boutique curated by Laurel. It wasn't a fashion house in New York. It didn't come with Hollywood cache.

Mom would have a fit. And Ashley...

Laurel didn't care whose boat she rocked.

Her vision filled her with joy.

CHAPTER FIFTEEN

"I PINNED YOUR quilt pieces." Odette ushered Laurel to the worktable later that afternoon. "If you'd taken any longer, I would've started stitching. I tacked down my friendship quilt top, which freed up my frame." Odette's baby quilt was now mounted on the quilting frame, ready for permanent stitches.

"You did all that? And you pinned mine?" Laurel had been gone less than three hours. She'd had lunch and napped. Clearly, Odette had done neither.

"It's amazing what you can do with a fancy quilt machine. Besides, yours is just a baby quilt." The old woman lowered herself into the rocking chair and closed her eyes. "Tuckered me out, though. If there's more to life than crafting, I don't know what it is."

There's more to life...

That was one of Grandpa Harlan's favorite starter sentences. Laurel glanced at the crazy quilt above the fireplace. Odette had said she was emotionally attached to it. Was Odette related to Harlan? If so, did her sister, Flip, have a valid claim on the mercantile? Laurel would have to make sure she was within her rights to open a business in the brick building.

That decided, she studied her pinned quilt. Traditional pink and lavender blocks that made sweet little triangular fish.

She didn't like it. The fish represented compromise and capitulation. Out of the limelight and behind the scenes. There was playful chaos in Odette's creation, a pinwheel quilt, while Laurel's was ho-hum.

You don't want boring, do you, Babies?

They most certainly did not.

Odette snored.

Laurel set the pinned fish quilt aside and dug in the basket of fabrics.

An hour later Laurel had her new blocks tacked in place. She stretched and drank from her water bottle. She was going to make a blackbird baby quilt. Granted, some of her blackbirds were various shades of dark gray, but the contrast with their yellow beaks and the shiny taupe background was striking.

"Flip was right." Odette leaned forward in her rocker, a sad look in her faded eyes. "She put her stamp on your quilt."

Laurel nodded. "Both of you pushed me to find…to be…" Impulsively, Laurel stood and gave the old woman a hug and a kiss to her cheek. "I've just realized what my imprint is—adding a bit of sparkle or a bit of shine to soften a bold statement or to bring glam to a traditional work." She'd found it. The drive behind whatever she created. Laurel's heart swelled.

The old woman huffed but didn't say more.

Laurel stared at her quilt once more—pleased, satisfied, delighted. She was grinning and couldn't wait to tell... Someone who wasn't Mitch.

She touched the fabric, refusing to be saddened in the midst of her epiphany. "But there's something to be said for color composition and your sister—"

"Stop right now." Odette walked slowly to the kitchen like a long-legged ostrich, stretching and picking up her feet in exaggerated motions. "If you give Flip too much credit, she'll take it all."

"Forewarned." Laurel held up a hand.

"You need to be on your way. It'll be dark soon." Odette opened a jar of almonds and began munching.

Eliciting a promise to leave her quilt be, Laurel bundled up—hat, scarf, jacket—and went outside to put on her snowshoes, pausing on the steps to look at the tracks Flip had left in the snow.

The sky was a subtle purple gray. The wind blew with its usual bite. She glanced to the highway and then to Flip's tracks.

Light glowed from Odette's windows, revealing her digging through a tub of brightly colored yarn. She might want strangers to think she was a crotchety old woman, but she was kind once you had the patience to get to know her. She suspected Flip was the same.

Both women were talented. Both had passion for their art. Both inspired Laurel to create, to reach beyond herself.

Her stomach gave a hungry growl. She was supposed to meet Sophie and the boys soon for dinner.

But she was curious about Flip and her cabin. And she wanted to tell Flip about her fabric choices.

But the biggest reason of all to talk to Odette's sister was the mercantile.

"The first part of any business relationship is seeing if you can get along outside the business world," Grandpa Harlan had told Laurel after she'd complained about her supervisor at Monroe Studios.

At his suggestion, she'd brought that woman coffee for a month, volunteered to sit her dog while she went on vacation and sat with her on lunch breaks, listening to her rave about her son's skill as a soccer player. In the end Laurel hadn't changed her supervisor's opinion of her as much as she'd understood what kind of person her supervisor was and how best to deal with her.

Laurel walked down the porch steps and turned to the right, certain that Flip's home couldn't be far.

"HAVE YOU SEEN LAUREL?" Holding a hand of each twin, Sophie hurried down the inn's stairs, looking frazzled. Her brown hair was staticky. Her red glasses had slipped down to the tip of her nose. "We were supposed to go to dinner half an hour ago."

At the check-in desk, Mitch turned the application paperwork for historical significance over, even as he felt a tremor of unease. Dr. Carlisle had said concussion symptoms sometimes showed up days later. "She's not in her room?"

I shouldn't have let her go to Odette's alone.

Sophie shook her head. "All I found was her phone."

Was Laurel wandering around, lost in the wilderness? Without her phone?

A trickle of fear slid down his spine.

"Mom, I'm hungry," the twin with the cowlick declared, tugging Sophie toward the door.

His statement and arm pulling was mirrored by the other twin. "I'm hungry. I want snacks." He tugged her in the direction of the alcove—the opposite direction from the door.

Sophie swayed between them. "Boys! Stop it. Aunt Laurel is missing."

They stopped their tug-of-war and gaped at her.

Mitch came to Sophie's rescue, doling out flashlights to the trio. Kids always liked flashlights. "Why don't we head over to the Bent Nickel and see if she's there?" He took a flashlight for himself. The sun had set, and it always paid to be careful. "I'll check in with Odette." He called her landline.

The twins made ghoulish faces with their lights, but Sophie looked relieved to be saved from being made a wishbone.

"Can I help?" Zeke wheeled across the room just as Shane came downstairs.

Sophie brought the two of them up to speed.

"Odette's not answering." Sometimes the old woman claimed to be too busy to bother with phone calls. Mitch grabbed his coat.

"Dad?" Gabby's concerned expression was more pronounced given her black-rimmed eyes. "Do you need help looking?"

"No, honey. You stay here with Zeke. Laurel probably went straight to the diner from Odette's." But the chill deep in his bones said otherwise. "Call me if she shows up." He pointed to their landline before Gabby could say something about not having a cell phone.

No one at the Bent Nickel had seen Laurel since lunchtime.

"We should call someone." Sophie wrung her hands.

"The sheriff?" Shane asked anxiously. "Search and rescue?"

"The sheriff lives on the north end of town." And let's face it, the old man should have retired years ago. Sending him out in all this snow would result in disaster. "And we don't call search and rescue until we're sure a person is lost."

"But she's not *here*," Sophie cried.

"Come on." Ivy led Sophie to a table where her boys were sitting. "I'll get you some tea. Mitch will be back with Laurel in no time." But Ivy's smile seemed as forced as her words sounded.

Outside the diner, Mitch strapped on his snowshoes. It was dark. It was cold. And Laurel was missing. Fear froze his lungs and leadened his limbs.

He wanted to find her, to wrap his arms

around her and tell her one of Harlan's stories, like the one about Harlan getting lost during a surprise spring blizzard. One of the stories Mitch had given his word not to tell.

That was how much she meant to him. If she was safe, he was willing to renege on a contract and go back on his word. If they hadn't gotten into an argument, she might be safe right now.

A few minutes later Odette ushered him inside, looking like she was settling in to binge-watch television outside. She wore a thick pair of gray sweats, mittens, an orange scarf and thick red knit socks. "What do you mean Laurel's missing? She left here over an hour ago before it was dark."

"She didn't show up for dinner."

It was chilly in her cabin. There was a stack of blankets on the couch as if Odette was going to burrow under them.

"That girl. I bet she went to Flip's." Odette picked up her phone and plugged the jack in, catching Mitch's startled expression. "Don't judge." She called Flip, but no one answered there, either. "Hers is probably unplugged, too." She reached for her coat.

"Stay here." The last thing he needed was for Odette to break a bone traipsing through the snow with no doctor in town. "I know the way."

Odette hesitated, arms halfway in her jacket. "Is it snowing outside?"

"No." The next storm was predicted to move in tomorrow night. The lack of falling snow was a blessing. It meant Mitch could follow Laurel's tracks, and could tell if she'd wandered into the woods.

Odette knew it, too. She nodded and hung her jacket back on its hook. "She's probably up there arguing with Flip. If Flip let her in. She's stubborn."

"Speaking of stubborn things." Mitch went to the thermostat, which was set at sixty, and edged it up to sixty-eight. "You can afford your electricity bill. I don't want to come looking for you and find you frozen over your sewing machine."

"I'm too stubborn to die of the cold." Odette opened the door and ushered him out. "Something else will get me, just like it got my man. That city girl of yours… She's not mountain folk. You find her. You find her right quick."

"I NEVER SHOULD have let you in." Flip paced the small kitchen.

"But you did let me in," Laurel said. "And then you let me look at your paintings." She'd been looking for a long time, thinking that Sophie would love to sort through Flip's work.

The paintings crowded her living room. There was no more space to store them, to hang them or to display them. Or to sit, for that matter, other than the kitchen table.

That would make me cranky.

"Have you always loved painting?"

"No. It's been an outlet. Nothing more. I'm not an artist."

"I beg to differ."

Each canvas was different. There was a corner in the back of the room with angry canvases filled with slashes of black paint depicting loosely formed subjects—speeding cars, sneering men, things hiding in the shadows. The couch was covered with more realistic paintings, carefully stroked studies of light and nature—the majestic Sawtooth Mountains, the sparkling Salmon River in spring, cabins nestled in pine-studded groves. Nearer the door, whimsy had taken hold. Flip's paint strokes were fewer, bigger, bolder. The pine groves were decorated with a blooming carpet of wildflowers. The moon illuminated many a red rose garden.

By looking at her work, Laurel felt as if she was peeking into Flip's emotional journey— from sadness to a happier place. Sophie would marvel at the collection's depth. But it left a different imprint on Laurel. Her work said there was hope.

"Look what I found." Laurel held up an unfinished portrait of Grandpa Harlan, hidden near the bottom of a series of moonlit rose garden paintings. "You have talent. I recognized my grandfather right away." Laurel admired the bold lines of the man's jaw. "He used to say he brought out the best in people."

"He would," Flip quipped.

They both laughed, but Laurel knew it was true. Grandpa Harlan had demanded perfection of himself, his family and his workforce. Those standards had made him a multimillionaire.

The last painting in the stack was a whimsical picture of a golden moon in an almost equally golden sky. "I'd love to have this one for my nursery. The moon has a face and that face is smiling." She turned it toward Flip, who'd stopped pacing and gripped the kitchen chair back.

"You're flattering me now." Her weathered face wavered from tentative pride to perplexed uncertainty as if she wanted to believe what Laurel said was true.

"I'm not." Laurel set the moon painting next to the one of her grandfather, and moved to stand near the old woman, gently prying her hands from the chair and giving them a reassuring squeeze. "If you let me, I could sell your paintings at the mercantile. That is, if you wouldn't mind me turning it into a place filled with beautiful things."

"Sell what you want." The old woman made a derisive noise. "Nobody wants my work. I paint for myself." Flip was determined not to take a compliment. But Laurel had been giving them since she'd arrived, and Flip looked… less angry, less distant. "I started painting in the mercantile because I ran out of room here. By rights, it's yours since I've only got a lease on this place."

"Thank you. It means a lot to get your blessing. But please think about letting me feature your work. Grandpa Harlan would have been thrilled if I brought your art to others to enjoy." Laurel was convinced of that. "I'd be honored, as well."

Flip turned away. "If I wanted to put my paintings up for sale, I could put them in the general store."

Laurel didn't feel right about that. The paintings deserved more than that, they deserved atmosphere, not apples and artichokes. They were art! She cast about her brain for a way to convince Flip. "Are there other artists in town? The mercantile could be a place we show off the talents that can only be found in Second Chance."

"You're Harlan's granddaughter all right." Flip brushed her gray-brown hair toward the back of her neck and sighed. "You never know when to give up."

"Then you'll agree?"

"If you get Odette to agree to sell some of her things—*which she won't*—I'll let you have a painting or two."

Laurel gushed her thanks.

Flip raised her head, looking through the dark window. "What's that noise?" She grabbed a shotgun.

THE LIGHTS WERE blazing in Flip's cabin and two figures could be seen through the kitchen window. On the porch a familiar pair of snow-shoes leaned against the wall near the front door.

His boots on the wooden steps announced him before he could knock.

Flip opened the door, frowning, holding a shotgun. "It's about time you came to collect this baggage. She's been trying to fill my head with all sorts of nonsense."

It had been years since Mitch had been in-side Flip's cabin. Back then he'd walked into her living room. He couldn't walk anywhere in her cabin today without knocking over stacks of paintings or unframed blank canvases. Her landline was nowhere in sight. If it had rung, it couldn't have been reached.

But he could worry about Flip later, because he'd found Laurel.

"Mitch?" Laurel had her jacket on. Her smile faded at the sight of him. "Is something wrong?"

The first rule of engagement with Laurel should've been not to look in her eyes. They used to shine bluer than the sky when she focused on him. Since he'd admitted he knew Harlan's disastrous Christmas story, they'd become a flat, pale blue and sorrowful.

He'd hurt her. But he'd lost something, too. Something he'd taken for granted. Something he had no right to ask for. A chance at winning her love.

"Mitch?" she said again.

"You missed your dinner with Sophie and left your phone at the inn, Miss Laurel." He wanted to kiss her. He wanted to hug her. He wanted to turn around and leave her at Flip's because the alternative was a long walk back to the town proper. Alone with Laurel. Under the stars.

Laurel said goodbye to Flip with a hug and

a promise to keep in touch, zipped up her jacket and stepped outside with him, closing the door to Flip's prying eyes. "Were you worried, Counselor?" She laid her gloved palm on his chest and stared up at him in a way he couldn't resist.

He hauled Laurel into his arms and tucked her head beneath his chin. "You can't imagine how relieved I am to find you safe." Mitch brought her closer. "Don't say anything just yet. Don't say anything about things we can't say to each other or dresses we can't leave behind or... Just...don't say anything."

She relaxed in his arms. "Oh, Mitch."

Mitch. Not Counselor.

He led her down the steps and then helped her put on her snowshoes.

They walked away from Flip's, their route illuminated by the moon and Mitch's flashlight. The northern part of town had only a few cabins interspersed with larger ranches that led up to the Bucking Bull. The smell of woodsmoke was faint, as were electric lights.

"We're taking the road back," Mitch said when Laurel tried to veer through the woods. "You should never stray off the road at night. You could get lost or injured. And without your cell phone..." They'd never find her. Or they'd find her too late.

"I never thought I'd get a lecture about not having my cell phone handy." A gentle tease.

"I never thought I'd give one." The tension in him eased as they slipped into familiar banter.

"Did my grandfather ever get lost in the snow?"

Her question broadsided him. "Is this a test?"

"It is if you still have the hots for me." She slid him a sideways glance and a hint of a smile. "You made quite the impression on me and the babies when Flip opened that door and our gazes connected."

He'd felt something, too. "I was a lawyer. Deep down, I still am. I want to tell you things…" He wanted to tell her everything. "But the terms of my silence last a full year after Harlan's death. I can't go against my word without a court order." Unlike Ivy. "If this is a deal breaker…"

The wind swirled past and their snowshoes crunched ice-crusted snow.

Laurel didn't say yes or no. She wasn't going to make this easy on him or maybe the decision was hard on her, too.

"You know," Mitch said, feeling a bit desperate, "there was a man who used to live out here. His parents were what someone in the big city might call dirt-poor. They worked hard for every penny they made." Mitch shifted his feet, but never took his eyes from her. "This man... He might have been barely eighteen. He could taste a snowstorm coming. The air was thick with cold and wet. But he needed to catch a fish to feed the family, so he stayed by the river casting his fly into a small hole in the snow and ice, unwilling to give up. And then the storm hit and Har..." Mitch swallowed. "And *he* still hadn't caught more than a bit of snow on that feathered hook of his. So he fought the wind and the cold and the hunger. And finally, he hooked a fish. And this young man turned to go home, only the snow was so thick he couldn't see more than a foot or two in front of his face."

A gust of wind blew snow from the pines above their heads.

"It took him over an hour to find his way home. He knew his family had to have food, because as you know, folks can get snowed in for days up here in Second Chance." The young man was Harlan, of course. But Mitch would deny it if she asked him.

The wind swirled, trying to throw him off balance.

Finally, she spoke. "My grandfather used to encourage me to reach for my dreams, wherever they might take me. It was nice to hear, but… I never had adequate time to explore my creativity." Her words were soft, quickly carried away by the wind. "Last year, if you'd have asked me what my dream was, I'd have said to be a red-carpet dress designer. But I had no vision of what my dresses would look like. No unique style in the way I dressed that said I was different than some other designer. I wanted to sew and create and have others love it." She glanced up at him and then away. "To have others love *me*."

Mitch clasped her gloved hand with his own.

"Is that the right motivation to choose a career?" She closed her eyes, seeming to gather herself before looking up at him again. "My grandfather once told me I was more than Ashley's twin. And I've gone through life wondering how to be more…*me*." Her gloved fingers gripped his. "It's hard to find yourself when you share a face with someone famous. When you have to wear another person's persona and leave yours behind."

"You've been very unselfish."

"I've been hiding." Laurel shook off his words. "Odette brings color to life. There's a warmth in her work that makes you want to hug something, which contradicts the facade she presents to the world." Laurel sniffed, but

Mitch wasn't sure if the cold had gotten to her nose or if her insight into Odette was choking her up. "And Flip... If I hadn't seen her full collection of work, I'd never have believed there was such depth to her soul, such beauty."

She was definitely choked up now. But she was also determined to keep moving forward, to push past adversity and unpleasantness the way she always did.

"I have so much to learn from them," Laurel said in a distant voice. "So much to learn about myself. And when I'm in search of joy and inspiration, how can I shut out one of the people who gives me both?" She stared up at him and said simply, "You."

Mitch's heart was full. The future seemed less uncertain. Because Laurel would be in it.

They reached the narrow ribbon of two-lane highway at a bend in the road. Moonlight stroked over the wide, rolling valley, washing it in blue and making it look like a calm and gentle ocean.

"Oh. It's stunning, like one of Flip's paintings." Laurel admired the view. "I've never seen the valley at night."

Her window faced the western mountains.

"I had an intense day today," Laurel continued. "And I have a lot to think about tomorrow. It's rare moments of beauty like this when I understand why my grandfather loved this place. Besides—" she wore a teary smile "—I'm partial to blue."

He stood next to her, resisting the impulse to take her into his arms again. "I'm partial to the blue of your eyes when you're laughing."

She gazed up at him, not laughing, wiping away a tear. "That's kind of you to say."

He wasn't feeling kind enough. "I should have said I prefer the blue of your eyes. *Period*." He rested his hands on her hips.

Mitch was in trouble. He could feel that trouble expanding in his chest, rising like a balloon, filling him with wonder. The trouble was love. And it was inescapable.

I love Laurel.

He loved her honesty. He loved her laughter. He loved her dogged need to negotiate peace. He loved her talent and tenacity. He loved how she wanted to protect her sister. He loved how she fitted into his arms and held on to his hand.

"We need to come to an agreement." His voice was gruff from emotion. "A peace accord in the midst of all these Monroes."

"What did you have in mind?" Her hands slid up his chest, giving him hope that she'd accept his terms for a truce.

But there wasn't just peace at stake. There

was love on the bargaining table. And as she'd said, love started with honesty. "Tell me what big secret is hanging over you." He covered her hands with his, closing his fingers protectively around hers. "Let me help you and those babies."

Her gloved hands fisted on his chest and her features stiffened, not in anger, but in anguish. "My life is tangled worse than a ball of half-unraveled yarn." He wanted there to be no barriers between them. He wanted to help her. He wanted to admit to Laurel that he'd fallen in love with her. He wanted her to love him in return.

All his wants pressed down on his shoulders. He had to be patient. Everything in due time as if he was preparing to win a long court case.

"If I could just unravel one piece…" She lifted her gaze to his. "If I was standing on solid ground personally, with my sister. Or professionally… I'd let you help. But it's all messy and I…I don't think you'd like what you found if you looked at my knots."

"You're wrong." He pressed her hands deeper into his jacket, over his heart. "I think you deserve to be happy, and maybe happiness is closer than you think." When the contract expired, when her problems had sorted themselves out, they'd be okay.

"Do you really think so?"

Instead of answering, he wrapped his arms around Laurel and kissed her.

A few minutes later, when they were both cold on the outside and warm on the inside, she drew back and stared at him in wonder.

He couldn't be sure because of the blustering wind whistling through the trees, but he thought she said, "You really think so," before she chuckled and tugged him toward home.

"I'M GETTING BETTER with snowshoes." Sophie passed Laurel going up the hill, singing her words instead of speaking them. "I'm so good, pretty soon we won't need our chaperone." She listed to one side, much as Laurel had done the other day. Only she righted herself with her poles and didn't fall.

Laurel had mixed feelings about their chaperone. For one thing, he was an excellent kisser. For another, he'd refused to let her out alone, worried Laurel would fall again, worried Laurel might develop a concussion or wander off through the lodgepole pines.

Laurel paused, glancing over her shoulder at him, the handsome, caring man she hoped would understand the Wyatt fiasco.

"First rule of snowshoeing, Miss Laurel. Don't stop in the middle of the hill." Mitch wore his kind smile, the one that brought back memories of warm kisses on cold nights. "Second rule of snowshoeing. Don't go into the wilderness without your phone."

Well, she was fairly certain no one was going to return her calls during the hour she was over here. "I'm right across the highway from help." From Mitch. If he'd chosen to stay back at the inn.

"I have my phone," Sophie reassured Mitch. "And we won't be here long. The boys might wear out their welcome at the diner." She'd left them with the schoolkids under the supervision of Eli Garland. Sophie reached the trading post porch and waited for Laurel, Mitch and his key. "Alexander and Andrew aren't due to start kindergarten until the fall. Mr. Garland gave me an hour." She checked her cell phone. "That was ten minutes ago."

"Can you open up the mercantile, Mitch? I want to show it to Sophie." Laurel reached the porch and stepped aside to allow him access to the door, bumping into a grinning Sophie.

"He's a keeper," Sophie whispered her favorite line.

"That I am." Mitch unlocked the trading post door and turned, his gaze colliding with

Laurel's. He was doing his best not to grin and she was doing her best not to tangle up their snowshoes as they'd done last night when she'd kissed him.

Sophie laughed. "I'm such a third wheel."

"You're not." Laurel's cheeks heated. She gave Mitch a gentle shove. "Let's go. I want to show you both something."

Mitch's brows quirked. He moved past Laurel and led them across the snowshoe trail they'd made the other day to the mercantile.

Laurel followed, hot on his heels, ridding herself of snowshoes and poles as soon as she reached the mercantile's porch. "Wait until you see the light in here, Sophie." She darted around Mitch to get inside.

Sophie peeked in while she removed her snow gear. "Why aren't there piles and piles of stuff in here?"

"Because of Flip, I think." Laurel peered into the glass case that held the bolts of faded fabric. "She had a painting of hers on display in here the other day. It was beautiful and angled to catch the light. She has so many paintings in her cabin and no room to paint or to step back and appreciate them."

"What did you want me to see?" Glancing around, Sophie wasn't as enthused as Laurel was. "It looks like it's been picked clean."

"No. It's been *cleaned*, Sophie. There's a difference." Laurel ran her gloved hand over the glass. "This was where ladies in town shopped. Unlike the trading post, there aren't any bear traps, for instance. No axes. No thermal wear. Look at this." She scurried around the display counter to point at a framed picture on the wall. "This is a fashion plate from over one hundred years ago. Women came in here to buy things that gave them joy. Just look around. Can you see it?"

Mitch smiled at Laurel, but she was fairly certain it wasn't because he saw her vision.

Sophie frowned. "See what?"

"What this could be." Laurel moved into the middle of the room and spread her arms. "I see a display of Odette's quilts here. And a few of Flip's paintings hanging on the wall there. Everything I sell would be handmade locally. Scarves, mittens, caps." A scarf or quilt with a bit of shine or sparkle. "Maybe some of that pottery and other rustic art pieces you rave about." There had to be other artisans in the area.

"A boutique?" Sophie pushed her glasses up her nose. "In Second Chance?"

Laurel came to a stop in front of the window overlooking the Lodgepole Inn and the valley beyond it, remembering the moonlit meadow and strong arms around her. "Yes, a boutique in Second Chance. *My* boutique." A joyous place. "All I have to do is convince Odette to let me sell some of her crafts." And maybe someday she'd sell some of her own.

"Well, if you could make that happen, I could open an antiques store in the trading post." Sophie stepped out onto the porch and looked at the log building. "It wouldn't be your average, stuffy mom-and-pop shop with tea-cups, Tiffany lamps and old books. I'm finding unusual pieces and there are bound to be more in the other buildings if what Shane told me is true."

"You can see it, can't you?" Laurel beamed at her cousin. "You can feel it?" The rightness of it all. "Us. Here. In Second Chance."

"Slow down." Mitch stepped between them. No smile on his face. No tease in his voice. "I'm not sure if anyone's told you, but we don't get many people stopping here to shop. Mack can back me up on this."

"Maybe that's because there's not much here to stop for," Sophie pointed out. "The town is charming. People would want to stop, get out and stretch their legs if they saw something interesting to stop and shop for."

"You've seen how little traffic goes through

during winter." Mitch extended an arm to Exhibit A: the empty highway.

"Lots of businesses are seasonal." Laurel leaned against the brick window ledge and regarded him levelly trying to discern the root of his protest.

Sophie nodded and put on her snowshoes. "I have lots of unique items to sell in the trading post. Some are worth a lot to the right collector."

Mitch shook his head. "I don't want to sound pessimistic, but since I've been here I've seen five or six businesses close, just in this part of town. Even with your grandfather's low leases."

"Well, they weren't Monroes running those businesses, were they?" Laurel raised her chin. "We Monroes have a saying—"

"To make money, you have to be passionate about what you do," Sophie finished for her.

"Because a passion for a business is like a rich cake with a cherry on top." Grandpa Harlan used to say that. "You have to eat cake when it's fresh."

"Because there's more to life than eating your greens." Sophie grinned. She was in. She was definitely in.

"Is this the right time to think about this?" Mitch tried to sound reasonable, but it was clear he had strong opinions about what they were doing. He wasn't convinced this was right for either of them. "Sophie has two young boys. You're pregnant and have things to unravel."

Laurel wanted to move closer, brush Mitch's dark, wind-tossed hair from his eyes, and press a reassuring kiss to his lips. "I'm going to do this."

"Me, too." Sophie looked just as determined as Laurel felt.

"I'm not going to be hurt." Laurel succumbed to the need to soothe. She stepped into Mitch's space and held on to his forearms. "The worst that could happen is we go out of business. And the best that could happen is our efforts entice more travelers to stop, eat at the diner, buy snacks and gasoline at the general store, maybe even stay the night at the inn."

He bent to press a tender kiss on her forehead.

Laurel wasn't fooled. He was worried.

She was worried, too. But not about the boutique succeeding. She was worried about her ability to convince Odette to sell her work.

And without both sisters, Laurel would only have a scarf or two of her own to sell.

CHAPTER SIXTEEN

"Dr. Carlisle?" Shane stood outside the clinic door in Ketchum with a twitchy Roy. They'd been waiting forty-five minutes in the cold for Laurel's doctor to emerge.

Forty-five minutes was enough time to get cold feet, literally and figuratively. Shane hoped he wouldn't be arrested tomorrow for kidnapping.

"Yes?" The woman blinked tired eyes at the two of them.

Shane swallowed his fears and introduced himself and Roy. "We had an appointment to talk about the job opening in Second Chance."

The doctor was tall, blonde and in her midthirties. She would've been a stunner had she been rested, bothered with some makeup, not been wearing black nerd glasses and not have a figure hidden behind a navy blue stadium jacket. She seemed a trifle bewildered as if she didn't remember agreeing to meet.

"We want to take you to dinner." Roy hooked his arm through hers and steered her toward Mitch's black Hummer parked at the curb.

"Coffee." Dr. Carlisle checked her phone. "I agreed to coffee."

"I know you've just finished a long shift," Shane said smoothly, falling into step beside her. "I bet you could use a good meal. Salad. Steak. Vegetables. A decadent dessert." A slam dunk unless she was a vegetarian or gluten-free.

There were so many ways this could go wrong.

Why did I let Roy talk me into this?

"Coffee." Dr. Carlisle freed her arm. She had big blue eyes, but she wasn't naive. "I'm going to be honest. I'm not looking for a new job. I like my work and… Frankly, I don't think Second Chance could afford me."

Shane named a figure that gave Dr. Carlisle pause.

"That can't be right." Her forehead creased. "Could you repeat that?"

Shane did, rocking back on his heels and staring down at his leather loafers, trying to look the epitome of innocence. Inside, his stomach lurched.

Roy propelled the doctor toward the Hummer again, which in typical kidnapper fashion had the motor running. "We have top-of-the-line facilities in Second Chance."

"We have facilities," Shane said under his breath, adding in a much louder voice, "and the last physician we employed treated about one person a day."

She glanced at Shane over her shoulder. "What did he do with the rest of his time?"

"Noah read a lot of books and enjoyed the view." Roy opened the back door, revealing Zeke in the backseat.

Dr. Carlisle's brow furrowed.

Not that Shane blamed her. She'd been expecting one man. Now she had three. "We brought Zeke in for his checkup."

"I graduated to a walking brace today." Zeke patted the seat next to him. He had the kind of features people tended to trust—ginger hair, lightly freckled, friendly smile. At first glance, no one would take him for a kidnapper.

"Achilles injury?" the doctor guessed, not budging from the sidewalk. She wasn't gullible. She'd gone to med school in New York City after all.

Shane had checked her credentials. He should have checked his own sanity.

"Tibia fracture. Broke through the skin and hurt like… Doc—" Zeke flashed his I'm-a-cowboy-you-can-trust-me grin. "Doc was our

last physician in Second Chance. Anyway...
he saved my life."

Dr. Carlisle grinned back at him. "I don't
doubt it."

"So, you'll go to dinner with us?" Roy
crowded behind her, trying to herd the poor
woman into the vehicle.

Once more, Dr. Carlisle didn't budge.

Shane gritted his teeth. Roy was going to
blow the whole thing with his strange vibe.
Shane dragged the town handyman back a foot
and repeated the salary figure.

"I...might be open to talking about this."
Dr. Carlisle glanced at her phone. "Is dinner
really necessary? I'm afraid I won't be a good
conversationalist after an eighteen-hour shift.
I delivered three babies today and I can barely
keep my eyes open."

"Dinner. Please." Zeke looked sorrowful.
"Take pity on me. I'm dying of hunger."

Shane winced. He'd fallen in with a bunch
of con artists. Was this what his grandfather
had intended for him when he left him a share
in Second Chance?

*Forget Grandpa. Do this for Laurel. And
Sophie. And the twins. Keep them safe.*

Girded, Shane resisted the urge to bolt.

"Bones need good food to heal." Dr. Carlisle relented and climbed into the backseat beside Zeke.

Now it was Shane who didn't budge. He couldn't go through with it. "On second thought, Dr. Carlisle—"

"Settle in." Roy elbowed Shane aside, sensing he was losing his nerve. "It'll be our pleasure to treat you, Doc." Roy closed the Hummer door behind her and glared at Shane.

"I think I'm going to be sick," Shane whispered.

"That's funny considering we're at a maternity clinic." Roy chuckled. "People'll think you're pregnant."

Shane scowled. "No. They won't."

"That was a joke, boy. Man up." Roy moved closer and whispered, "She's in the car. It's time to make our getaway."

Shane had taken risks in his life, but he'd never committed a felony. At some point Dr. Carlisle would realize they were driving her to Second Chance, not a restaurant in Ketchum.

"Use that phone of yours to tell Zeke not to talk much." Roy nudged Shane toward the driver's door, still whispering, "She's exhausted and the way this thing rides, she'll be rocked to sleep in no time."

"WOULD YOUR BABY daddy be jealous of my dad?"

Laurel nearly dropped her knitting needles. Her latest stitch slipped. She pulled the coppery yarn and the silver thread she'd been using, unraveling a few stitches.

It took her a moment to rearrange her yarn and needles. Only then did she look up at Gabby, sitting across the couch from her in the common room at the inn. Mitch had invited the Monroes to dinner. They were just waiting for Shane to return from his trip to Ketchum to eat.

"Gabby," Laurel said quietly. "You shouldn't ask people personal questions like that."

Gabby's knitting sat forgotten in her lap. She was frowning, an expression that looked fierce given her purplish-red bruises. "I'm only asking for my dad."

Laurel raised her eyebrows, challenging that defense.

"You know, to protect him." Gabby leaned forward and lowered her voice. "Because you're practically famous. If your baby daddy is a famous person, too, and he showed up here, you'd choose him over my dad."

The needles slid out of Laurel's hands. "Isn't that undervaluing your father?"

"Get real." Gabby raised her fingers to her

nose as if gauging how swollen it was. "Why would you stay here with my dad if you had a chance to be with someone really rich and really talented?"

"Hang on. Your dad is great." It was true. "But that doesn't mean he and I are...will..."

"That's just stupid." Gabby's knitting fell to the floor. "I saw you kissing. I've seen movies. I know lots of kissing means forever is in your future. At least, until someone better comes along."

Laurel covered Gabby's hand with her own. "Kissing doesn't mean forever." If it did, she'd have a forever with Wyatt, which would have meant she'd never have Mitch in her life. Or Gabby. She'd never have found inspiration in a sparkle. Or planned to open a boutique featuring local artisans, who at this point were all women.

There's an angle. Her inner voice sounded a lot like Grandpa Harlan.

"But..." Gabby frowned. "You love my dad, don't you?"

Laurel fell back on the couch cushion. *Love?*

"What's wrong with your face, Gabby?" Alexander asked, saving Laurel from answering. "Is that a mask?"

Love? She'd known she was falling, but... Did she love Mitch?

Laurel felt comfortable with him and excited at the same time. When he was near, he was never near enough. She made excuses to touch him, to brush her hand over his. That was all physical stuff.

And emotionally?

Emotionally, she enjoyed his company, she valued his opinion, she trusted him with details of her life she'd never told anyone else. He had a way of looking into her eyes that seemed like he saw to her very soul. And she didn't mind. She didn't mind one bit. Because she loved him.

"It's not a mask, Alexander. I ran into a wall, remember?" Gabby rolled her eyes. "Note to self, little man. Watch where you're going at all times."

Love. Laurel hugged the thought closer.

Love. She loved Mitch.

She sat up taller, wanting to see Mitch, wanting to tell Mitch, because she was suddenly sure he felt the same way.

A vehicle pulled up outside. Doors opened and closed. Voices murmured and got louder. Someone climbed the porch steps.

Laurel turned, eager to see how Shane had fared on his doctor hunt, interested to hear an update on Zeke's leg.

"This can't possibly be it." Her mother's

voice spilled into the room as she opened the inn's door. And then she was standing there, staring at Laurel wearing a gray wool A-line skirt, a white silk blouse, boots and pearls. Her short red hair was perfectly coifed. "Or I could be wrong."

Laurel got to her feet so fast she experienced a head rush. She willed herself not to sway, not to back down, not to pass out in shock. "Mom?"

"Are you...*knitting*?" Her mother couldn't have sounded more disgusted if Laurel had been caught shoplifting at Nieman's.

"Mom." Laurel set her knitting on the coffee table. "You should have told me you were coming."

"Look at yourself. It's worse than I thought." Her mother leaned out the door and encouraged someone to get inside quickly.

Ashley?

A man's heavy tread came up the stairs. Broad shoulders appeared behind her mother.

Wyatt?

Laurel's knees buckled. She leaned on the arm of the couch.

The man moved past her mother and came inside, shutting the door behind him.

Not Wyatt.

"Cousin Holden?" Laurel couldn't believe it.

In a true indicator of Holden's popularity in the Monroe family, Alexander and Andrew didn't greet him. They exchanged silent glances instead.

"Where's Shane?" Holden surveyed the inn with a frown. He wore an expensive puffy jacket, blue jeans, an oatmeal-colored knit sweater and mukluks—sensible mountain attire that would put Shane's city clothes to shame. Had he gone gray since the funeral? Silver streaked his temples. "This town is worse than we thought, Aunt Genevieve. I mean, log cabins?"

"Where's Ashley?" Laurel demanded when it was clear no one else was coming through that door.

"She's shooting a guest spot on a sitcom." Mom surveyed Laurel the way horse trainers surveyed racing prospects. "Have you gained weight?"

Holden approached the check-in desk and rang the service bell.

Ding-ding-ding.

The door to the apartment was closed. Mitch and Sophie were in the kitchen, cooking a special meal to celebrate the reopening of the mercantile and trading post.

The bell grated on Laurel's frayed nerves. "Shane should be here any minute."

Holden reached for the bell to ring it again when Gabby snatched it away.

"Can I help you?" Gabby said with preteen scorn.

Holden stared down his nose at Gabby much the same way Shane had stared down his nose at Gabby and Mitch the day they'd first arrived.

"Is he hard of hearing?" Gabby asked Laurel when her cousin didn't answer. She turned back to Holden and raised her voice. "Do you want a room?"

"We won't be staying the night." Mom marched over to Laurel, skirt swaying with purpose. "We're all leaving." She took hold of Laurel's arm. "Pack your things. We have lives to lead and contracts to sign."

"No?" Laurel would have liked her refusal to come out like she meant it. Instead, she sounded indecisive.

The babies practiced kickboxing in her stomach. Which, in reality, was an overstatement, but Laurel imagined they were upset at their grandmother treating her like a spineless rag doll.

"What happened to your face? Were you in some sort of accident?" Holden scowled at Gabby. "Is the labor pool here so weak Shane has to hire kids?"

"Hey! Mr. Monroe," Gabby called, waving her hands at him, "my dad and I own this place, okay?"

"Sweetheart, *I* own this place." Holden winked at her. "And from where I'm standing, it's a teardown."

Mitch came out of his apartment. He took stock of the room. He took stock of Laurel's face. His dark eyes took stock of her mother's hand on her arm. "Now, that just won't do." He gestured to Laurel's arm, but he didn't come to her rescue, because...

Because he'd been encouraging her to take charge of her life for days. Because he knew she could stand up to her mother. Not for Ashley's sake, but for her own.

"Mom, I'm *not* leaving." There. That sounded believable.

"What's in the water here that would make you want to stay?" Mom's fingers squeezed Laurel's arm. She looked at Laurel's waist, hidden behind a loose tunic sweater. She looked at Laurel's knitting, made from soft coppery yarn. She released Laurel as if she'd been scalded. "Don't tell me. You're pregnant. You've figured another way to ruin everything for us."

Reality Check Number One. Forget wondering if Mom would be happy to learn she was going to be a grandmother.

"Yes, I'm pregnant." Laurel stepped back. "With twins."

Mom clutched her pearls.

Mitch looked Holden up and down. "Would you like a room? It's getting late and the mountain roads are treacherous at night, especially during a snowstorm. We take all forms of credit and cash."

"You want me to *pay* for a room?" Holden was jerkier than Shane at his jerkiest. "Have you looked at this place? You should be paying me to stay here."

"Holden." Sophie stepped in before Laurel could, coming out of the kitchen and pushing up her glasses. "The people in this town lease their businesses from us. That means nothing is comped. So get out your wallet if you want to stay."

Holden turned on his heel and left.

"Was it him?" Mom jabbed a finger in Mitch's direction. "Is this the man who got you pregnant?" She marched over to the desk and rose up into Mitch's face. "Are you going to make an honest woman of my daughter?"

"That's entirely up to your daughter."

Mitch's gaze met Laurel's. The shock was, he might have been serious.

He wants to marry me?

The babies cheered.

Reality Check Number Two. If this was a proposal, it was sadly lacking.

She'd always dreamed of candlelight and roses.

"If this guy didn't do it, who did?" Mom circled back around to Laurel.

"Mom, I didn't mean for it to happen." Laurel sat on the arm of the couch and gripped her knees, because she had to hold on to something. "It's never happened on a date before. And it goes without saying it won't happen again because I can't be Ashley's double anymore." She hoped Ashley would forgive her for that.

"Are you saying… *Wyatt?*" Mom shrieked at the top of her lungs. "Those are Wyatt Halford's babies? But…he had a date with *Ashley!*"

"And therein lies the problem." Laurel slid off the couch arm to the couch cushion, wishing she could slide out of sight.

"Wyatt Halford? The sexiest man alive?" Gabby jumped up and fist pumped the air.

"Gabby, go to your room." Mitch didn't look

happy. And he didn't look at Laurel. "This isn't funny, nor is it behavior I want you to model."

Mitch's reaction clawed at Laurel's insides. It was all she could do to keep herself upright. Her chest ached and tears pressed at the backs of her eyes. He'd told her he'd stand by her side when the knots unraveled.

He doesn't love me.

"Oh, Dad. Reality check." Gabby took hold of his arm. "There's no way Laurel will pick you over the sexiest man alive."

He can't even look at me.

"You were supposed to *date him* as Ashley, not…" Mom's hand waved in the air as if she held a wand. "I can't believe you told him who you were."

Oh, boy. "Mom."

"I can't believe you told him our secret."

Oh, man. "Mom."

"What do you think Wyatt's going to do with *that* information?"

"Mom!" Laurel shouted, her cheeks burning with embarrassment because now everyone knew who'd gotten her pregnant and under what circumstances. "I didn't tell Wyatt who I was."

"But that means… He still thinks you were Ashley." Mom collapsed on the couch next to

Laurel, ashen. "As soon as we tell him, we're ruined."

Reality Check Number Three. For once, Mom was right.

CHAPTER SEVENTEEN

"WE WERE SUPPOSED to go to dinner in Ketchum!" Dr. Carlisle was not as susceptible to Shane's smile as most of the elderly women in Second Chance. She swung her big black purse at Shane, connecting with his shoulder.

"Ow." Shane stepped out of range. It felt like she had a brick in her bag. Snow fell thick and fast around them as they stood outside the Bent Nickel. And it was so cold, the snow wasn't melting on either one of them. "We just thought you'd give our offer more consideration if you visited the town."

Dr. Carlisle had fallen asleep soon after they left the clinic, waking up when they reached the summit and berating them all the way down the road into Second Chance. As soon as he'd parked in front of the diner, Roy had helped Zeke out of the Hummer and left Shane to dig them all out of this hole.

Dr. Carlisle growled like a cornered cougar and swung again, missing Shane's snowflake-frosted head by inches. "After this caper, there is no way I'm working for you people."

"Technically, you'd be working for Second Chance, Inc."

She swung her bag at him again.

He dodged her swing by leaping sideways, landed wrong and fell onto his hip. The pain paralyzed him. "I need a doctor."

"Fat chance," Dr. Carlisle shouted at him.

There is no way things could get worse.

"There you are." The masculine voice of doom.

Things just got worse.

Cousin Holden stood near the gas pumps in front of the general store, scowling at Shane as he bore down upon him.

In his head Shane had a colorful conversation with his grandfather, who'd gotten him into this mess. But Grandpa Harlan didn't answer back.

"Hey, Holden." Getting slowly to his feet, trying to ignore the pain, Shane pasted on a smile and waved to his cousin. "Come on over. There's someone I want you to meet." He introduced Dr. Carlisle to his family nemesis. "I was just going to show Dr. Carlisle the medical clinic. She's interested in the position of town doctor."

"I'm not." Dr. Carlisle swung her bag at

Shane again, but it lacked the energy of her previous attempts. Perhaps due to pity. Her gaze glanced off Shane's hip. "I was kidnapped."

"You were *invited* to dinner and you accepted."

"There was your first mistake." Holden grinned at the doctor, clearly enjoying this. "You accepted Shane's invitation."

"I was coerced." Dr. Carlisle slung her bag to her shoulder. "It was supposed to be a coffee meeting."

Since she'd holstered her weapon, Shane decided to show her the million-dollar view. "The clinic is over here." He marched across the plowed, narrow highway and up the packed trail Roy had made a few days ago when the snow had stopped.

Behind him, Dr. Carlisle and Holden were bonding over their mutual dislike of Shane.

"You can't trust a word out of his mouth," Holden was saying, helping the attractive doctor over a rough patch of snow. "My aunt called me to accompany her here because she felt Shane was influencing her daughter to stay."

"Despicable."

"And the part about me is completely untrue." Shane stepped onto the porch of the clinic and moved out of purse-striking range. "If you've never been to Second Chance, now's the time to stop and smell the roses."

The sun was setting behind them and its warm orange rays reached across the valley to light the top of the Sawtooth Mountains like a beacon.

Holden helped Dr. Carlisle to the porch. In the diminishing light, the gray at his temples looked like blond highlights, taking a good eight years off his age. And look at that! Holden had that glimmer in his eye, the one that said he had an interesting woman in his sights.

In this light, Dr. Carlisle was a striking woman. Shane suddenly appreciated her looks, including her long blond hair. Not because he preferred blondes, but because Holden did.

"It's gorgeous," Dr. Carlisle said.

"Beautiful," Holden agreed, but he wasn't looking at the view.

Shane opened the door and led them inside. "But the best thing about working here is this." Shane came to stand to one side of the plate-glass window overlooking the valley, allowing Dr. Carlisle and Holden space. "With only a patient or two a day, you'd have plenty of time to enjoy this."

The three of them stood in silence in front

of the window, looking out on the broad, flat valley blanketed in glistening snow. Flakes drifted past slowly. Peacefully. Romantically.

Without moving his head, Shane glanced at the couple next to him.

The couple.

There were sparks between them, all right. Holden wasn't huffing and puffing like the big, bad wolf. And the good doctor? She was standing very still, fingering the bracelet around her wrist, not her purse strap.

"I promised you'd be back by midnight, Dr. Carlisle." Shane decided it was time to go and let nature—Mother Nature or Holden's nature—take its course. "I'll be waiting in the lobby at the inn whenever you're ready for that ride."

Shane hurried out, shutting the door behind him. Only when he reached the bottom of the slope and had his feet firmly on the highway did he turn and look back.

Holden and Dr. Carlisle stood at the plate-glass window, smiling and laughing as if they were on a date and hitting it off.

Not exactly what I had in mind.

But it'll do.

"Laurel's mom isn't very nice," Gabby told Mitch quietly over dinner.

They sat in the common room with Zeke, Shane, Sophie and the twins, while Laurel and her mother ate at the kitchen table in the apartment. The pair hadn't requested privacy. No one had wanted to eat with Mrs. Monroe.

Genevieve was what Mitch had expected Harlan's family to be. She wore flawless, thick makeup and expensive jewelry. Her clothes were as inappropriate for the mountains as Shane's clothes were. She was entitled and scornful.

"And she's loud," Gabby said. "Laurel winces when she's loud."

"I'm loud, too," Mitch admitted, remembering the times he'd lost his temper recently.

"It's your bark, Dad." Gabby shrugged, not taking her eyes off the pair in the kitchen. "You've always had it."

"Even old dogs can learn new tricks." His love for Laurel made him feel different on the inside. Or it had until he'd learned the truth about her pregnancy.

Or should I say the lies?

Parents and role models were supposed to make good choices. When Laurel had described taking the place of her twin, he hadn't thought through the implications. He hadn't taken the hint. She hadn't told her baby daddy about her babies because he thought she was someone else. There was no defense for that.

Was there?

"I'm sorry I've been bad lately." Gabby looked at Mitch sheepishly. "Laurel said you needed to hear my apology. Can you forgive me?"

"Of course." Apologies were tough at any age, but tougher for preteens. His chest should have swelled with pride. Instead, he wrestled with Laurel encouraging his daughter to do the right thing when Laurel had been unable to do so herself.

When in the course of a one-night stand is it appropriate to correctly identify oneself?

Mitch was in defense attorney mode, trying to formulate an argument that would justify Laurel's behavior. He stared at Gabby. How could he condone what Laurel had done?

"Dad, I'm warning you now. I'm going to experiment with makeup sometimes." Gabby's cheeks flushed. "And I might wear a dress once in a while come spring. Laurel said she'd help me pick some out. Don't freak about it, okay?"

"I won't." He was too busy freaking out about Laurel's complicated knots.

Laurel had changed before dinner. Her red locks were brushed and down, fanning across her shoulders. She wore a flowing blue skirt that reached her ankles and a creamy lace off-the-shoulder blouse.

She looks like a Monroe.

Mitch drew a deep breath, trying to listen to the small voice in his head that said Laurel was still Laurel. So she'd made a mistake?

She lied.

Laurel entered the common room, avoiding Mitch's gaze.

That sharp pain in my chest? It's my heart breaking.

Laurel's mother joined them.

"How'd it go with the doctor?" Laurel asked Shane, who was sitting on the hearth.

"The jury's still out." Shane stared at the fire.

"I may have to disappear and take up an alias in Mexico," Zeke murmured cryptically.

"What did you guys say to Dr. Carlisle?" Mitch demanded, welcoming a non-Laurel crisis.

"There's that bark, Dad." But Gabby was grinning.

"Oh, it wasn't anything we *said*," Zeke admitted. "More like something we did."

Shane ran a hand through his hair and stared out the window in the general direction of the medical clinic. It being dark outside, there wasn't much to see but the reflection of his worried expression.

"Laurel, we're not finished talking." Her mother crossed her arms over her chest.

"We're done for today, Mom. I'm tired."

Mitch's breaking heart panged. Laurel looked as distraught as he felt.

Genevieve cast her finger over the assembled. "I'll need everyone here to sign a confidentiality agreement."

Everyone groaned.

"Aunt Gee, that's not happening." For once, Shane said something Mitch agreed with.

"I have to protect my daughter's reputation." Genevieve frowned.

"She means she has to protect *my sister's* reputation," Laurel clarified in a defeated voice.

"Objection," Mitch protested reflexively. "Don't let her rob you of your joy."

"That's right." Sophie picked up one of her kids and plopped him into her lap. She grinned. "We mommies have to protect our happiness. I'm going to open an antiques shop in the trading post across the street."

"Bully for you," Genevieve said flatly.

"And I'm going to open a boutique in the mercantile next to it." Laurel threw her shoulders back.

"No." Genevieve stomped her high-heeled boot. "I forbid it."

"You can't." Laurel's tone offered no room for argument.

"What are you going to sell in your boutique?" Gabby asked Laurel. "Clothes? Like your pink dress?"

"No. Nothing that fancy." Laurel smiled, some of her sparkle returning. "Quilts. Paintings. A scarf or two."

Gabby leaned forward, excitement in her bruise-rimmed eyes. "You mean, if I knit scarves, I could sell them in the store?" At Laurel's nod, she turned to Mitch. "I could save to buy my own phone."

"Yep." No harm in agreeing to that. At the pace Gabby knit, she'd be lucky to produce one scarf a year. "Yep," he said again, because his brain blipped when Laurel's gaze bounced to him and away.

"When you say antiques, sister dear..." Shane regarded Sophie with skepticism. "You're not talking about a sea scroll or a fancy clock some English lord owned, are you?"

"This is not the Monroe art collection." Instead of getting defensive, Sophie became more animated. "There's an old pedal sewing machine in there and I think it works. I found a scale in the back. You put in a nickel and it gives you your weight and your fortune. Plus, there are boxes of collections. Hood ornaments, brooches, skeleton keys."

The snort of disgust Laurel's mother made was largely ignored.

Shane still looked dubious. "Are you sure this isn't yard sale junk?"

Sophie reached over and slugged her twin in the arm, not hard, but a slug nonetheless. "I can sell each key for twenty-five bucks and—"

"You can *price them* for twenty-five bucks," Shane clarified. "Whether you sell them for list or not depends upon what kind of person walks into your store."

"Or shops my website." Sophie pushed her red glasses up and lifted her nose in the air.

Shane shook his head. "All I'm saying is you're located at a crossroads of a couple highways. People who come through town are headed elsewhere. Their cars and SUVs are going to be loaded. There won't be room for antique sewing machines or nickel scales."

Sophie sniffed. "Those are the people who'll buy a skeleton key."

"Oh, for the love of Mike." Genevieve glared at Laurel. "You want to stay for this?"

"Yes." Laurel's nose joined Sophie's in the air.

She can go anywhere she wants to. Harlan's voice.

Mitch frowned. Not unless she found a good lawyer. Someone who understood she'd gone on the date for the right reasons and then... That was as far as Mitch could take the case.

What case broke you? Harlan's voice again.

Mitch rubbed his temples, trying to force the old man out of his head. Because it had been a combination of cases and a bad marriage and an increasing intolerance for clients who lied.

This case. This case will break me.

And it wasn't even being tried in court!

Sophie wasn't giving up trying to sway her brother. "You're such a hypocrite, Shane."

Her boys stared at their mother with wide eyes. Sophie rarely lost her temper or raised her voice.

She shook her finger at Shane. "When you took over the Monroe Resort in Las Vegas, you complained bitterly about the blue-collar clientele. And then you set about bringing in high rollers, luxury shoppers and people wanting to get married in style. We're going to do the same thing."

"Don't hold your breath," Genevieve muttered.

"Knit scarves and skeleton keys," Shane

mumbled, crossing his arms over his chest. "You can send updates to me in prison."

Mitch's frown deepened. Shane was going to need a good lawyer, too.

"My grandmother used to collect skeleton keys." Zeke's admission was inadmissible in Mitch's book, because increasingly, he had a feeling Zeke had the hots for Sophie. "Lots of people do."

Shane might have had the same impression as Mitch, because he scowled at the cowboy.

"If Grandpa Harlan was here," Laurel said to Shane, "he'd hear the excitement in our voices."

"That coldhearted pig?" Genevieve scoffed. "He's the reason you're all unemployed and wasting your time in run-down shacks. Well, I've got news for you, Laurel. You're set to make millions off this design contract. All you have to do is sign on the dotted line."

Mitch held his breath. It was one thing to acknowledge to himself that Laurel didn't check the boxes he'd made when he thought about marrying again. It was another to hear her dreams of being a designer were in reach. No more quilts or scarves for her. It'd be back to silk and rhinestones.

"Mom, let it go," Laurel said wearily.

"Millions?" Gabby gaped.

Mitch shushed her.

While Genevieve gave Laurel all the reasons she shouldn't dismiss the offer, Mitch's phone buzzed with a notification. He drew it from his back pocket and then interrupted Mrs. Monroe's rant. "The passes are officially closed."

Shane groaned and exchanged a glance with Zeke. "That's not good."

"Mexico, here I come," Zeke murmured with a love-struck glance Sophie's way.

"Closed?" Genevieve shrieked. "Tell me that doesn't mean I'm stuck here. Where's Holden? He has four-wheel drive."

"Holden is on a date," Shane said, regaining some of his perpetually good humor.

"A date?" Genevieve stomped her boot. "Impossible. He just got here."

Shane shrugged. "You know how he is, Aunt Gee."

Apparently, she did, because she quit whining. About that, at least.

"Mom, I'm not signing."

"Oh, come on." Laurel's mother had followed Laurel to her room. She fanned the pages of the thick document in front of Laurel and singsonged, *"You'll be a millionaire."*

"And what will this deal make you?" Laurel demanded, hoping standing up for herself would earn her some alone time. She and the babies needed to mourn the loss of Mitch. "And what will this deal make Ashley? Because when you told me about this contract you kept saying *we*."

Cold blue eyes glittering, Mom replied, "I'm taking what I'm worth, since there would be no contract without me."

"A figure, Mom." Laurel was calm. There was no joy to be found here. "Let's hear the number."

"I deserve every penny." Her mother shuddered. "In fact, I deserve more, considering the mess you've left me to straighten out with Wyatt."

Laurel knew she'd have to come to her question another way. "Can we focus on the positive for a minute?" She took one of her mother's hands and placed it on her baby bump. "You're going to be a grandmother."

Mom snatched her hand back, aghast. "Don't remind me. Hot on the heels of the grandmother title comes menopause and death."

"Mom," Laurel chastised, trying not to let her rejection sting, trying not to let loose the flood of grief and disappointment that pressed at the back of her throat at the knowledge that

Mitch didn't love her enough to get past her deceit.

"Laurel, pregnant or not, you don't pass up deals like this." Mom's shrewd gaze searched for a weakness. It didn't take long for her to find one. "A month ago you were a salaried nobody."

"I don't care about fame."

"Then this is the deal for you. You can stay here and open your little shop while you make red-carpet gowns."

"*Mother*. The terms?"

"If you must know…" Mom's gaze swept the worn brown carpet with a look of concern. "I'm taking twenty-five percent." At Laurel's gasp, she added, "And Ashley will license her name to your designs for an additional five."

They want thirty percent of the value of my designs?

The babies drew back in horror.

How could Ashley do this to me?

"I may be a salaried nobody," Laurel said in a stiff voice that didn't sound like her own. "But even I know a bad deal when I hear it." She turned away, fingering the fuzzy copper yarn ball on her bedside table, remembering how warm she'd felt in Mitch's arms. But memories did her no good now. She had to think. She had to fill in the gaps Mom had so conveniently left out. Laurel faced her mother. "Did you tell Ashley about this?"

A little shrug. A little turning up of the nose. "A good manager doesn't bother their client with small details."

Ashley doesn't know.

"This isn't a *small* detail."

"Laurel, your up-front money is a million dollars." Mom glanced around the simple room. "That'll go a long way here. Think this over carefully. Maybe you'll miss the comforts of modern life. I can negotiate an apartment in LA or New York into the deal. This could be the first step toward your dream of owning a shop on Rodeo Drive."

"A shop with Ashley's name on it." Laurel couldn't let that small detail pass.

"You need Ashley's name to get the deal." Mom tsk-tsked. "You did this to yourself. If we tell the world you made the dress, people will question Ashley's integrity and your name becomes irrelevant."

"They're going to question Ashley's integrity anyway once the truth about my situation gets out." Laurel sighed, filled with regret that her sister was collateral damage to her pregnancy, and unable to shake the suspicion that she'd lost any chance with Mitch over this.

"By rights, Wyatt should pay child support. Why don't you negotiate that?"

"We are *not* telling that man about this yet!" Mom jabbed a finger toward Laurel's stomach, her expression fierce. "Much less ask him for money first thing! You'll look like you're scheming. Is that what you want?"

Laurel stumbled back, numb.

"This is a delicate matter. For once, Laurel… *For once!*" Mom tossed the contract on Laurel's bed and stomped out the door. "Do what I say when I say it!"

"LAUREL," MITCH CALLED SOFTLY, tapping her door lightly just after midnight.

She opened the door and tugged him inside. "What are you doing here? My mother will have a meltdown—another one—if she finds you here."

"We need to talk." He wanted to brush a lock of hair from her shoulder. He wanted to kiss the worry lines on her forehead. He kept his distance. "I've been thinking."

Laurel stared at him in silence. Behind her, the door to the closet stood open, revealing her pink dress.

"It looks bad for you. This thing with Wyatt…the actor. When he finds out… When the world finds out he thought he was with

Ashley, but you wound up pregnant..." In his head, this conversation had made him sound heroic. In reality...

"Say what you came here for." Laurel crossed her arms, but she couldn't hide the tears in her eyes.

Whatever they'd had... Whatever he'd hoped they had... It wasn't in the room with them.

He tapped his chest. "I can coordinate your defense." Technically, he couldn't be her attorney. He wasn't licensed to practice in either Idaho or California.

"You want to lead my legal team." Her shoulders hunched. Her features threatened to crumple. "You're offering to stand by me as my attorney."

Mitch raised his hands. "I know that sounds bad."

She took a step back, a grim reminder that he did indeed sound bad. "Let's not do this. I get it. You didn't like my wardrobe. You didn't like my dress. And now you don't like the mistake I made. I get it. I'm not the kind of person you want as a role model for Gabby."

His mouth wouldn't open to argue. But his heart... His heart was pounding like a trapped man in a sinking ship.

"I'll make this easy on you. On both of us." She stepped around him and opened the door.

When he hesitated to leave, she added, "For Gabby. Leave for Gabby."

He did.

He let her release him.

He let her shut the door.

She was making it easy on him and doing the right thing, but his heart still pounded and his chest ached.

And her mother watched him from the end of the hall.

CHAPTER EIGHTEEN

A VIOLENT DOOR slam shook the Lodgepole Inn.

That, combined with a gust of icy wind, woke Shane. He swung his legs around and nearly fell off the couch in the common room.

A table lamp next to him came on, blinding him.

"You."

"Dr. Carlisle." Shane turned to keep a wary eye on the purse-wielding doctor and rubbed his face with both hands. "I lost track of you. What time is it?"

"Five o'clock in the morning." She was dusted with snow from head to toe, and her dark slacks looked wet as if she'd fallen into a snowdrift. "I dozed off talking to your cousin, who's still sound asleep by the way." She assumed the position of a batter, only her bat was that big black bag. "You had better give me a ride back to Ketchum right now or I'll press charges!"

"Don't hit me." Shane got to his feet. "I'm up. I'm moving."

"Where's the fire?" The door to one of the downstairs guest rooms opened and Zeke hobbled into view. He squinted in the light, bumped his injured leg against the wall and howled.

"What's the emergency?" Mitch opened the door to his apartment.

"Mr. Monroe?" Dr. Carlisle seemed confused. She was staring at Mitch, not Shane.

There's a question to ask later.

"Dad, is everything okay?" Gabby appeared behind her father, wearing a blue flannel nightgown and reddish-green shiners.

There was a moment of silence where everyone looked at everyone else.

"Oh, for the love of bicycles!" Dr. Carlisle dropped her bag, shrugged out of her jacket and rushed to Zeke's side. "You should be in bed. Come on."

"Dr. Carlisle." The cowboy opened his eyes wider. "I've been waiting my entire life for a woman to say that to me."

"I'm not the woman you've been waiting for." She set one of his crutches against the wall and coached him on the one-crutch hobble around his folded wheelchair. "You may have graduated to a walking cast, but you'd do best to keep to that wheelchair for a few more weeks."

"You really know how to crush a man's ego, Doc." But the cowboy didn't sound as if he was complaining.

Dr. Carlisle shut the bedroom door behind them.

"I need coffee and a toothbrush." Shane hurried to the stairs.

"And a good lawyer." Mitch grabbed hold of Shane's arm before he'd reached the first step. "Don't forget, the passes are closed."

Shane looked up, not heavenward but to where his room was, wondering if he could hide from Dr. Carlisle for twenty-four hours or until one of the three mountain passes opened again.

"*I'm* not going to tell her," Mitch said in that firm voice of his.

"Since you're the mayor and my defense attorney," Shane countered, jerking from his hold. "I think you should give her the news."

"As owner of the town and the originator of this cockamamy plan," Mitch said, "you should tell her."

Shane flirted with the idea of getting Holden to tell the doctor the news. Where was he anyway? "I say we have Gabby tell her."

"Tell her what?" Gabby asked, clearly not following the nuances of the conversation.

"Nothing." Mitch scowled.

"She's in doctor mode, Mitch." Shane smiled at Gabby. "And the next person she's going to treat is your daughter. Your beautiful, sweet, innocent daughter."

Dr. Carlisle would never hit Gabby with a brick-loaded purse.

Gabby put her hands on her slim hips. "Is there something the adults in the room forgot to tell me?"

"Okay, change of plan. Even I can't do that to you." Shane's brain moved on to plan B. "Get the good doctor a room, preferably with a view of the Sawtooth Mountains. I'll text my lothario cousin her whereabouts in case he wakes up and worries about her."

Forgoing a toothbrush, Shane darted into the small kitchen alcove at the bottom of the stairs and set the coffee brewing.

Mitch lingered. "About Laurel."

"What about her?" Shane spared a glance at the innkeeper's face. "Oh, don't tell me you dumped her."

The man gave Shane the weakest of smiles. "She beat me to it."

Shane shook his head. "I know you know what my grandfather would say about that."

Mitch nodded. "Everybody deserves a second chance." To his credit, he looked miserable.

At any other time, Shane would've reveled in his pain. But Mitch had broken Laurel's heart because he couldn't see honest regret staring him in the face. "She deserves better than you."

Mitch didn't argue.

The coffee finished and footsteps heralded the doctor's return.

"I thought you could use a cup to get your day started." Turning his back on Mitch, Shane held out his peace offering. "The teen with the black eyes is Gabby."

Dr. Carlisle scowled at Shane but accepted the mug. "What happened to you, kiddo?"

Gabby patted the door frame. "I was texting and bumped into this wall."

Dr. Carlisle's slender blond eyebrows shot up. "You have a cell phone."

"Not anymore." Gabby's shoulders drooped. "I suppose this is life's way of telling me I was too young to have one in the first place."

"That's my girl," Mitch said with pride.

Dr. Carlisle spotted the sink in the alcove and washed her hands. "Can I take a closer look at your colorful life lesson, Gabby?"

The teen brightened. "Dad said I didn't break my nose, but I'd like a second opinion." She added in a whisper, "I didn't realize how much I like my nose until it became a schnoz."

Dr. Carlisle cradled Gabby's face and gently turned it to and fro, peering at her bruises and staring into her eyes. "And you can breathe all right?"

"Yes."

"And afterward, you never passed out or dozed off when you shouldn't have?"

"No."

"Your father is correct about it not being broken." She smoothed Gabby's strawberry blond hair over her shoulders. "I don't want to alarm you, but some of that excess fluid may drop to your jawline in the next day or so before it dissipates completely from your face. It'll look like you have bruises on either side of your mouth."

"Fantastic," Gabby said, yawning. "My dad would say this is the punishment fitting the crime."

Mitch enfolded his daughter into a gentle hug. "The hardest of life's lessons always leave a painful mark."

Dr. Carlisle's pleasant bedside manner disappeared. "I'm ready to leave now." Her eyes sought to burn holes in Shane's face.

"Ah, yeah. Here's the unfortunate news about that." Shane didn't know how to soften the blow. "We've just learned we're snowed in. No one can get in or out of the valley."

"No one?" Her gaze drifted toward the window. She'd walked through the snow to get to the inn. She'd know he wasn't lying about that.

"No one," Shane said firmly.

"Can I get you a complimentary room?" Mitch came to Shane's aid. "We have plenty of hot water for a bath or a shower. Will a queen bed do?"

Her shoulders drooped. "Can I put a hold on my calls and a do-not-disturb sign on my door?"

"We'll put you in the Ponderosa Room." Gabby handed her a key attached to a four-inch piece of wood into which the word *Ponderosa* had been carved. "Give me a few minutes to get some fresh towels up there." She hurried into her and Mitch's apartment and banged around in cupboards.

"If you need anything, the general store and the Bent Nickel Diner open at seven." Mitch smiled kindly at her, but then again, he'd had no part in the kidnapping so he could manage a tranquil smile.

"Charge anything you want to my account," Shane added.

"You'd be amazed what a woman needs in the mountains," Dr. Carlisle deadpanned.

Arms filled with towels, Gabby scampered up the steps to the second floor.

Mitch moved at a much slower pace to the stairs. "While you're here, I'd appreciate it if you could examine Laurel."

"Oh, yes. She fell the other day." It was a little scary how Dr. Carlisle could swing easily from angry, kidnapped woman to caring physician. She followed Mitch upstairs. "How's she been feeling?"

"Good. But it would ease my mind if you'd take a look."

"Of course." She glanced over her shoulder at Shane, eyes narrowing even if her tone was cheerful. "It seems I have an abundance of time on my hands."

The moment they disappeared, Shane pulled out his cell phone to check the weather report. If luck was with him, the storm would blow through today.

Silently, he swore.

Luck wasn't with him.

As soon as the Bent Nickel was open, Shane took up residence at a booth near the front windows.

He wanted Holden to see him when he descended from the clinic. He wanted to interrogate his cousin on what had happened.

Not that he wanted details. An overview would do. Starting with: What did you talk about all night? And ending with: Can you work a little more of your magic on Dr. Carlisle and convince her to stay?

Aunt Genevieve entered the diner, wearing the same clothes from yesterday and the same sour expression. She paused inside the door to finger comb her short red hair, which allowed her time to spot Shane.

"Where is Holden?" she demanded, taking a seat across from him. "His vehicle is out in front, but he didn't check into the motel."

Shane cradled his coffee cup. "He's around."

"Is he?" His aunt craned her neck and waved at Ivy. "It's like I'm in a horror movie and he's the first to disappear."

Well, this was an unexpected bright spot in the morning. Shane grinned, grateful for the distracting opportunity to tease. "You know the first person to die in a horror movie is always the most clueless." He rather liked that adjective attached to Holden.

Order for coffee given, she settled back in her seat. "I haven't seen Holden since he went looking for *you*, Shane. If my son was writing the script, he'd list you as a suspect."

"*I* haven't slashed Holden to ribbons and stuffed him in someone's basement, if that's what you mean." It was tough to drink his coffee around his widening grin.

Ivy appeared with a coffee mug and a pot of coffee.

"So glib," his aunt muttered. "I may have married into the Hollywood branch of the Monroe family, but I've always admired Holden and his siblings. You never catch any of them making a scandal."

Shane nearly spit out his coffee.

Poor Aunt Genevieve and her selective memory.

Shane glanced across the road to the dim glow of the window at the medical cabin. He couldn't wait for Holden and Dr. Carlisle to be in the same room as his aunt.

"Shane, Roy mentioned you…*brought* a doctor home last night." Ivy set a water glass and menu for Genevieve on the table. She put her hand on her hip. "Where is she?"

"Is someone else missing?" Aunt Genevieve demanded, holding true to her difficult nature. "Does someone need to send out a search party?"

"No," Shane said quickly. A partial explanation was in order. "We're in contract negotiations with a doctor for our clinic. And Holden is—"

"An expert when it comes to money." His aunt finished Shane's sentence. She beamed up at Ivy. "I'm sure they're off somewhere negotiating."

"They were negotiating something." Shane tried hard not to smile. "I'm waiting on an update." He hoped Holden wasn't a deal breaker as well as a heartbreaker.

Ivy gave Shane a dubious look.

"I'll have an egg-white omelet with quinoa, tomato and kale." Aunt Genevieve hadn't looked at the menu.

"We don't have quinoa or kale." Ivy looked at Genevieve the way she used to look at Shane.

"I passed a store on my way here." Genevieve gestured toward it.

Ivy's forehead crinkled. "Mack doesn't stock quinoa or kale."

Before his aunt could say something completely insensitive, Shane said, "She'll have oatmeal."

Now it was Aunt Genevieve who frowned. After a moment she nodded. "Steel cut, of course."

"Oatmeal," Shane said again when Ivy might have mentioned her oatmeal came in a small pouch she added hot water to. "You'll like the oatmeal."

It was practically guaranteed his aunt wouldn't like much else in Second Chance.

CHAPTER NINETEEN

THE SNOW MIGHT have trapped them in the valley, but life in Second Chance always went on despite the nonstop precipitation.

Wrapped in a jacket, her teal scarf swathed about her face, Laurel entered the Bent Nickel. It was lunchtime. It hadn't stopped snowing all morning. But nearly every booth and table was full. The second wave of Monroes had bought them out.

Hunched over, nursing a broken heart, Laurel considered a hasty retreat.

What if they know the truth about me?

What if they do? That was her grandfather's voice. Strong and confident. *Won't change who you are inside.*

He was right. She lifted her chin and squared her shoulders. She might not have been good enough for the likes of Mitch Kincaid, but she wasn't a bad person.

From a booth in the back, Holden gestured for her to join him.

Holden wasn't her first choice for a lunch

partner, but she felt sorry for him since he was alone.

"Laurel." Odette grabbed the hem of her coat as she passed. She sat with Flip. "Is it true there's a doctor in town?"

She nodded. "But she's sleeping." Gabby had told her that.

Odette's features smoothed into a satisfied smile.

"I can't promise she's staying," Laurel added, rubbing Odette's back when her smile fell into a mopey frown. "Hey, I wanted to talk to you about the boutique I'm opening in the mercantile. Flip has agreed to allow me to sell some of her paintings. You want to be featured, too, don't you?"

"I don't sell anything," Odette growled.

Flip laughed, but it lacked her usual spitefulness. She'd be disappointed if Laurel couldn't convince Odette to participate.

Laurel knelt near her mentor. "Imagine families with babies passing through, ones who didn't pack warm clothes for their kids. They'll stop to play in the snow and need a knit cap to keep their little ones warm. Or a thick, dry sweater for the car ride home."

"Not for sale." Odette pulled her knit cap around her ears.

"Speaking of car rides, perhaps now is the

time to remind you of the Lee family motto." Flip pointed to a yellowed map of Second Chance that was framed and hung above their table.

"The only motto I know is to make money you have to be passionate about what you do." Laurel tried to move on.

But Flip caught her jacket in the same way Odette had. "The most difficult path is finding the truth in your heart."

Laurel squinted at the map. She couldn't read the script on the bottom. "It says that?"

"Yes." Flip nodded.

"Laurel!" Holden called impatiently from the back booth.

With heavy steps, Laurel went to join him.

"Will you be by later to sew?" Odette called after her.

Laurel shrugged without turning.

"I didn't take you for a quitter." Odette was in one of her moods.

Laurel kept her mouth closed. If she'd learned anything from coming to Second Chance, it was how to have the patience of a saint.

Holden nodded a greeting as she approached. He was a natural-born leader, like Shane, but lacked Shane's creativity and endearing wit. That made Holden seem like a wet blanket on some occasions and a stuck-up pain in the butt on others.

This morning Laurel had some sympathy for him because he looked a bit green. "I recommend the soup, crackers and club soda."

"Thanks." He laid his cell phone faceup on the table, the sure sign of a man who considered whatever might happen in the world more important than the person they were dining with. "What's your take on this town?"

"I love it," Laurel said without thinking.

Holden cleared his throat. "I hear they need a doctor."

"I hear you...*interviewed* one." Holden might be intimidating on Wall Street, but he was just her cousin after all. Laurel remembered him when he had acne and braces.

Holden straightened his flatware on the paper napkin. "She's overqualified for the position."

"But not overqualified for you. Or vice versa." Laurel reached across the table, placing her hand over his to stop his fidgeting. "This is Idaho, not New York. It's a small world and relationship expectations are sometimes different here."

Case in point: Mitch.

"It's not like I plan to live here." Holden worked his jaw.

"You'd tell me if she never wants to hear your name again, though, right?" Laurel paused, but Holden said nothing. "She's my doctor. You may not have to see her on a regular basis, but I have an appointment with her in three weeks."

Holden withdrew his hand. "She's only your doctor if you stay here. Go home, Laurel. You're having twins. You can get top-notch medical care in California."

Laurel sat back. He was right, of course. But California didn't have Sophie and Shane. Or Odette and Flip. Or Gabby and...

"Your mother negotiated a deal of a lifetime for you."

Laurel might not have been schooled in legalese, but she was sure that wasn't true.

"I'm not going to leave this town without you," he said firmly, expecting no argument.

There was the Holden she knew and loved.

Ivy refilled Holden's coffee cup. "I'll be right back for your lunch order."

"She's taking a deal and leaving us. What a sellout," Odette said in a loud voice. "And she showed so much promise."

Holden leaned to one side to look at the elderly eavesdroppers. "Is that woman referring to you?"

Laurel nodded and kicked her voice up a

notch as she said, "But she's mistaken. Sophie and I are opening retail shops here. I'm going to feature artisan textiles—local paintings, quilts, knit items."

"Don't ask me to invest." Holden slurped his steaming coffee. "In fact, we should probably talk about your portfolio." He managed Laurel's savings.

Laurel closed her eyes and tried to recall how she'd felt in the mercantile. Joyful. Certain.

"Sign the contract, Laurel, and we'll devise a new way to protect your assets."

"I've found a place here, Holden. No financial plan can protect my heart." Her chest constricted. Truer words were never spoken.

"Putting your heart in a business?" He sipped his coffee. "That's old-school."

"It's how Grandpa Harlan made his fortune." Multiple times over.

"And how hundreds of thousands of entrepreneurs go bankrupt every year." Holden held her gaze. "Second Chance isn't for Monroes."

He was so wrong.

"I'm not hungry." Laurel got up.

She needed to find Mitch. But she couldn't pass Odette and Flip without saying something.

"You are both strong, talented women. And

if you're too afraid to put your work on display and put a price on it, so be it. The joy you create will go unnoticed."

"Well…the nerve," Odette harrumphed.

"Yep." Flip laughed. "The nerve."

"WHAT ARE YOU going to do, Dad?" Gabby asked as she changed the sheets on Laurel's bed. "How are you going to fight for Laurel?"

"I'm not. In not so many words, we broke up." He scrubbed Laurel's toilet harder. "She's going to be a fancy dress designer in Hollywood, make lots of money and forget us."

"You barked at her, didn't you?" The mattress squeaked as Gabby sat on the bed. "Because of the sexiest man alive? Dad, you're almost as attractive as Wyatt Halford."

"This has nothing to do with that actor." He'd never be able to watch one of his movies or shows again. "And everything to do with the choices Laurel made."

"Her choices?" Gabby's voice sounded small. "You think she'd pretend to be Ashley again and get pregnant by another famous hottie?"

"No." Mitch scowled, grateful he was in the bathroom and Gabby couldn't see his face. His cheeks were heating. This was practically a discussion about the birds and the bees. "Laurel isn't like that."

"Then what's the problem?"

Mitch's chest squeezed.

What's the problem?

He stopped scrubbing and leaned against the door frame, removing his plastic gloves and tossing them into his supply bucket. "Have I told you lately how brilliant you are?"

"No?"

He sat on the bed next to her and gave her a hug. "Why don't you go downstairs and call your mother? She hasn't heard from you in days."

Gabby didn't wait for him to think twice. She hightailed it out of there.

Outside the window, the day was as gray as his mood. The clouds were thick and low, and snow fell hurriedly to earth, guaranteeing another day of the passes being closed.

Facts were facts. Laurel was having the babies of the sexiest man alive. Mitch didn't have any problem imagining what Wyatt could give those girls. Private school. Tuition to a prestigious college. A ski lodge in Aspen. A gap year in Europe. Mitch didn't even know where he'd be next year. Much as he wanted to trust Shane, Second Chance might not earn historical significance, and even so, the Monroes might sell the town off anyway.

Mitch stared at his hands.

What kind of man couldn't promise a stable future for his little girl?

He got to his feet, intending to finish Laurel's bathroom, but his leg brushed a clipped stack of papers on the bedside table. They fell to the carpet.

The stack had been turned upside down. He righted them.

It was a contract.

He hadn't seen it when he came in. It might have been under Laurel's pillow or beneath the blankets.

He read the first page.

It was the contract Laurel's mother had brought.

He read the last page.

Laurel hadn't signed it.

His heart soared with hope.

Mitch sat back down and began to read the contract from the beginning.

CHAPTER TWENTY

"LAUREL." MITCH SAT on the couch in the common room opposite her mother. He had a serious expression on his face and her design contract in his hands. "Come join us."

Chilled, Laurel removed her jacket but put up her guard.

Her mother didn't look happy and neither did Mitch.

"You hired a lawyer?" Mom scowled. Her clothes were as rumpled as her temper. "Does this mean you don't trust me? Your own mother?"

"What do you think?" Laurel asked vaguely because she had no clue what was going on. She sat on the hearth and glanced at Mitch, at stern features and square shoulders. He gave nothing away. "Counselor."

Mitch allowed the briefest of nods. "I looked at the contract as a favor to Laurel." His words were as stiff as his backbone. "She doesn't have to take my advice."

"Good." Her mother slapped her hands on

her thighs. "I don't need to hear anything from you, then."

"But I'd like to hear what Mitch has to say." Laurel's fingers knotted in her lap.

Mitch dropped the thick contract on the coffee table. It landed with a resounding thud. "I wouldn't sign it. This deal leaves the door open for Ashley to fire Laurel and hire another designer. *Any* other designer at *any* time."

Despite the fire nearby, Laurel didn't feel warm.

"It's a good deal," Mom said through gritted teeth. "She should be grateful."

"It goes without saying that agents usually take fifteen percent," Mitch continued.

"This is a very complicated situation." Mom snatched up the contract, hugging it to her chest.

"You could design a dozen dresses and if this Xuri person isn't happy, she doesn't have to pay you any more than the initial signing bonus." Mitch tsk-tsked. "If you sign this, you should go into the deal thinking you won't see a dime more than your advance." He leaned toward Laurel, his gaze serious and yet nonjudgmental. "Or rather seven cents more since your mom and sister are entitled to part of the pot."

"Thank you for your *opinion*." Mom stood, making it easier to look down her nose at

Mitch and Laurel. "But this is between my daughters and me, and—"

"What would you suggest as an alternative?" Laurel asked Mitch.

"We can't present an alternative," Mom sputtered. "This contract was approved by Xuri herself!"

"But it wasn't approved by me." Laurel didn't look at her mother. She was more interested in the guarded kindness in Mitch's eyes.

Above them, the floor creaked. Behind Laurel, the fire crackled and a log fell apart.

"You know what I'd suggest," Mitch said slowly.

Laurel nodded. She knew. He wasn't suggesting marriage to him. "Protect my happiness." *Protect my heart.*

Too late on the latter.

"Of all the foolish notions." Her mother came to stand in front of Laurel, came to stare down on her with a look designed to defeat dissent. "Happiness? A million dollars won't make you happy?"

A million dollars wouldn't make her happy if she couldn't be with Mitch.

"Mom, the only way I'll sign that deal is if Ashley's name isn't attached and your take is fifteen percent." And even then, Laurel wasn't sure she wanted to sign the deal. She had no

dress design ideas lingering at the back of
her brain. Although ideas for baby quilts? Of
those, she had plenty.

Mom glared at Mitch. Mitch bared his teeth
at Mom.

No one seemed interested in Laurel. She
stood, thanking Mitch for his input.

"Not so fast." Mom caught her arm. "We
need to talk about something else." She shooed
Mitch away, or perhaps she hoped he'd budge
at her sweeping hand motion. "In private."

He didn't make a move to stand.

Her mother huffed. "Tell your guard dog
that we need to discuss Wyatt in private."

Mitch's gaze darted to Laurel.

"I'll be fine." Laurel shook off her mother's
hold and gave Mitch the reprieve he was no
doubt looking for.

When he'd shut his apartment door behind
him, Mom leaned forward. "I need you to return to Hollywood with me and face the music.
We'll tell Wyatt first and see how it shakes out
with his people. Then you and Ashley can do
an interview together, one where you admit
this was the first and only time you pretended
to be your sister."

Laurel dug her heels into the hardwood. "I
can't lie." Not anymore.

Mom's head bobbled around, although not

a red hair on her head moved. "I don't care about your recently rediscovered morals. We have Ashley's career to think about."

Laurel's throat threatened to close. "A lie put me into this situation. I'm not going to get out of it with another one."

"Are you saying Wyatt isn't the father of those babies?"

"No. I'm talking about saying this was *the first and only time*—" air quotes "—I did the Twin Switch."

Mom's eyes narrowed. "You're making this impossible to pull off without hurting Ashley's career."

"And I'm sorry about that." It made her sick to her stomach. "But if you talk to Ashley, I know she'd feel the same way. No more lies."

"Let me get this straight." Her mother's eyes narrowed. "You think having Wyatt Halford's babies is going to be something people won't care about? That there will be no need for interviews to explain it away? That you'll write his name on their birth certificates and it won't be seen and leaked to the press?" Mom fell back on the couch and laughed in brittle chunks. "Even if I allowed you to hide out here, do you think reporters won't find you? Do you think your lawyer friend can protect you from people who get paid thousands of dollars for photographs? You have a famous face. You can't hide from this in some boutique in the boonies."

Laurel swallowed thickly. "No more lies."

Her mother was a master manipulator. She recognized the dead end they'd come to and took on a new attack as smoothly as a shark circled back for the kill. "Okay. What about your lawyer friend?"

Laurel glanced toward Mitch's apartment.

"You care about him." Her mother got up and sat next to Laurel on the hearth. "Him and that spark plug of a little girl." She rubbed Laurel's forearm. "Don't do this to them. They'll resent you for it. Those two and all the people in this sleepy little town."

Odette, who eyed strangers suspiciously. She'd never emerge from her cabin.

Ivy, whose diner hosted schoolkids most of the day. Where would they go when the paparazzi descended?

Mack, the entrepreneur, would probably create and sell maps of places Laurel had been in town, assuming it was more by then.

And Mitch? He'd lock up the inn and refrain from telling Laurel she'd ruined the town. But it would be there in his eyes.

What about Gabby? She'd rebel against her loss of independence. Mitch would be forced to leave Second Chance. And it would all be because of Laurel.

She couldn't do that to him. She couldn't do that to anyone in town.

Laurel stood on shaky legs. "If I do this your way…"

"I'll make adjustments to the contract." Mom nodded, eyes glittering with triumph.

The thought of signing any design deal sent the fear of failure churning in Laurel's stomach, but it wasn't as sickening as the pain her obstinance would cause. "I won't promise to sign anything."

"Oh, you'll sign. You can't have Wyatt Halford's babies without some financial leverage." She brushed Laurel's hair from her shoulders as if she was the most caring mother in Second Chance. "You need money in case Wyatt decides a woman who'd pretend to be someone else in order to sleep with him isn't good enough to raise his kids."

Laurel cringed in fear, turning away.

He can't have my babies.

"We'll talk more about this on the way back to California."

IT WAS SATURDAY. And Saturday meant Mitch was making tuna casserole.

He'd expected Laurel to come talk with him

after her mother chased him off, but she hadn't shown up.

He boiled water and opened cans of tuna, mushrooms and peas.

Still no Laurel.

He put the noodles in the boiling pot and got out milk and cheese from the refrigerator.

Still no Laurel.

He drained the noodles, mixed everything together, topped it with bread crumbs and put it in the oven.

He heard voices in the common room and ventured out to see if it was the Dragon Lady, aka Laurel's mother, or anyone else staying at his inn—anyone else being much preferable to talk to than Mrs. Monroe.

The Dragon Lady sat next to Gabby. "That is a gorgeous nose." She admired a framed photo of Gabby from last Christmas that had been sitting on the check-in desk.

Mitch's vision blurred.

"I know, right?" Gabby gingerly touched her still-swollen nose. "Everybody says it's going to look just the same when the bruises go away, but I'm not convinced."

Genevieve spotted Mitch, her nicey-nice smile hardening for a second before returning to nicey-nice. "Girls with noses like this land lots of television roles in Hollywood."

Hollywood? Mitch nearly vomited in his throat.

"Really?" Gabby gushed.

"Gabby." It was the pink dress all over again. His vision cleared. He successfully swallowed bile.

"Yeah, Dad?" She beamed at him with those raccoon eyes.

"I need you to make a salad."

Gabby's hand fluttered in Genevieve's direction. "But—"

"Now." He didn't apologize for his bark.

His daughter flounced his way as if intent to make a dramatic exit. Instead, she stopped next to him and raised up on her toes to give him a kiss. "I know what she is, Dad. Give me some credit."

He slanted her a grin, cupping her cheek. "Have I told you lately how brilliant you are?"

"Not nearly enough." She skipped off.

Mitch waited until Gabby went into their apartment and closed the door before he confronted the Dragon Lady verbally, without barking.

"I suppose you don't want me to put ideas in your daughter's head." Laurel's mother was a shrewd operator, able to smile warmly as she read his mind.

Mitch hadn't survived years in the court

system to back down at the first challenge. "I suppose you'd like to sleep in a bed tonight and not out in Holden's car."

She kept smiling, the way opposing council sometimes did when they thought their next play overruled Mitch's defense. "We can do a deal. I won't put ideas into Gabby's head if you won't put ideas in Laurel's."

He shook his finger at her. "You underestimate Laurel's intelligence and her talent."

"And you underestimate her need to protect people, like Ashley...her children... and your sweet, sweet little girl." Genevieve sighed. "Gabby would shine like a diamond on-screen."

Mitch couldn't look at Mrs. Monroe. She didn't get it and regrettably, never would. He stared out the window at the delicate snowflakes and the snow-covered pines. He had to remind himself that there was beauty in the world that power-hungry people like Genevieve Monroe couldn't touch. Because if he didn't remind himself, he might lose his cool and say things he didn't want his daughter to hear.

Mitch forced himself to face her. "I have a sleeping bag I can loan you, but you might want to buy a pair of snow pants from the general store before it closes."

"You're bluffing." She fidgeted, unsure.

The door to Zeke's bedroom opened and the cowboy hobbled out on one crutch. "He's not bluffing. And after having to listen to you all afternoon, I'd be happy to escort you outside."

The Dragon Lady took in Zeke's walking cast and his single cowboy boot, and shook her head. She stood and headed for the stairs.

"Mark my words, gentlemen. When the roads are clear, I'm taking Laurel home to California. Don't test me or I'll make sure Holden sells this place to a developer who'll make me look like Glinda the Good Witch."

Her footsteps receded.

Mitch caught Zeke's eye. "Tell me everything you heard."

"You stole my keys." Mitch climbed the slope to reach Laurel midmorning on Valentine's Day.

Laurel had known she couldn't leave town without talking to Mitch one more time, but she'd been avoiding him.

He reached her, standing tall, his dark hair ruffling in the breeze. "Please tell me you didn't shovel snow off this porch."

"I asked Roy first thing this morning." And then Laurel had pulled a small bench onto the mercantile porch so she could stare out at the valley, enjoying the breathtaking beauty one last time.

"You didn't answer your door last night when I knocked." Mitch settled onto the bench next to her.

"I'm going home with my mother." Leaving happiness and hotness behind.

The babies were I-smell-bacon unhappy.

"Please don't tell me that decision makes you feel better." When she didn't deny it, Mitch put his arm around her, resting his hand on her hip. "It doesn't make me feel better. For the record, it makes me want to shout at something."

Laurel refused to look at him, at the good man she was giving up for the good of all involved. "Mitch, you don't understand."

"Oh, I understand all right. In your head…" He touched her temple with his. "You believe going back is the best way to protect everyone you care about. Ashley and her career. Your babies. Maybe even me and Gabby."

He read her all too well. "But if you know this, then you realize it isn't the right thing to do."

"Have you forgotten what's important in life? The joy of becoming a mother? The passion for a business in a place that your grandfather loved? Putting the needs of your kids first? Thinking about what makes you happy?" He whispered in her ear. "Like the love of a good man?"

"Mitch, it's much more complicated than you make it sound."

"Is it?" He pulled her closer, his voice enticing. "You're up here because you love this spot and you don't want to leave."

"Yes, but—"

"You're in my arms because you love me and you don't want to leave."

"Yes, but—"

"If your biological baby daddy was Joe Schmo from Cleveland, you wouldn't leave." He edged apart from her so he could turn and take her gloved hands in his, so he could stare into her eyes and she could see into his. "You wouldn't leave this valley. You wouldn't leave Second Chance." His voice dropped to a whisper. "You wouldn't leave *me*."

He was right.

He was right, and he knew it. But that didn't change anything.

Tears filled her eyes. "You don't know what a circus my life could become if the situation with Wyatt isn't handled right. He could call me unfit. He could try to take my babies away from me. He could ruin Ashley's reputation, her credibility, her career."

"Laurel Monroe, I'm here to tell you that's not going to happen." He sounded so certain. "And if by chance it does, I don't care. I love you. I love how you like to dress up. I love that you're creative enough to make things from scratch. I love that you want everyone to be happy and get along."

"But—"

"I love you. That's all that matters." His gaze was kind and yet filled with regret. "I should have remembered how much I loved you when all your knots unraveled. I underestimated you, how good a person you truly are and what a positive example you've been. I also underestimated Gabby. I'll be apologizing to you both for the rest of my life."

The babies fluttered happily.

"The point is, I love you. I can't live without you." Mitch dropped down on one knee. "And I'm no slouch in the legal department. Your mother has a plan? So what." He shrugged. "Shane and I have a plan, too. And do you know what it involves?"

"Please don't tell me you're going to kidnap Wyatt and bring him to Second Chance." She was joking through her tears. Mitch loved her. He was willing to endure the circus that came with the Hollywood Monroes.

Not that she was going to let him, but she loved him for suggesting it.

"Kidnapping? That's close, but no. I want to marry you. Let me rephrase. I *have* to marry you, because I can't live without you. And when Ashley brings Wyatt to our wedding— *as her date*—"

"Oh, Mitch. No. He'll think that they... That he... And then she..."

"Ashley can handle herself," he reassured her. "At least, that's what she told Shane when we spoke on the phone this morning."

Laurel's spine straightened. "You called Ashley?"

"Technically, Shane called Ashley. Woke her up at 5:00 a.m. Explained that you needed her help, for once, and she was ready to put Wyatt on a plane tomorrow." His gaze turned sly. "That is, if we were going to get married tomorrow."

"Oh, Mitch." He stole her breath.

"That is, she could have gotten him on a plane if Wyatt was in town."

"He's not in LA?"

"Nope. Apparently, he just left to shoot an action movie in South America and won't be back for four months." He squeezed her hands. "So you see, if you let your mother drag you back to California, it would've been for nothing. The man isn't even there."

If he thought that relieved her stress, he was wrong. "Four months." Her voice rose louder than his had ever done since she'd come to Second Chance. "I'm going to have to live with uncertainty for four months?" She stood. "I need to fly to South America."

"Hold up." Mitch drew her into his lap. "I've been talking about love and marriage, and you've said nothing."

She kissed his cheek. "I said a lot."

"Nothing about love," he grumbled.

He loves us. The babies swooned.

"I love you, Mitch." Laurel removed her gloves and framed his cheeks with her hands, needing to touch him skin to skin. And then she pressed her lips to his, needing the reassurance of his kiss. "Why wouldn't I love you? You remind me of what's important when I get all tangled up in protecting others and keeping the peace. You remind me that *I'm* important."

"You're one of the most important people in my life," he murmured, touching her nose with his. "Let me help you with this. We can face this together, I promise."

She closed her eyes, knowing she should refuse, but unable to do so. "All right, Mitch. I love you. I love that you aren't afraid to stand up to people in power. And I love that you aren't afraid to extend an olive branch and admit that you're wrong."

He drew back slightly. "I was wrong? When?"

"You were wrong about me opening a boutique in the mercantile. If I stay, it can't fail. Even if it doesn't make much money, it'll be a place that brings happiness to me."

"I *was* wrong," Mitch admitted with a broad grin. "If it brings you happiness, it is a huge success." He kissed her briefly. "Are you sure you don't want to pursue that dress design contract?"

"There will have to be a new set of terms." His eyes softened, and his smile was the kind one that had won her heart weeks ago.

"Now, that's exactly what a lawyer would say."

He made her forget complications. He reminded her to be happy. How could she ever have considered leaving him?

"Marry me, Mitch Kincaid. Marry me and my babies."

His smile turned wicked. "I thought I was the one doing the asking."

"Humor me."

"Yes." He lowered his lips to hers and kissed

her long and slow, as if they sat on a warm beach in the Bahamas and not on a cold, snowy slope in Second Chance, Idaho. "Yes."

EPILOGUE

THE EMAIL IN Mitch's inbox was from the historical society.

It was a reply back to his query from two weeks ago.

Since Laurel had agreed to marry him, or him her, depending upon who you asked, Holden had left as soon as the pass to Boise was open, taking the sulking Dragon Lady with him.

Although Dr. Carlisle hadn't accepted the position of town physician, she hadn't had Shane, Zeke or Roy arrested. In fact, she claimed the two days she was at the inn were the best two days of sleep she'd had in months.

Gabby's nose had emerged from the bruises, as small and pert as ever. Those bruises had earned her the respect of her elementary school peers, but she was glad to have her old face return. She hadn't worn makeup since. What she had done was dedicate her evenings to knitting scarves. She might make enough to buy a phone yet.

Laurel and Sophie were making slow progress on their retail endeavors across the road. During breaks in the snow, others in Second Chance came to help put the buildings in order. Flip and Odette had agreed to sell their work, and Roy had agreed to help Sophie go through other buildings to find items to sell.

Laurel entered the inn with Shane and the twins. The boys shucked their boots and jackets and ran across the room to Zeke, begging him for a game of checkers. Shane was wearing a new pair of sensible snow boots. He had yet to wear a pair of blue jeans or snow pants, but there was hope for him yet.

Laurel came to stand beside Mitch, wrapping her arms around him. "Shane, I don't want you to drive me to my doctor's appointment. The last thing I need is my doctor upset to see her would-be kidnapper."

Mitch covered one of her arms with one of his as his heart filled with the love of her presence, especially at the feel of an ever-growing baby bump. "Since I'm going to be Laurel's labor coach, I'm the only one allowed to drive her to the doctor."

"Dr. Carlisle was our best and only lead." Shane flopped onto the couch. "We have to keep things running smoothly here if we want to convince Holden that Second Chance is worth preserving. My consultant's report is due in three weeks and who knows what he'll recommend."

Mitch opened the email. He had to read it three times before the words sank in: Second Chance was a candidate for historical protection.

"Does that email say…?" Laurel leaned over his shoulder to read the missive.

"Uh, Shane." Mitch grinned. "You might want to come over here. I found just what we need to save Second Chance."

* * * * *

*In case you missed the first installment of
The Mountain Monroes, check out*
Kissed by the Country Doc
*by Melinda Curtis,
available at www.Harlequin.com!*

*Coming next, sparks fly for
Sophie and Zeke in*
Rescued by the Perfect Cowboy*!*

Get 4 FREE REWARDS!

We'll send you 2 FREE Books plus 2 FREE Mystery Gifts.

Love Inspired® books feature contemporary inspirational romances with Christian characters facing the challenges of life and love.

FREE Value Over **$20**

Get 4 FREE REWARDS!

We'll send you 2 FREE Books plus 2 FREE Mystery Gifts.

Love Inspired® Suspense books feature Christian characters facing challenges to their faith... and lives.

FREE Value Over $20

BETTY NEELS COLLECTION!

Buy 3 and get 1 FREE!

Experience one of the most celebrated and beloved authors in romance! Betty Neels will delight you with her signature brand of storytelling: happy romances, memorable couples and timeless tales of lasting love. These classics have been combined in 2-in-1 books for your reading pleasure!

YES! Please send me the **Betty Neels Collection**. This collection begins with 4 books, 1 of which is FREE! Plus a FREE gift – an elegant simulated Pearl Necklace & Earring Set (approx. retail value of $13.99). I may either return the shipment and owe nothing or keep for the low members-only discount price of $17.97 U.S./$20.25 CDN plus $1.99 U.S./$2.99 CDN for shipping and handling per shipment.* If I decide to continue, I'll receive two more shipments, each about a month apart, each containing four more two-in-one books, one of which will be free, until I own the entire 12-book collection. Each shipment is mine to keep for the same members-only discount price plus shipping and handling. I understand that no purchase is required. I may keep the free book no matter what I decide.

☐ 275 HCN 4623　　　　☐ 475 HCN 4623

Name (please print)

Address　　　　　　　　　　　　　　　　　　　　　　　　　　Apt. #

City　　　　　　　　　　State/Province　　　　　　　　Zip/Postal Code

Mail to the **Reader Service:**
IN U.S.A.: P.O. Box 1341, Buffalo, NY. 14240-8531
IN CANADA: P.O. Box 603, Fort Erie, Ontario L2A 5X3

MBN19

Get 4 FREE REWARDS!

We'll send you 2 FREE Books plus 2 FREE Mystery Gifts.

FREE
Value Over
$20

Both the **Romance** and **Suspense** collections feature compelling novels written by many of today's best-selling authors.

Get 4 FREE REWARDS!

We'll send you 2 FREE Books plus 2 FREE Mystery Gifts.

Harlequin® Special Edition books feature heroines finding the balance between their work life and personal life on the way to finding true love.

FREE
Value Over
$20

YES! Please send me 2 FREE Harlequin® Special Edition novels and my 2 FREE gifts (gifts are worth about $10 retail). After receiving them, if I don't wish to receive any more books, I can return the shipping statement marked "cancel." If I don't cancel, I will receive 6 brand-new novels every month and be billed just $4.99 per book in the U.S. or $5.74 per book in Canada. That's a savings of at least 12% off the cover price! It's quite a bargain! Shipping and handling is just 50¢ per book in the U.S. and 75¢ per book in Canada.* I understand that accepting the 2 free books and gifts places me under no obligation to buy anything. I can always return a shipment and cancel at any time. The free books and gifts are mine to keep no matter what I decide.

235/335 HDN GMY2

Name (please print)

Address   Apt. #

City   State/Province   Zip/Postal Code

Mail to the Reader Service:
IN U.S.A.: P.O. Box 1341, Buffalo, NY 14240-8531
IN CANADA: P.O. Box 603, Fort Erie, Ontario L2A 5X3

Want to try 2 free books from another series! Call 1-800-873-8635 or visit www.ReaderService.com.

---

*Terms and prices subject to change without notice. Prices do not include sales taxes, which will be charged (if applicable) based on your state or country of residence. Canadian residents will be charged applicable taxes. Offer not valid in Quebec. This offer is limited to one order per household. Books received may not be as shown. Not valid for current subscribers to Harlequin® Special Edition books. All orders subject to approval. Credit or debit balances in a customer's account(s) may be offset by any other outstanding balance owed by or to the customer. Please allow 4 to 6 weeks for delivery. Offer available while quantities last.

Your Privacy—The Reader Service is committed to protecting your privacy. Our Privacy Policy is available online at www.ReaderService.com or upon request from the Reader Service. We make a portion of our mailing list available to reputable third parties that offer products we believe may interest you. If you prefer that we not exchange your name with third parties, or if you wish to clarify or modify your communication preferences, please visit us at www.ReaderService.com/consumerschoice or write to us at Reader Service Preference Service, P.O. Box 9062, Buffalo, NY 14240-9062. Include your complete name and address.

HSE19R2